Sand & Water

A Novel

Michael Hoerning

BookLocker
Saint Petersburg, Florida

Paperback ISBN: 978-1-64438-939-3
Hardcover ISBN: 978-1-64438-940-9

Published by BookLocker.com, Inc., St. Petersburg, Florida.

Printed on acid-free paper.

BookLocker.com, Inc.
2019

First Edition

Library of Congress Cataloging in Publication Data
Hoerning, Michael
Sand & Water by Michael Hoerning
FICTION / Medical | FICTION / Magical Realism | FICTION / Romance / Medical
Library of Congress Control Number: 2019913211

For Martha

Acknowledgements

I give thanks to my parents, Jerry and Annette, may they have many lives. To my wife, Michelle, my daughters, Katia and Kir, and my sons, Zacarias, Nicolas and Theo, for boundless love, laughter, and chaos.

To my assistant and editor, Tamara Lichtenstein for spirited dedication to this project. To my editor, Beth Hill, for her skillful support and encouragement. To the on-the-ball publishing team at BookLocker.

To my friends and motivators, Sasha Lazard and Michael Mailer.
To Lenny Pensler, funny man, gone but not forgotten, and to his daughter, Elisa Gabrielli, the first to tell me to write this book. To Maria Benitez, *duende* incarnate.

To readers Kristin Ellingson, Laura Hays, and Christopher Hagen; to all of my readers for your insights and opinions, passion, compassion, and thoughtfulness.

To friends, old and new, partners in crime, fellow travelers: Jere Corlett, Dr. Gary Frank, Emi Grimm, Devon Jackson, Nick Klonis, Yoost Lammers, Janis Lyon, Randy Montoya, Charlie Newton, Cindy Romero, Scott Valentine, and Stephanie Yiannias. Thank you for taking this journey with me.

Part 1

Music

Marc

April 2, 1993

You can go through it crawling on your hands and knees. Or you can go through it walking tall, head high, eyes clear. One way or another you'll have to get through it.

The words marched into Marc's mind as if uttered by an invisible coach. He shook his head, struggled for balance against shifting blasts of subterranean wind. Eyes clear? His eyes were squeezed shut, prickling with sand and ash.

His hand gripped the cold, slippery rail, felt the rough texture of chipped paint. He took another step down, and another, making tentative contact with each wet stair.

The wind grew fiercer.

A metallic whine bore into his ears from the deep distance, and under the concrete and metal of the stairs, thunder rattled the illusion of solid earth. Nothing was solid. Everything vibrated and the vibrations jarred his bones, drummed his skull. Down and down into liquefied, shaking earth.

Walk tall. He tried to straighten his back, hunched under a burden that grew with each step. His knees crackled and threatened to fail, threatened to shoot him into a never ending and shattering fall.

At long last, he arrived at a dimly lit, low-ceilinged subway platform. But to his left, where the train tunnel and rails should have been, a pool of emerald water lapped a few inches below the platform's edge.

The wind gusted erratically, causing him to stumble as he attempted to clear the grit from his eyes and take in the unexpected scene. Amid the filth and neglect of the subway station, the pool looked clean and inviting, its surface barely rippling, as if the wind couldn't touch it. Marc sank to his burning knees, staring.

A woman's head and bare shoulders emerged from the water, another unexpected vision of loveliness in this grimy pit. She raised a hand, fingers curled in a little wave—welcoming or wistful, he couldn't tell.

He felt overwhelmed by a desire to follow her into the water, but his body was now frozen or turned to stone, bowed by the crushing weight upon his back. Couldn't move his feet, couldn't even open his lips to speak as he watched her disappear. Blood pounded in his ears. His hands splayed uselessly on the cold concrete.

You can go through it crawling on your hands and knees. Or you can go through it walking tall, head high, eyes clear. One way or another you'll have to get through it.

Marc Hochstaff was bargaining his way through. Staggering, not walking tall. The body he dragged through his dream was his own. This morning he was sleeping off one more big night before the kids came home—the sleep of the shitfaced.

Across his bedroom, the shadow of a hawk slipped through floor-to-ceiling glass, drifted over an expanse of hand-troweled plaster wall and the empty Stoli bottle standing upon the dresser. There, it paused above a jumble of desiccated lemon quarters before reaching Marc's thoroughly thrashed king-size bed. It hovered upon his exposed thigh and vanished over the bed's edge.

"Marc, hey, I'm leaving." A woman's voice, level, no-nonsense.

Squinting through coppery lashes, Marc swam to consciousness, losing the dream, struggling to hold on to its words. His sluggish senses pulled him in both directions, back into dream darkness to replay its message, up into daylight and someone speaking aloud. He recognized a blur of color and movement, the rustle of fabric, soft footsteps, the brisk scent of his shampoo.

A feminine hand alighted on his leg, tugged at a sheet to cover it. Touched by the sweetness of the gesture, he strove to remember her name. She moved in and out of sight gathering whatever she'd been wearing the night before, her slim figure draped in a florid caftan that once belonged to his ex. He'd never liked that thing. With any luck, it would walk out the door this time.

The bed creaked as she sat. She pulled the caftan over her head, fastened her bra, and slipped into a blouse. Wet black hair hung past her shoulders. Her head disappeared again for a moment when she bent to scoop two martini glasses from the floor; she set them on a nightstand.

He watched her fish a twist of lemon peel from one of the glasses, pop it into her mouth and chew, the fine muscles in her jaw moving in unconscious rhythm. Maybe she felt his attention. She turned, pinned him with green almond eyes, throat bobbing as she swallowed the peel.

"Hi, um… Clara. Good morning." Marc's tongue felt like a thick foreign object in his mouth, and entirely too much light flooded the room, but there was no way to turn it off—the skylight and solar windows just doing their jobs. He rubbed his eyes and pulled distractedly at the elastic holding his ponytail, loosening tangled hair. The headache didn't budge. "Shit, I'm a jerk. Sorry."

She zipped into a skirt. Sat on the bed again to slide her feet into cowboy boots. Marc's feet, sticking out from under the sheet, felt iced.

"No, you're not a jerk. You're an asshole." Her tone was warm, and so were her hands as she took one of his feet into her lap and gave it a perfunctory rub. "Look, it's not like anyone died. It's a divorce. Get over it."

Pushing his foot from her lap, she leaned in to kiss his cheek, a hint of resignation and bitter lemon scent on her breath. "Call me sometime. I've never gone home with the band, much less the drummer. You're good. Very good."

The carpet silenced her descent from the loft, but when she reached the tile-floored living room, an unholy, echoing racket struck Marc's ears. The front door opened and closed with finality. To sleep longer would be heaven, but he should have been heading out the door already, too. Between half-shuttered eyes he noticed a shadow playing over the undulating wall. A hawk, slow and purposeful, circling in the morning air outside the window.

The kitchen sink, counters, and table were filled with what looked like every dish and glass from the cupboards. Kata would show up any minute to restore a semblance of order, as she had done once a week for the past several months. Marc called the unrelenting mess her job security.

He drained the dregs of yesterday's coffee from the pot into a thermos, added a splash of milk and a handful of ice cubes, and grabbed a freckling banana from the fruit bowl.

Stooping to rescue a stray drumstick from his kit, stashed haphazardly after last night's gig at Evangelo's, he winced at the amplified pounding in his head. He trudged back to the sink to chug a glass of water, then another. The dogs barked from the back porch, but Kata would take care of them also. No time for dog play now.

Marc slid into his gray Mercedes sedan parked in the gravel outside his door and noticed a scrap of paper tucked under one of the windshield wipers—a cocktail napkin with *Clara* and a phone number penned in neat, rounded cursive. He barely glanced at it before shoving it into the console to get lost amid a raft of receipts and restaurant napkins, then he maneuvered his sunglasses over his nose with one hand, steering the car with the other. His tires raised a smoky haze of dust behind him from the unpaved road to the nearby two-lane highway.

Turquoise Trail, Highway 14, was notoriously treacherous, but Marc enjoyed its curves and picturesque views of hilly desert dotted with piñon and juniper trees, and in the fall, the chamisa blooms that sent artists scurrying for cadmium yellow paint—a brilliant, toxic pigment to depict a brilliant, toxically annoying plant. The only good chamisa was in a painting, as far as he was concerned. He'd just learned that the raging allergies he suffered every year now were due to pollen from the charming chamisa bushes and juniper trees. He cursed the damned things every chance he got.

A sneeze-powered expletive burst from his throat. After swerving back into his lane, he glanced into the rearview mirror and accelerated.

Law enforcement was as usual, which was to say, no cops in sight—the good and the bad of living in one of the poorest areas of one of the poorest states in the U.S. Easy to understand why some folks got confused, thinking New Mexico was foreign territory.

No, you don't need a passport to get here, Grandma, but you can buy New Mexico parody passports at Woolworth's on the Santa Fe Plaza—souvenirs for tourists, and potentially useful documents for New Mexicans traveling out of state. Woolworth's sold Mexican jumping beans alongside candy bars and hot chile chewing gum, apple pie, Frito pie, enormous sombreros, and howling coyote tchotchkes, together with the usual toothpaste, T-shirts, snacks, and sundries. Marc had been asked more than once, when visiting friends back in New York, what it was like to live south of the border. Old Mexico, New Mexico—he would find himself giving impromptu lessons in history and geography.

The traffic, including Marc's car, was, snagged by a string of red lights once he hit town. He sneezed and swore again, running ever later. His eyes stung with phantom sand from the unsettling morning dream—what did it mean? Crawling, walking, one way or another—a horn blared behind him. *Drive.* His tires shrieked as he turned left and immediately right.

The Santa Fe Gym sat on a hill across from the National Cemetery, and was accessed by the last signal light before the highway humped north out of Santa Fe. Marc's physical therapy clinic hummed inside, a symbiotic arrangement produced by the fortuitous fall of an icicle. The gym owner, nearly impaled by that errant spike as he exited a grocery store, had been sent to a clinic for therapy on his banged-up shoulder. A business opportunity immediately became obvious when he unfolded his first bill for therapy services—put a PT clinic in the gym, a no-brainer. Marc was happy to oblige, said goodbye to working in a traditional setting and opened Santa Fe Physical Therapy. Business boomed from the first day, bringing in more therapists, assistants, and aides. Marc was ringmaster.

He swung through the gym's double doors, pushed his sunglasses to the top of his head, nodded at the teenage boy manning the front desk, and strode the length of the bustling club toward his clinic in the rear, returning greetings as he went.

Also discreetly checking out women, pausing for no one except for his friend Dez, an attractive personal trainer—hispana, as she had corrected him when he was a newcomer, not 'Latina,' not 'Hispanic,' not 'Chicana,' and definitely not 'spic,' unless you fancied a hospital vacation with your jaw wired shut. Northern New Mexican, deep-rooted, proud and badass woman.

Dez read the hangover in his eyes and deftly intercepted him.

"Dude, too much lovin' goin' on," she said in a low, playful tone. "Take it easy."

"Always some left for you, sweetheart." He returned her smile with a wince.

"Thanks, baby, you know you'd be the one if…"

A shapely, athletic woman strolled by, exactly Dez's taste. Marc's too.

"Yeah, baby, I know. I'll shave extra close for you." His usual plea.

Dez chuckled. "I know you too well. Here." She opened her hand to offer a couple of ibuprofen capsules and a vitamin C tablet.

Marc hesitated a moment but took them, swallowing the pills with a slug of iced coffee from his thermos.

"Go on. Ruby's ticked off, so watch your own ass," Dez said, swatting him smartly on the butt.

"Her bark's worse than her bite."

"Not today."

Marc entered the clinic, greeted his secretary, a middle-aged hispana wearing a fierce expression on her pit bull face. Scarlet nails beat in 4/4 time against arms folded under her jutting bosom. A tiny figure on a cross, suspended by a chain at her throat, sank into her cleavage. Her rolling desk chair squeaked as it rocked.

"Hi, Ruby. Sorry."

She rose from the chair, which skittered behind her and rebounded from a file cabinet, to hiss, "Mrs. Alvarez is pissed. She's been waiting a half hour. I told her to start on the bike like you usually do. She won't listen to me."

"Sorry, rough night." He turned toward a plump, older woman in full makeup and an expensive tracksuit sitting behind him across the clinic waiting room.

"Mrs. Alvarez, if you don't do what Ruby says, *I'm* the one who gets my ass chewed. Please?"

Mrs. Alvarez's gaze lingered a moment on his rear end before her expression softened. She sighed, but climbed obediently onto the nearby stationary bike and began to pedal, giving him an approval-seeking smile.

"Thanks, doll!" He flashed a grin.

"How are the kids?" Ruby asked, softening as well.

He pulled the appointment book from the desktop in front of her to scan the schedule. Friday, TGIF. "Oh, you know—good. They're with their mom."

"I can tell. You're not late when they're staying with you. What happened with that nice French girl, Corinne? I liked her."

"Visa was up. She wanted a wedding."

"Think of the kids; there are worse things."

"I *am* thinking of the kids. I let her get too close to them. From now on, separation of church and state. Women and kids, church and state."

Ruby shook her head.

At that moment, a pretty brunette, her face contorted, limped into the clinic. "Could someone help me? It's my knee."

Marc steadied her. "Ruby, is treatment room three open?"

She nodded.

"Okay, let's take a look." He helped the woman hobble around the corner; they exchanged introductions, and then he popped back to address Mrs. Alvarez, who was pedaling in extreme slow motion.

"I want fifteen minutes on there, and I want you to sweat! Come on, doll baby, you know you can do it."

Mrs. Alvarez frowned and glanced at Ruby. The velour-clad knees lifted, drove down, lifted again. *Varoom. Brava, Mrs. Alvarez.*

Marc's urgent patient was sitting on the padded table when he returned. After examining her, he handed her a tissue and said, "Okay, you have, like, no ACL, and now it's kind of subluxed out of alignment. There's a manipulation that will help. Ready?"

Radiating pain, she barely nodded.

"Hold on. This is gonna hurt you more than it hurts"—he quickly manipulated the knee—"me."

"Aghhh!"

"Sorry, but that actually should help. Keep it iced for fifteen minutes, and again tonight before bed." He draped the knee with an ice pack.

She gulped, looking cautiously relieved. "Thanks. What do I owe you?"

"Dinner tonight?"

"You're kidding, right? Aren't you violating some professional code? Besides, I have a date."

"Breakfast then." He smoothed on his no-shame game face.

Before she could respond, the door flew open and Ruby beckoned him into the hallway, her tone terse. "Someone in the gym went down—maybe a heart attack."

He dashed from the clinic into the gym, where a knot of people stood around a figure lying near the free weights. A man—late forties, reasonably fit, face ashen, lip a gory mess, eyes closed.

Dez pulled Marc close. "They said he dropped like a rock—hit his face on the weight rack."

Marc knelt to check for a pulse. "Anyone call an ambulance?"

Feet shuffled, throats cleared.

"Call 9-1-1!"

"Got it!" Dez rushed away.

The gap she left in the circle of bystanders was immediately filled by another young woman, this one blond-haired and flushed. Her face had a deer-in-the-headlights look, yet her voice was calm. "I know CPR," she announced.

Marc locked eyes with her. No time to waste, but the intensity of her blue eyes... He felt himself lingering way too long, an eternal nanosecond—

"He's not breathing!"

Her words slapped Marc into action. "I'll take the head. Begin two-man CPR."

"Ready? Go," said the woman, already kneeling at the stricken man's side. She started rhythmic compressions of his chest while Marc gave mouth-to-mouth resuscitation without regard for the blood.

"Switch!" she ordered after a couple of minutes.

"No switch," Marc said. "Blood."

"I don't care about the blood. Switch!"

The victim began to breathe on his own before Marc could argue further, and the paramedics arrived a moment later. Marc regained his feet, gave a hand to his CPR partner, and backed out of the way as the crew took over. He felt the woman's appraising gaze on him and attempted a modest smile.

Instead of smiling back, she looked alarmed and mimed wiping her mouth. "Um."

Marc copied her movement and grimaced, his fingers sticky, his face heavily smeared by the stranger's blood. "First time ever... Think I'm gonna be sick. Pardon me."

He hoped to make it to the men's locker room before spewing. Toilet or sink? Didn't matter—banana, coffee, blood—all churning. When the heaving stopped, he washed his face in cold water until his normal color returned. He rinsed his mouth, cupping his hands repeatedly under the faucet, and patted his face dry. He made himself spend quality time with the drinking fountain, rehydrating.

MC Hammer's "U Can't Touch This" thumped from the adjacent aerobics class when he left the locker room. He could hear Armando Gallegos, the charismatic instructor, singing along as he led a group that was probably loaded with beautiful women, as usual. Was Armando's hangover the same as, better, or worse than his own? While Marc had played hard onstage at Evangelo's, he'd seen Armando playing hard at the bar. Marc gingerly shook his head. Mrs. Alvarez would be waiting to feel his healing hands on her neck and lower back.

It proved a hectic day without counting the mouth-to-mouth resuscitation: two new evals, an elite athlete training for competition, four princesses—patients of any gender needing an extra measure of personal attention—and three unscheduled drop-ins. Marc was looking forward to getting off his feet later that evening, when Armando hurried in, anxious and excited, his black hair, dark eyes, and white teeth all glittering.

"Man, I need a really big favor."

Marc raised an eyebrow. "Don't have much cash on me."

"Twins!" Armando said in an exaggerated, pleading tone.

"Twins?"

"Two new girls in town. Twins. I was thinking threesome, but they say four for dinner."

Marc felt a twinge of nostalgia. Ten years older than Armando, he'd mentored the kid in developing a professional attitude, but at this moment, Armando represented carefree, youthful energy—something Marc felt in short supply of tonight. "I'm actually bushed."

"Twiiins, Marc."

"I got my kiddos back tomorrow, can't do a late one tonight but— *Okaaay*, El Farol. Seven o'clock."

Armando smacked a triumphant high five. "Bro, don't be late. You won't be sorry!"

"Hope not," Marc said, his palm stinging as Armando flew out the door.

He said a grateful thanks to Ruby, who'd already left for the day, as he poured a cup of lukewarm coffee from the pot she'd made midafternoon. Pulled a gym bag with a change of clothes from one of the desk drawers. Time to rev up with a stint on the stationary bike, do a couple of sets on the bench press, shower and steam, maybe sauna.

Twins, that would be a first. He ran a hand through his hair. Hangover? What hangover? Ancient history. The night was young.

The Lantern

Canyon Road, Santa Fe's tourist dream of shops and galleries, shared its charms with locals as well as visitors. During the summer, vivid colors spilled from flowerboxes and from the paint boxes of plein-air artists memorializing its scenes. On Christmas Eve, twinkle lights, bonfires, and *farolitos* turned the narrow street into a homespun, miniature Great White Way, as jammed as New Year's Eve at Times Square.

El Farol perched just above the heart of Canyon Road's gallery district. True to its name, which meant *the lantern*, it was an iconic watering hole drawing human moths to its flame. Tables on its street-side porch overlooked Canyon Road's descent from the watershed, a view of streaming turquoise and silver, boots and buckles, broomstick skirts with concha belts and western shirts with bolo ties, hefty cameras, thick wallets. Tourist greenbacks flowed up and down the road, chasing fine art, fine dining, and fine entertainment. Good times.

The bar was thronged when Marc arrived, blues rocking the PA system. He found Armando sitting at a table for four with a half-empty green Dos Equis bottle, two full shots of tequila, and little dishes of tapas: squid in bright red sauce, olives, cheese slices, bread. Armando was happily munching, a scarlet dribble on his chin. Marc dropped into a chair across from him and tossed back one of the shots.

"Hey, heard about your mouth to mouth today," Armando said, offering a tapas plate.

Marc took one look at the heap of squid tentacles—which he normally would have relished—and pushed it away.

"Don't remind me. I threw up after. Mouth to mouth is bullshit—stops fearful people from doing CPR. It's about the heart, anyway. Always the heart."

Armando raised his glass, well into a cheerful mood already. "I'm hoping for a little mouth to mouth myself tonight. These girls are hot!"

He rubbed his chin, checked his watch. "Late. They'd better make it."
He looked up again, scanning the place, then grinned broadly and
stood with a wave.

Marc turned to see two women approaching the table. He
recognized them both. What the—

The women abruptly halted, clearly recognizing him as well,
causing a waitress behind them to slam on her brakes. The bottles and
glasses on her laden tray wobbled precariously.

"*These* are the twins?"

"Fraternal, bro. Chardonnay and Cabernet. Cheers!" Armando's
eyes unabashedly devoured the two women, a blonde and a brunette,
now standing just a few feet from the table.

With a single voice, both women and Marc targeted Armando.
"*Did you know?*"

"What?" Armando said, smiling cluelessly.

"That you fixed me up with the smartass who *propositioned me* on
his treatment table?" said the dark-haired twin, sweeping dagger eyes
from Armando to Marc.

"*This* is the physical therapist?" the blonde asked. "I thought you
were a muscle head who happened to know CPR. You're the cheesy
player that hit on my sister?"

Before he could say *ouch*, the sister chimed in, acid-toned.
"Wait— This is the *hero* who did CPR with you?"

Marc offered a hand to his CPR partner, hoping she'd take it again.
"Didn't catch your name—the mouth-to-mouth thing. Marc Hochstaff,
physical therapist. Hero? Well, thanks, but that's a little over the top.
Can we start over?" He gave her what he hoped was a winning smile.

"Marina White," she said evenly, her handshake brief and firm.

He turned to her twin. "Nicole, right? So, how's the knee now?
Better?"

"Not gonna get down on the dance floor tonight but yeah, it's
actually better. Thanks, Muscle Head." She looked slightly amused. "I
could use a drink."

The waitress had delivered her cargo to an adjacent table. She
efficiently took their orders for beer, shots and more tapas.

"Glad you made it," Armando said, offering Marina a plate of
squid.

She skewered a gnarly tentacle with a toothpick and chewed with enthusiasm before reaching for a hunk of bread. "Thanks. I made Nicole take me to the hospital to check on the man with the heart attack; that's why we're late. They said you"—she turned to Marc—"the two of us, made a big difference."

"CPR's something you want to know *how* to do but never *have* to do. Glad he made it."

"We did well together." She lifted the bottle placed in front of her by the waitress, and took a swig.

Armando and Nicole tossed back shots and ordered another round before the waitress finished serving. The driving rock music on the PA system quieted. Lights dimmed except onstage, where spotlights fell on two long-haired men, a guitarist and a vocalist seated on stools. The guitarist began a purposeful strum on a flamenco guitar while the vocalist, a mountain of a man, launched into a passionate flamenco *cante*, face upturned as if he were lost in worship.

Marc moved his chair closer to Marina's to get a better view of the stage. He sensed her body tense in anticipation.

Offstage, behind a baby grand piano, a young female dancer in a flowing, white dress approached, clapping in rhythm. With deliberate steps she rounded the piano, striding up into her own spotlight upon the stage, where she struck a pose and held it, tapping a single foot slowly, seductively, capturing the crowd's attention. She moved with sustained self-assurance as her dance built in intensity. Suddenly she froze.

Another dancer emerged from the shadows, her figure slim and muscular in a crimson dress, her face mature, the expression severe, even menacing. She mirrored the young dancer's pose. Both remained still for a long moment before initiating a duet, by turns dueling and collaborating. The vocalist clapped along, his voice soaring, and other voices in the darkness of the audience made *jaleo*, calls of encouragement and approval.

In a shocking image of triumph, the older dancer in red leapt to the piano top, pummeling its protected surface with a display of percussive footwork. Her arresting gaze turned from the young dancer to look out into the audience.

Marc caught his breath as if smacked in the chest; he glanced at Marina, who seemed struck by the same blow, and back to the dancer, whose lips pulled into almost a smile. Silence swelled in the room and then broke, as cries of *brava* erupted.

Marc raised his bottle in a toast to the performers, who bowed solemnly. Marina tapped her bottle against his, and each took a swallow.

"I need a smoke!" Marc joked, stirred by a mixture of unease and afterglow. He wasn't even a smoker.

Marina's air was dreamy, rapt. "I've never seen flamenco before," she said, her words soft with wonder.

"I have, but not like this. This was..."

"*Duende*," Armando said.

"What's that?" Marina asked.

"The soul of flamenco. *Duende.* Blood... darkness... spirit... passion."

Marc gaped at his friend.

"Dude, that girl in white—she's my cousin," Armando explained nonchalantly. "She's been dancing since she could walk. Everyone in my family sings or dances."

The PA started up again, shifting the mood with lively seventies rock.

Nicole leaned in toward Marc, her voice raised over the music. "You aren't from here originally, are you? New York?"

"Yeah," he said, returning to earth like a skydiver. "Been here five years. My wife—ex-wife—was Caribbean. She wanted to live in the most Spanish part of the country. She thought New Mexico would feel more like home to her; guess it did for a while. We went from a one-bedroom on Fifty-First Street to Rome, Italy, for a couple of years—great city, Rome—then to fifteen acres complete with a stable, snakes and coyotes. Quiet country life."

"Horses?" Marina asked.

"Chickens and dogs, no horses."

"A stable with no horses? Shame..."

"You like to ride?" Armando asked with a suggestive tone.

"I love it, and miss it. I had a horse for twelve years."

"She left a wall full of ribbons back home. You should see her jump," Nicole said.

"Marc's got that stable..." said Armando brightly.

"And *kids*," Marc interjected. "Chelsea and Zane, seven and four. I have, like, a double life," he explained. "Two weeks with the kids, two weeks without 'em. Kinda Jekyll and Hyde."

"Who am I talking to now?" Nicole asked, leaning closer, with a coquettish grin.

He chuckled. "So, where's home?"

"Chatham, Mass," the sisters replied together.

"Cape Cod, right? You hang out with the Kennedys?"

"Just the dead ones!" Nicole rolled her eyes. "Dead Kennedys concert at the Channel, Boston. Marina dragged me. She's into the punk scene."

"*Was* into it," her sister corrected.

"Up to maybe two weeks ago, when we left," Nicole argued.

Marc interrupted to say, "Yeah, the Channel? I saw Alice in Chains there over Thanksgiving. Great venue." He was gearing up to gab music, but the beat in the club shifted, livelier and louder, and Marina tugged him into the dancing crowd.

The rhythms of the night, not to mention the entrancing movements of his partner, energized him. Grunge, alternative rock, R & B. When a romantic ballad slowed things down, sorting dancers into swaying, entwined couples, he sought her eyes for permission and took a step closer.

"I don't like to meet men in bars anymore," she said, hugging her elbows.

He read her wariness, gave her space. "I get it. But you and I," he pointed toward her collarbone, and touched his own, "we met on the gym floor, saving a man's life. Now we're on a dance floor. Let's keep dancing."

He waited for her nod, waited for her to step toward him, before gently pulling her close, guiding her body with his hand at the small of her back. Her hand rested lightly on his shoulder. By the end of the song, her fingers were making themselves at home upon that shoulder and her lips hovered near his neck. The room was warm.

"You want to step outside, get some air?" he asked as an upbeat song kicked off.

She allowed him to lead her to the cantina's weathered porch. High desert evening had drained the heat from the day. Somewhere up the canyon, the shrill cry of a coyote was answered by another and another. Marina looked startled.

"What was that?"

"Just coyotes," Marc said. "You worried?"

She looked worried. "No…" She moved closer, leaning on the porch railing.

"You want another beer?" he offered.

"No, thanks, I've had enough." And then matter-of-factly, she explained, "I'm actually the heavy drinker in the family—or I used to be. Used to have green hair too." She gave a short laugh. "Needed a change—a bunch of changes."

"So, you're a rare natural green-head, but you decided that blondes have more fun? That's one change. That's huge!" He studied her hair. "Not seeing any green. Good job on the roots, girl."

She laughed again, batting his fingers away from her scalp. "Stop. This is my real color."

"Okay, if you say so." Watching her steam a little was fun. "You have great teeth."

"My dad's a dentist. Are you checking me out like a horse? Hooves next?"

"Please, let's see those hooves."

"Not on a first date," she mock-chided. "Too ticklish."

"Really? You can tickle mine till the cows come home. Don't hate me 'cause I'm not ticklish."

"That's so unfair."

"I know. Life's unfair. I'll keep your ticklish feet in mind if you ever show up in my clinic with plantar fasciitis. I like to avoid getting kicked in the schnoz."

"So why did you become a physical therapist?" Her eyes searched his with unexpected intensity. "How did you know that's what you wanted to do?"

Why does anyone do what they do? He disliked cynicism, so he gave her honesty. "I was headed to med school to be an orthopedic surgeon, but didn't want to kill anybody."

"*What?*"

"An orthopedic surgeon asked me if I was prepared to kill someone. He wasn't kidding, and neither am I. He said, 'Sooner or later you'll make a mistake.' I didn't like those odds, so I went into physical therapy. I knew I wanted to help people. I get to do that, and avoid killing them, at least in a therapeutic setting.

"The other person who influenced me was my cousin Leo. He was born with muscular dystrophy and died when he was only twenty-two. Leo was cool. My buddies and I would take him to concerts and shows. Leo in his wheelchair would get a pity pass, which meant we'd all get to skip ahead on line, get good seats and the girls." He chuckled at the expression on Marina's face.

"I know, it sounds terrible," he agreed. "We *were* terrible. But we had great times together, all of us. Friends told me after he died how much it had meant to them, hanging out with him." Marc's throat tightened unexpectedly.

"I was with him when he was dying," he continued. "The two of us alone, his eyes wide open, the first time I'd ever seen him really afraid, which is saying something with all the shit we used to get into. He couldn't speak anymore by then—used blinks to communicate. I told him he got stuck with a bad body this time around and the next one would be much better, he would be floating… I told him 'no fear,' and his face relaxed."

"You told him he would get another body?"

"I've believed in aliens, other lives, and ghosts since I was a little kid—big imagination, biggest TV in the neighborhood—but *no fear*? I didn't know what the hell I was talking about. He trusted me, that's all. My aunt, his mom, tore me a new one when I told her about that conversation afterwards. She had fear."

He blinked hard, cleared his throat. "Leo got stuck with a serious handicap that eventually killed him. He wasn't a saint, a figure on a pedestal. His condition was a thing he had; it didn't define him. Like you aren't defined by your ticklish toes."

Marina was staring at him, speechless.

"Okay, enough about me and my cousin and his wheelchair—see how I used him again, to get a front row seat with you? Thanks, Leo." Marc turned his eyes up theatrically, then looked back to Marina. "Meanwhile, what about these changes you're making? Kind of weird to be a horsewoman in the East and come west to give it up, don't you think? What brought you to Santa Fe?"

"A dream. Probably sounds silly, but it was so real, and it helped me decide to come here. I'll ride again, but it'll be different. I learned that from the dream." She glanced up the dark road as another chorus of coyote howls rose yip, yip, yipping to the stars, an eerie mix of laughter and lamentation.

"Tell me about it."

"How much time do you have?"

"As much as you got."

"Don't worry—it's short." She smiled, but then grew serious. "Nicole's on vacation. I'm on the rest of my life."

Dyeing Ends

Two Weeks Earlier
Chatham, Massachusetts

Marina tipped her head under the pouring water. Green dye trickled from her wet hair, bright as a plastic shamrock, a ballsier tint than the weak green of the beer she had served all day. Lime lines ran down her neck and over fingerprint bruises on her shoulder, fanned across the slick territory of her back and hips, diverged to trace her legs, and rejoined to swirl into the shower drain.

When she stepped from the tub at last, turbaned in a towel, diluted dye dribbled like spilled mouthwash onto the white bath rug.

"Shit!" She grabbed a washcloth to blot the blooming spots. No need to give Nicole another reason to regret the invitation to stay at her place. It wouldn't be for long. Couldn't be for long.

She tiptoed into the narrow hall to the small, dark guest room illuminated only by the glowing face of the clock radio, one of the few possessions she'd brought with her from her own apartment—or, rather, her ex-apartment. The pad she'd shared with Eric was his alone now, though for safety's sake she'd left him a note assuring him that her absence was temporary. *A few days to help Sis, on crutches with a sprained ankle. Back soon.* She was a poor liar, however, and she knew that Eric knew. The clock was ticking.

Eric was out partying hard with his biker pals for the night, but he would come looking for her as soon as today's score and cash ran out. Her job at the pub was all about cash; St. Patty's Day had put a nice green stash in her pocket. She made sure to leave half of it with the note, an insurance policy to keep his party going, keep him out of her hair.

It was already four a.m. Nicole would be waking in a couple of hours to get ready for work in their father's dental office. Marina turned the clock to the wall, tired, but too wired to sleep. That line she'd done at midnight in the pub bathroom had to be the last one.

Restless sleep morphed straight to dreams. Or to something else, somewhere else. She was herself, but different. No gaudy dye colored the blond hair hanging loose down her back, and she wore jeans, cowboy boots and a western shirt with pearled buttons—nothing like the breeches and jacket she used to wear for show jumping before Eric moved into her life. And she was with a horse, but not a sleek, dark creature with meticulously braided mane and English saddle. No, this fellow was white and spotted, wild and proud as he stood alone in a western landscape of red rock and soft sage, violet and deep blue mountains in the distance. She walked up to the creature, stroked its face.

"Hi, boy, I've been looking for you." The horse dipped its nose in greeting, then allowed her to mount its bare back in an effortless move, her fingers in its mane for a handhold. It began to trot and then canter over the sandy plain. A man in a cowboy hat stood waving at her in the distance, his face shadowed, but she knew he was smiling. The horse's muscular surge felt like her own. *Run, boy.* They ran.

She awoke with a start, disappointed to have missed what happened next in the dream. She closed her eyes to seek the horse, the cowboy, and the exhilarating run, but the smell of coffee made slipping back into the dream impossible. It also reminded her of what she wanted to tell Nicole.

She swung her legs over the side of the bed and went to the bathroom, where she flossed and brushed her teeth, aggressively professional. Most of the green was gone from her hair; a few more washings should do it. She shrugged into a bathrobe and strolled to the kitchen, hairbrush in hand.

Nicole sat at the table, a cup of steaming coffee in front of her, and greeted Marina with a smile.

"Good morning, sunshine. Feeling any better?"

"Thanks for letting me stay," Marina said, running the brush through her hair. She winced as it glanced over a tender spot. "He's never laying a hand on me again."

"Or your sister will beat the crap out of him. What are you going to do?"

"It's over. He's history. I can't take it anymore. The blow, the fucking lifestyle, they're eating me alive. I'm sick of making excuses for myself. I want to do something big." Her voice wobbled, damn it. Nicole had been born just minutes before her, but those minutes counted for a lot. Nicole was the big sister, the voice of authority.

"Big?" Nicole's gaze shifted from her face to her hair. "Did you dye—"

"Temporary this time. It'll wash out."

Nicole looked relieved. "Sit. Have coffee with me."

Marina shook her head. "I'm kinda jittery already—not what you think. Well, yeah, but not anymore. I promise." She took a calming breath. "I'm done here. I want… maybe Colorado… New Mexico. Santa Fe." The name floated like a ribbon of cloud across the blue sky in her mind's eye. "Santa Fe seems perfect for me. I have to get out of here." Her hands fluttered to the back of an empty chair, gripped the smooth curve of oak as if it were a steering wheel.

"Whatever we have to do, we'll do. You know I'm here for you. I'll work on getting Dad to let me go with you, to help you get settled, okay?"

Marina threw her arms around her sister in a tight embrace. "I love you. I really do."

"I know." Nicole beamed. "Don't let Dad see your hair. Put it up in a scarf or something."

Marina flinched, then sputtered. "I've been a full-fledged adult— *we've* been—for over ten years! I can do what I want with my hair—"

"Hon, if you want to be treated like an adult, time to start acting like one. It's not about green dye. It's about taking responsibility for your life. Turning over a new leaf. That is exactly what you are going to do. And that's what I'm going to tell him this trip is about. You *have* to live up to the billing I'm giving you, so don't let me down. I'm the one that'll be stuck working for a grumpy old dentist. *Please* make him smile."

"Did I say I love you? You're the best sister in the world."

Marina's white Isuzu Trooper stood packed with suitcases and a large cooler in the driveway below Nicole's attic apartment. The break from Eric had gone better than expected, chiefly because his Harley had been absent when they went to gather her belongings. No need for Nicole to beat the crap out of him, or for Marina to repeat what she had told him over the phone, to which he had responded with slurred and cursing disbelief. They took no furnishings, no bearers of bad memories, only her favorite clothing and basic necessities. Their movements were swift, their ears alert for the roar of his return.

"I told Mom and Dad we'll call every night from the road to let them know where we are, and that we're okay," Nicole said. "Dinner together last night, all of us, like old times—it meant a lot to them. They worry about you so much, even if they don't show it."

"I actually had a good time," Marina said. "Dad didn't even mention my hair."

"I gave him advance warning and told him to forget about superficial stuff like that. Change that matters is on the inside, even if we can't see it. You're making a great change—I can feel it." Nicole glanced at her wristwatch. "Come on; we have to say goodbye to the beach. I'll drive."

As they passed through the picturesque seaside town, their home since infancy, Marina considered whether she ought to be feeling regrets about leaving, or any incipient homesickness. The image of the waving cowboy filled her mind; this time she could see his smile. No, no regrets. A wave of childlike pleasure rose in her chest, and a song twanged from her lips, soaring out the open window.

"I'm gonna get me a horse and ride him wherever I want. I'm gonna marry me a cowboy and ride him whenever I want!"

"Really?" Nicole gave a transparent pretense of shock.

"Really." Marina giggled. "I am so out of here. Ain't gonna do Harleys anymore. No more machos, no more drugs, no more crazies, no more thugs. Clean... Life's going to be clean. Healthy."

Nicole pulled the car to a stop before a stretch of sand and water unpopulated by anyone but a handful of gulls. A stream of pewter-edged clouds rolled fast and low over the choppy waves. The sisters stepped from the car, their hair whipped by humid gusts of wind. Three gulls landed together near their feet.

"Ugh, they're so pesky," Nicole said, scurrying back. "Shoo!"

The gulls ignored her.

"Caw, caw!" Marina called.

The birds eyed her and edged closer.

Nicole grimaced. "For twins, we certainly are different. Say goodbye to your obnoxious friends."

"Until we meet again," Marina said, nodding at the gulls. They flapped their broad wings and sailed away. She turned back to the car. "I'll drive now."

Truck-stop postcards flew eastward over the following several days as they took a meandering route west, initially sticking to the major highways for efficiency's sake. Nicole didn't want to miss more days of work than necessary, but curiosity, plus the large atlas their parents had given them and Marina's edginess about Eric's potential pursuit, drove them off the beaten track and onto the blue roads. They stopped in Niles, Illinois, to see a half-size replica of the Leaning Tower of Pisa and to eat pizza; Marina insisted they order and converse in exaggerated Italian accents.

Later, in a disorienting moment of déjà vu, they came upon a sign for the village of Chatham, an Illinois version of their hometown on the Mother Road, old Route 66.

In Missouri and Oklahoma, the route was dotted with ghost towns: Albatross, Rescue, Plew, Fallis, Foss and Canute, and possibly ghosts, if stories about the Hornet Spook Light could be believed. They sought out the Spook Light, a mysterious ball of light reputed to travel along a dirt road near Quapaw known as the Devil's Promenade. Marina was convinced they would have seen it had they stayed past midnight, but after a couple of hours sitting in the deserted lane, Nicole ruled that they return to Joplin to find a room for the rest of the night. Another Oklahoma detour took them to Dead Women Crossing, a reputedly haunted site of a turn-of-the-century unsolved murder.

After further stops at the petrified wood gas station in Decatur, Texas, the down-on-its-luck town of Shamrock, also in Texas, and the ghost town of Cuervo, New Mexico, they arrived in Albuquerque and turned north for Santa Fe.

The ascent of La Bajada at dusk was followed by glorious confirmation of the city's existence, its twinkling presence cupped by the Sangre de Cristo Mountains, when the highway curved into a leisurely descent toward the lights. Marina knew she would never forget that first sight. She rolled down her window to take a deep breath of dry, desert air.

They ended up on the main commercial drag, Cerrillos Road, similar to franchise-lined strips in other towns across the country but with notable exceptions: funky adobe-style motels and restaurants; neon images of cowboys and horses, cactus and chile peppers; and the Yucca Drive-In movie theater. The back of its big screen, visible from the road, was bizarrely decorated with what looked like the graphic silhouette of an enormous erect phallus and testicles. That one should have been on a list of Route 66 tourist attractions.

The Silver Saddle Motel, picturesque on the outside, comfortably musty on the inside, was the endpoint of the long drive. Exhausted and exhilarated, they dropped onto the beds, kicked off their shoes, and considered what to do about dinner.

"So, that's how I learned that the official New Mexico state question is '*Red or green?*'" Marina told Marc, hugging herself as the night grew chilly on Canyon Road. "My first taste of chile at Tomasita's."

"Which did you choose?" he asked.

"Christmas. Both!"

"I'm more of a green guy, myself."

"The state bird is the roadrunner, state flower is the yucca," she continued. "We had a very informative waitress. That reminds me, speaking of yucca—what is *up* with the Yucca Drive-In?"

"You mean the biggest penis west of the Mississippi?"

She laughed. "Talk about an erection. And it's *blue!* Who had the balls to do that, to think people would believe it represents a yucca plant? I went back and looked at it in the daytime. The little white 'flowers' in its head? Fireworks! Oh my God, it's an *orgasm!*"

Marc was delighted by her frankness. "Yeah, I'd like to meet the guy—or gal—who designed it," he said. "Whoever it was had *huevos*. It probably dwarfs the cathedral downtown. Hey, let's go back inside and warm up. Your sister must be wondering what I've done with you—hope she's getting on all right with Armando. He can be a handful. Harmless. Well, kinda."

"Nicole's great at taking care of herself; she's always been the strong one. I'm going to miss her when she goes home."

"Yeah, change, even good change, can be hard. But I think you're wrong about who's the strong one. Look what you've done already, climbing into a new saddle, not falling back into the old one."

He wrapped her in a light bear hug. The arms hugging him back were trim and spirited. She pulled away slightly, gave him a shy little smile.

"No more mouth to mouth today," he said, holding a finger to his lips. "I met my quota already."

She giggled. "They won't believe it."

"Let them think what they want. The truth will be our secret."

"What exactly is the truth?"

"Exactly." He led her back to the table, where shots of tequila had transformed Nicole's and Armando's faces into brightly shining *faroles*.

"Got a morning class to teach, don't you?" Marc reminded Armando.

Armando's bleary smile didn't budge. "Yeah, man, eight. Don't worry, I'll be there."

"I'm driving you home," Marc said. "I'll pick you up at seven to get your car."

Armando began to protest, but Marc, bigger and taller by far, and several shots behind him, made clear the plan wasn't up for debate.

"Marina, you're the designated driver tonight too," he added. "Right, Nicole?"

Nicole considered for a moment. "Yes, she is." She opened her purse and dug out the keys.

"Ice that knee tonight, doll. G'night, ladies, be safe," Marc said, guiding Armando to the door. He shot Marina a wink and walked out into the night.

"Mouth to mouth…" Armando mumbled. "You get any? Did I get any?"

"A gentleman doesn't tell," Marc replied.

"Right, right… Thanks, bro. Thanks for everything." Armando tripped.

Marc knew he'd not only be driving Armando; he'd be hauling him to bed and setting his alarm clock. He hoped there was orange juice in Armando's fridge—the guy was going to need it in the morning.

By the time he'd taken care of Armando and arrived home himself, it was late indeed. But the fatigue he felt was a surprising pleasure, different from the usual.

It had been a lovely evening, with the talking and dancing and the show. The date had been corny and old-fashioned—not even a goodnight kiss. Right off the bat she'd called him a cheesy player, and *that* had been the game changer. Had he bet on himself going into this date, he would have lost. Turned out, he wasn't a player after all.

He was reminded of being seven years old and playing the board game Trouble with his first love, vivacious Viviana. She would blow bubble gum bubbles and pop them while she banged the plastic bubble on the game board—pop goes the Pop-O-Matic—making the die jump around inside and enthusiastically sending his playing piece back to start over. Back to the beginning…

Nope, player wasn't the right word. He was play*ful*. *Play*ful. He'd forgotten how good *playing* felt.

Stretched out in bed, relaxing into sleep, he startled himself with his next thought. Damn, he didn't get her phone number. She probably didn't even have a phone yet. *Damn.*

Chelsea and Zane

Marc was putting the finishing touches on a gourmet Italian meal the following night when high-pitched voices rose outside. His heart leaped. The kids were back, finally. His sun, his moon, his gravity. An hour and a half late and no phone call from their mom, Rosana. He had grown to expect this lack of consideration from his former wife, but still—

"Dad!"

They ran into the kitchen like rambunctious puppies, laughing, hugging, kissing, both heads covered in mops of curly hair.

"Chels! Z-boy! Missed you guys. Love you!" He washed and dried his hands.

"How are you, Daddy? Whatcha been up to?" Chelsea asked.

"Worked a lot, Bible studies, soup kitchen." He rapped a large wooden spoon inside the lip of a pot on the stove, shook off a bean, and laid the spoon on the tiled counter. "How's your mom?"

"Late, we know… She's okay, a little stressed," Chelsea reported.

It was easy to forget that Chelsea was only seven years old; she was precocious, motherly, and wise beyond her years. *Wicked smart*, Kata, a Mainer, called her. A good big sister to Zane, whose boy energy and wide brown eyes made him a chick magnet. Luckily, Chelsea looked out for him and kept him in line. She was already helping him wash his hands for dinner at the kitchen sink, making sure he used soap.

From atop a turquoise stool, Zane called out to Marc.

"Any girlfriends, Daddy?"

"Kind of, but it's none of your business."

"How many?" Zane persisted.

"Seventeen."

"Years old?" Chelsea asked.

"Watch it," Marc warned.

"Wow, Dad, we haven't been gone that long," said Chelsea. "You must be exhausted. Really, are you dating?" She helped Zane to dry his hands.

Marc dipped the spoon back into the pot and lifted it to her mouth. "Here and there. Taste," he said, aiming to shut her up. "Blow on it first—it's hot."

She blew, then sampled. "Needs green chile. And, Daddy? I have a new rule for you. Your girlfriend—or girlfriends, whoever they are—they have to respect our hair." She brushed a curl from her brow. It fell right back into her eyes.

"Respect your hair? Like this?" He bowed formally.

"I mean like, leave it alone! That what's-her-name you went out with—Darlene—she wanted to *straighten* my hair. As *if!*"

"As *if*—okay—respect your hair." He reached for a notepad by the telephone on the wall, scribbled a note.

"And she shouldn't laugh like a hyena," Chelsea continued. "Or treat us like babies." She shifted into Texas-accented baby talk. "*Lookie what I brought fer yewww, sugar, this sweet little tea set.* What a *phony*, pretending she liked us just so you would like her."

"Ginger?" Marc asked, fuzzily recalling Ginger's attributes.

Chelsea's brows scrunched as she nodded vehemently. "Fake eyelashes, fake smile, and fake—"

"I get the picture," he interrupted, pencil scratching on paper. "Must be real."

"And pretty and nice and not call me a stinky little boy!" Zane chimed in.

"Who did that? That wasn't very nice," Marc said.

"You know, the one that got mad when the dogs slobbered on her," Chelsea said. "And, Zane, to be fair, you *were* stinky that day. The dogs got skunked, and you rolled around with them."

"Pretty and nice and not call you stinky. Got a list going here. Guys, I'm not in the market for Mary Poppins. But if you have anything you want to add, I'm *list*-ening."

"Why don't you let us meet anyone anymore?" Zane asked.

Marc made a smart-ass face in answer, and turned to Chelsea. "As for you, my budding food critic, Little Grandma would roll over in her *grave* if she heard you talk that way about her Italian Wedding Soup. *Chile?* Sacrilege!"

"But everything tastes better with green chile," Chelsea insisted, a true New Mexican as well as an Italian.

Marc filled three bowls, set them on the table and opened the fridge as the kids seated themselves. "All right, monkeys, *mangia!*"

"Do you like being not married to Mom?"

Chelsea's question stopped him cold, a finger probing a still-open wound. He exhaled, taking the time to collect himself. He took a jug of juice from the fridge and filled two cups. "Well... it was pretty crummy there toward the end. As much as I can't live with your mother anymore, it feels like I failed. I don't like to fail."

"I'd still like to meet your girlfriend," Zane insisted, swinging his legs, jarring the table.

"You mean girlfriends." Marc gave him a high-five as Chelsea rolled her eyes. They joined hands, bowing heads to say grace. "Zane, you do the honors."

"Rub a dub, dub, here comes the grub."

"Yay, God!" was the group chorus. They thrust their joined hands into the air.

Marc opened his eyes the next Monday morning to find his son perched like a cat upon his chest.

"Daddy, please, please, please, can I bring Hamlet home with me today? Ryan got to take him twice already. I want it to be my turn."

"If Hamlet is a pig, the answer is no."

"A *guinea* pig, Daddy."

"He's Italian?"

"Silly! The class pet! I want to take care of him tonight."

"Okay, get off and let me think a moment." Marc yawned as he sat up in bed, before glancing at the clock. Chelsea needed to be delivered to school and Zane to preschool, both accompanied by knapsacks, sweaters, water bottles, lunches, snacks, homework—

"Dad! I need you to sign my permission slip!" Now Chelsea was on the bed next to Zane. "We have a field trip and Mom forgot to sign it and"—her words tumbled out in an anxious rush— "I can't go if you don't sign and I really, really want to go, please, Daddy." She shoved a crumpled piece of paper at him. "It's the zoo! Today!"

Met and Jet, the family mutts, added their panting, drooling, and hair-shedding bodies to the bed. The dogs were rowdy and playful, and it didn't matter which you called—they both came.

"You *live* in a zoo; you really need a permission slip? Take it down to the kitchen table before these mutts munch it—your teacher wouldn't believe that story. I'll meet you there in a sec. Get dressed. Did your mom pack clean clothes?"

"Sort of," Chelsea said. "Some clean, some not clean. I spilled grape juice on my shirt yesterday, but there wasn't time to wash it."

"Put the dirty stuff in the hamper. Help Zane with his."

Marc pulled himself together and headed downstairs after the kids.

"There's no Froot Loops, Dad! I need Froot Loops!" Chelsea's wail sounded tragic.

"There are six kinds of cereal in the cupboard."

"But not Froot Loops! I need them, and Mom wouldn't buy them."

"I won't either; that's something we agree on. Breakfast has to be more than colored sugar blobs."

"But, Daddy—"

"No buts. Here, this one's full of nuts. Like this house," he added, pulling a cereal box from the cupboard.

"No, it's not. Don't you read the ingredients?"

"Honey Nut Cheerios," Marc said, pouring some into a bowl.

"It doesn't have any nuts," Chelsea maintained. "We're studying cereals in class. That's why I have to bring Froot Loops. Graciela is bringing Honey Nut Cheerios."

Marc picked up the box and examined the ingredient list. She was right—no nuts. Who knew?

"Hey," he said, grabbing a fork and striking a wild-eyed pose. "What am I?" He reared back, stabbed the box several times with maniacal energy. Cereal burst from the package to scatter around the kitchen, a treat for Met and Jet. "Psycho serial *cereal* killer! Don't tell your mom I let you watch *Psycho*, okay?"

"Okay, Daddy. Hey, Daddy, what am I?" Now Chelsea struck a pose, arms out. She swung an arm across her body, tapping a fist to the inside of her elbow, then swung wide again, finishing by turning sideways, one arm up, the other bent.

"A little teapot!" Marc said, suppressing a smile, knowing what she was up to.

"No, Daddy, Jets! Jets, Jets, Jets! See, look, I'll do it again with the chant."

Not to be outdone, Zane sang out, "Meet the Mets, greet the Mets—what am I?"

"Your father's son, a Mets fan." Marc ruffled Zane's uncombed hair.

"Daddy, can I bring the psycho cereal killer box?" Chelsea asked, waving the ravaged box.

"Let's not test your teacher's tolerance on this one. She probably already thinks I'm a nut case. Here, your permission slip is signed; I'm putting it in your lunchbox. Bring me back a souvenir. How about a hippo?"

"Too dry for a hippo. A llama! *Could* we get a llama? Sage's family has *three* llamas."

"Well, we'll have to visit Sage when you want to hang out with llamas, then. Plenty of dog drool around here—let's not add llama spit."

"I wish I could go to the zoo," Zane piped up. "Can't I go with Chelsea?"

"When you go to big-kid school, you'll get to have field trips too. Meanwhile, we *could* swing a visit to a special little zoo closer to home, the petting zoo in Cerrillos. Remember the donkey, the turkeys?"

"Yes!"

"Okay, next weekend, I promise."

He watched the children gobble their breakfasts. *What am I?* The question was easy to answer today; he was back in Daddy mode. His heart felt light, full, and naturally sweetened.

Cinco de Mayo

Healthcare in America meant bureaucracy and paperwork, loads of it. Marc was examining charts at Ruby's desk at the end of the day, when a friendly voice caught his attention.

"Hi, hero."

Marina stood before him, her smile mischievous, yet bashful. She looked fantastic as she pushed a lock of hair behind her ear. He thought of his first sight of her over the fallen man, pale blue eyes open wide, and he realized that the tables were turned. *He* was the deer in the headlights.

"Um, hey, stranger." His voice came out sounding rusty. He sprang to his feet, rocketing the chair with a bang against the filing cabinet. "Been thinking of you. I never got your phone number, and you haven't been back to the gym. It's been, what, a month since El Farol? I wondered if you changed your mind. You know, about Santa Fe. You okay?"

"Great, I'm great. I finally got a phone. Turned out to be more complicated than I expected. I'm learning a thing or two about Santa Fe." She chuckled. "And I've been so busy, I haven't had time for the gym, sorry. Nicole and I found an apartment, and she helped me settle in. I couldn't have done it without her. She went home a week ago. And I," she pointed at her chest, "I started a job at the Santa Fe Opera."

"Congratulations!"

"Thanks! The hours are intense, but the work's really interesting. I feel like things are starting to come together."

She lowered her voice, glanced around the empty clinic lobby. "To be perfectly honest, I kinda fell for you at El Farol that night. It scared me—the timing—with me just starting out, trying to get on my feet. Too many changes too fast." She took a breath. "I'm better now, and free at the moment. It's Cinco de Mayo. Can I buy you—"

"—a beer?" Marc grabbed some charts, turning his back to hide the goofy smile he could feel taking over his face. He stuck the charts in the file cabinet and pivoted, still smiling, but hopefully in a calm and professional way. "Yes, but I have the kids again. Got an hour, tops."

"Great!" Her cheeks went pink. "I think I'd be too nervous to spend more than an hour with you."

Really? Here he was, trying to hide his feelings, and she was brave enough to show hers. *She* is *the strong one*. He felt humbled and happy. "I'll drive," he said, closing and locking the clinic door behind them, taking her elbow and enjoying the spontaneity of the moment. It was clear that she was, too. That stunning smile.

A few minutes later, they had parked downtown and were strolling on San Francisco Street. Marc took Marina's hand and swung it playfully as they passed the Trading Post Curio Shop, its entrance flanked by stereotypical wooden sculptures of Indian men standing on drums.

They were about to cross the street when a biker roared up with the unmistakable thunder of a Harley and U-turned in front of them, forcing them to step back. Marina gasped; Marc's grip tightened. The biker was heavily tattooed, wearing a black leather vest, black wrap-around sunglasses, and a bandana on his head.

Marc felt the man's stare through the sunglasses and returned it with equal ferocity. Flute, drum, harmonica *wah-wahs*—the iconic spaghetti western soundtrack from his childhood filled his head. Wah-*wah*-wah-*wah*-wah… Wah-*wah*-wah…

The biker slowly, deliberately, dismounted, without averting his masked gaze. He pushed around to the front of the motorcycle, his body rocking back and forth in a scissoring, impaired gait, and halted inches from Marc, hands on his hips as he swayed unsteadily.

"Hey, asshole!" Marc bellowed.

"Who you calling asshole?" responded the biker, his raspy voice belligerent.

Marc released Marina's hand and enveloped the dude in a bro-hug. He grinned widely, leaning to support the shorter man.

"Herb, man, look at you! It's been ages. How's it hanging?"

"Since you got me walking again, always left," said the biker, performing a bawdy gesture with his index finger in front of his crotch. "But that's okay. Got me a new ol' lady, and she's a southpaw!" He pushed his sunglasses up over his head, revealing dark, dancing eyes.

"Glad to hear it, man. You keeping her happy?"

"We're great. Clean eight months now." His smile dropped. "I'd be dead without you."

"You got off the meds yourself. That was all you, bro. Herb, this is Marina. Marina, Herb." Marc turned to Marina, who had gone pale. "Having cerebral palsy wasn't enough of a challenge for this guy, so he got himself hit by a train, shattered his pelvis."

Herb picked up the story, speaking with earnest gruffness. "Addicted to pain meds. Left for dead in a nursing home for six months. This guy's my hero. Saved my life."

"He seems to make a habit of that," Marina said, as color returned to her face.

"Herb, join us for a beer at Evangelo's." Marc indicated a bar across the street.

"Thanks, man, but I'm not drinking anymore. Almost done with vices. Almost! I'm a sex addict now!" He shook with laughter and wiped his eyes. After another hug with Marc and a handshake with Marina, Herb scissored back to his bike and rumbled away.

Marc made a show of checking for traffic, then he stepped off the curb and back on again, making Marina dance a cowboy cha-cha. Giggling in exasperation, she yanked him off the curb with unexpected strength and pulled him across to Evangelo's.

The saloon wasn't busy yet, and Nikos was behind the bar, as usual. Black-haired with a thick mustache, well-muscled, an excellent soccer player, as he liked to remind his customers, he was regularly mistaken for Spanish but was Greek, like a handful of other downtown business owners.

When Marc had first visited the bar, he thought this guy was excessively vain, what with framed photos of himself in army fatigues all over the place. But eventually Marc got the story; it wasn't Nikos in the pics, and it wasn't Nam. The pictures were of Nikos's father, a WW II hero. He'd been featured in a black and white spread in Life Magazine. The most well-known image hung in the middle of the bar: an alert, unshaven, and helmeted young man, movie-star handsome, rifle on his back, cigarette at his lip. Nikos's pop had opened the place in 1969, and died on the same date twenty years later.

Nikos now ran Evangelo's Cocktail Lounge alone, for his mother. The atmosphere was simpatico and smoky, no matter the time of day or year.

Marc waved at Nikos before turning to Marina. "That's Nick. Ask him for a couple of Buds. Here's my card; I'll be right back."

She started to object. "I wanted to invite you—"

"This one's on me," he said firmly, handing her the card and stepping away, pretending to search his pocket for coins for the jukebox. He snuck a peek as she approached the bar.

Nikos gave her an appraising look. "You with him?" He indicated Marc with a tilt of his chin.

She nodded.

Nikos's brows pushed together like hands in prayer. "Honey, never date the drummer."

"I didn't know he was a musician."

"He's not. He's a *drummer*. Drummers hang out with musicians. What can I get you?"

"Two Budweisers, and you can put them on this card."

The barman shook his head. "Marco, *malaka!*" he barked. "Marc put you up to that, didn't he? Sweetheart, I hate Bud, I don't serve it, and this is a cash-only bar. Dos Equis green is his usual."

Marina took the joke with good humor. "I get the credit card thing—and I like Dos Equis, so I'll have the same. But why no Bud?"

Marc sidled up to her. "Evangelo's folklore, a secret. You won't get a straight answer out of him." He put cash on the bar. "Okay, you can leave the tip. How about that?"

Nikos served the beers and moved away to restock glasses. Marina plunked down a generous tip, Marc noted with approval. It figured that after working the bar and restaurant biz in her hometown, she'd be a good tipper.

"Cincin," he said, Italian style. "To your health."

She clinked back and grinned. "So, a prankster and a musician. Or should I say drummer. You're in a band?"

"Yeah, we play around—"

"I'll *bet* you do."

"Played here a few weeks ago. Gets a little tough to coordinate with kid care, but we have a good time."

She looked suddenly thoughtful, her eyes cloudy and distant.

He touched her hand. "You had a scare back there. It wasn't just about a Harley climbing the sidewalk."

"Yeah. I know he's in the past. Eric, I mean. I thought I was afraid of him, but that's not it."

She tilted the bottom of her bottle, circled it on the bar, drawing wet orbits across the varnished wood. "How do you reinvent yourself when your old self keeps hanging around?"

"Good question. I'm working on that one, too. Divorce, watching the kids grow and change, my business—I ask myself who I am today, and some days the question's hard to answer. We're nautiluses, growing new chambers in our shells, moving into them without losing the old ones. Yet we don't go back into the old ones. Those are sealed."

"And each new chamber is bigger than the last," she said softly. "So beautiful…" She looked away.

Marc waited, watching her. "Where did you just go?"

"Not sure, but not backwards," she replied, returning her focus to his face.

He felt her gaze like a gentle touch probing his features, her own exquisite features more relaxed now.

"Where did you say you live?" she asked.

"About twenty, twenty-five minutes south of town. Garden of the Gods."

"Sounds heavenly. Still no horses?"

"Chickens, dogs, cats, and kids are plenty for now." He drank.

"How about women? My sister kinda liked you."

"I like your twin's twin."

She ducked her head, playing with her bottle. When she faced him again, she was so *present*. It made his next words feel inevitable, though he hadn't planned them.

"Here's the thing. I have my kids, so between them and the clinic, I'm pretty busy. But would you have lunch with me every day till they go back to their mom?"

She didn't blink but puffed out her cheeks, said, "We're gonna get fat," and smiled like an angel.

They emerged from Evangelo's to the festive, brassy strains of mariachi music. A roving band in splendid traditional attire was moving up the street toward the plaza. Another band headed their way from the opposite direction. What could have been a cacophony of dueling mariachis became a bigger band when they stopped in the middle of the street and merged to play the same piece of music, filling the air with harmony and infectious good will.

"Cinco de Mayo. There *will* be mariachis," Marc said, taking Marina's hand, and taking in the scene.

"'*Malagueña.*' It could have been '*La Marseillaise,*' you know?" he mused. "A little Mexican army beat what was supposed to be the best army in the world at the time, the French, Cinco de Mayo, 1861. And France had been looking to help the Confederates against Lincoln. We have a looong way to go with civil rights in this country—no question—but Jesus, just imagine, the slave states might have won the Civil War. Gotta thank these guys! Viva Mexico!" he shouted, raising an imaginary glass to the mariachis. "*Gracias, amigos!*"

He turned back to Marina. "Sorry for the rant," he said, feeling sheepish. "Don't know what's got into me—mariachi music, Dos Equis, you."

Beaming, Marina said, "Don't apologize. I didn't know that about Cinco de Mayo. All the more reason to celebrate."

They applauded vigorously when the musicians finished their piece, and began to walk arm in arm down the street toward Marc's car. Just before getting in, they moved together and kissed, a mutual, spontaneous impulse.

"You're scaring me," Marc said. The energy of the kiss, racing from his toes on up and bursting from his scalp, gave new meaning to the word *buzz*.

"You should be scared."

Sweet

Over the next ten days, Marc and Marina created a daily oasis, meeting for lunch at Tía Sofía's, Plaza Café, the Shed, the Guadalupe Café, La Choza, and at the Sheraton's restaurant at the hotel next to the gym. They ate take-out in a shady stretch of the river park, downtown.

Marc was impressed with Marina's pluck—her job as an administrative assistant at the opera was demanding and complex. Her previous work in her father's office and in the restaurant and bar scene had honed her organizational and public relations skills, but the opera environment was another order of magnitude. There was international scheduling and communications to deal with; accommodations, transportation, and assistance to line up for apprentices; there was trouble-shooting, ego-soothing, ass-covering for higher-ups. The fast-approaching start of performance season heightened stakes and stress. She began her days early, finished late, took no days off.

Meanwhile, Marc's clinic bustled with the addition of Santa Fe's summer residents, twisting ankles on hiking trails, straining knees and elbows playing tennis and golf. The end of the school year brought a slew of activities requiring his participation. Chelsea was finishing first grade, and Zane's preschool program was ending.

It took creative scheduling on Ruby's part and extra duties for Kata to make it all work. He didn't tell Ruby about Marina, but enjoyed her approval of his regular lunches outside of the clinic.

Before Marina, he'd skipped meals or wolfed down a bite on the fly, sitting on top of Ruby's desk, shedding crumbs into her files while gabbing with Dez. He fended off Dez's and Armando's inquisitions about his absences. This thing, whatever it was, needed to be protected from even the most well-meaning friends—it was new and tentative and unexpectedly serious, which was funny. Funny weird and even funny amusing. He wondered sometimes who was reinventing whom. Who *was* this guy doing lunch dates?

Marina was turning out to be serious and funny in her own ways. She intrigued him further the more time they spent together. She was smart, no question about that, as well as blindingly gorgeous, which she seemed to forget. As much as she loved and depended upon her twin, this move to independence had been a positive step in her life.

Marc felt privileged to witness her transformation, to be someone with whom she could share vulnerabilities and successes. His professional life had been on an upward trend for years, an emotional bulwark against the choppy turmoil of his private life. He was able to offer workplace advice, not that she needed much. She was a quick study.

They fell in love over lunches and kisses in the park and in Marc's car, risking chile spills on their work clothes. Their time together was romantic, friendly, profoundly joyful, even including a few tears. The day of their last lunch, finishing their meal at Tía Sofía's, Marina declared, "I haven't gained a pound. You make me light. When do you pick up the kids?"

"Their mom is picking them up at three."

"That means that we are…"

"We are!"

Marina, her face alight with the pleasure of her successful surprise, handed him a room key for the Eldorado Hotel. "It's a suite."

"Sweet! Check, José." He signaled the mustachioed waiter and leaned toward Marina. "I'll call Ruby to reschedule the rest of my afternoon." They hustled out the door like schoolchildren anticipating summer vacation.

The nearby Eldorado was the largest and most impressive hotel in town, catering to visitors accustomed to tasteful luxury. Its grand yet comfortable lobby displayed museum-quality works of Native art. Entering the place felt like stepping into another world, one hushed and plush.

The elevator gave them an opportunity to fondle each other, security cameras be damned. When Marc opened the door to their room, his jaw dropped. They would be spending the night in one of the most opulent suites. Clearly Marina had made excellent use of her opera connections. He shook his head.

She pretended to look disappointed. "Is that a 'no,' you don't like it?"

"No! I mean it's a 'yes,' yes!" He pulled her close. "Yes, I like it very much. You are something else, sweetheart."

Marc felt as if time slowed and flowed back on itself. Her flush reminded him of their first meeting. His lips met her cheek, jaw, throat, the nape of her neck. He savored the scents of her skin and hair, began to unbutton her blouse.

Her fingers tugged at his belt, unbuckling it with ease. She slid his pants down over his hips, caressing.

Desire spiked in him, desire to join skin to skin, to explore and marvel in each other's bodies as they'd been doing with each other's hearts and minds. Marc kissed every inch of that woman, a tender devotion she returned with equal ardor, leaving them drained, dazed, breathless.

Both king-size beds ended up rumpled over an afternoon and evening of pillow talk and lovemaking.

"Ten daytime dates before we made love. That's a record for me," Marina revealed, as she lay sprawled across the sheets, enjoying their room service meal.

"Me too." Marc stared at the ceiling, still shaken by the day's leap of faith, and ready to propose another. "Let's do this. The weekend the kids get back, I'll cook us a nice Italian dinner, and you can meet my menagerie. Oh, boy… Church and state."

"Church and state?"

"Separation of. Don't worry about it. Reinventing myself. Growing pains."

"I hear you. But remember the nautilus shell; the next chamber is roomier."

His breath came deeper, more easily. "Yes." He sought his own strength in her eyes, those steady, glowing eyes.

Kneeling before him, she took both of his hands, holding them in a kind of communion. "It's going to be okay, Marc."

The movement of her breasts, full and glorious, made him feel giddy, and then hypnotized, and finally, stable. He matched the rhythm of his breathing to hers. They sat for wordless minutes, until she led him back to the other bed.

Garden of the Gods

Sunday, May 30, 1993
Santa Fe, New Mexico

One of the positives about being divorced—and there were a few—was getting to make a huge mess in the kitchen with no one complaining. Marc loved to cook, and like a painter throwing paint around, he loved losing himself in the process.

Zappa's "Dinah-Moe Humm" throbbed from the sound system as he chopped, diced, pounded, sliced, and sang along, turning it into a cooking song.

"A little *more uh*—oregano, that is…"

Marina was going to experience authentic Sicilian-style cooking tonight; the anticipation of feeding her filled him with pleasure. The garlic press was in his hand when the familiar commentary began.

"How many cloves is he using? That's not enough."

"Yes, it is, Zizzi. Count them."

"Count them? Never. I never count them. I use the whole head."

"That press is no good. It's just shredding, not pressing."

There they were, in his mind if not in the flesh, the women who had introduced him to the arts of the Sicilian kitchen starting when he was six years old. They came as an invisible Greek chorus—after all, Sicilians were basically Greek—to comment, kibitz, and coach the culinary action and rate the results. It happened whenever he cooked the old homestyle dishes. But unlike the traditional Greek chorus, as lockstep as the Rockettes, they did not speak with a collective voice. On the contrary, these Sicilian women conducted themselves more like dueling, highly opinionated sportscasters.

"Put a little pepper in it!"

"What's he doing with the tenderizer, tickling the scaloppine? Figlio, *pound it! You aren't going to hurt it—it's dead already!"*

"Look at those bread crumbs. They have to be just right. Too small and they're sawdust, they get soggy; too coarse and they fall off."

"Did he pound the scaloppini? It doesn't look thin enough to me. Pound again."

"Pat them dry, don't rub. They're still wet. This is importante, *so pay attention."*

"Now the eggs; beat them well. Make schiuma di mare. *"*

"Too much flour; you aren't powdering a baby's culetto, bicciuridu! *A dusting, basta."*

"Chop the onion this way, not that way. Who showed him to do it that way?"

"More capers!"

"Too many capers, you'll sour the sauce."

"More lemon."

"A pinch of sugar, I said. That's not a pinch, that's a bucket. Oh, Dio mio."

"Did he seed the tomatoes?"

"I always seed the tomatoes—why isn't he seeding them?"

To seed or not to seed. He'd flip a coin: Auntie Fortunata or Grandma Delfina? Heads. Delfina wins. She was top seed anyway, the one who'd given him most of his cooking lessons.

Marc's mom was a businesswoman who'd been growing her own direct mail advertising company when he was growing up; both she and his dad spent their days outside the home. His dad kept bakers' hours, driving a bread delivery truck. His mother's mother, Grandma Delfina, lived in a basement apartment beneath the kitchen. She did most of the cooking, teaching Marc not only basic skills but imbuing him with an appreciation for the intrinsic pleasures of the process. He remembered Grandma Delfina placing her strong, knobby brown hand over his small white one as she taught him to slice and chop an onion.

Other members of the extended Sicilian side of the family lived within shouting distance in the neighborhood, which meant frequent group feasts for holidays, confirmations, baptisms, graduations, weddings, funerals, and picnics. Any excuse for a party, any reason to cook and share.

"Okay, Delfina, you win—I'm seeding the tomatoes," Marc said aloud to the voice in his head. His grandmother was still alive and cooking, but she now lived in Texas with his cousin Leo's parents.

Meanwhile, as Marc spoke to the women in his head, steam was rising from a stainless-steel pot on the stove and a plate of plump sardines awaited dressing.

The kids had made themselves scarce. Nothing for him to do but hope for the best. Of the two, Zane was most likely to go along to get along, but Chelsea... He stirred a saucepot too vigorously, splattering his T-shirt. Time was short and he needed to shower and change. Marina was a punctual person.

Barking ten minutes later alerted him to Marina's arrival. The dogs scooted from the courtyard with a happy-yappy ruckus, danced up a dust storm around her car and, duty done, trotted back through the gate.

Marc made his own dash downstairs to the front door, wearing a loose, white long-sleeve shirt with the sleeves partly rolled up, his hair pulled into a ponytail. He stretched his lips into a confidence-boosting smile before opening the door, hoping to silence the whir of nerves, regretting his decision to forgo wine with the meal. A swallow or two—or ten—might have eased the evening's tensions.

And there she was, in tight jeans and sleeveless blouse, one tanned, silver-bangled arm raised to knock. She was a dazzling knockout, leaving Marc's *hi* stuck to the roof of his mouth, like peanut butter to a dog's palate.

Her eyes widened when she grinned, and she hugged him lightly, craning her neck to look into the house. "Are the kids here?"

"Inside," he said, his mouth barely functioning. Her loveliness temporarily dislodged his worry about the kids. "Let's take a look at the stable first." He draped an arm around her waist and guided her down the driveway, stealing glances, attuned to her every reaction, overcome by the swell of love rising in his throat.

"Marc, this place is truly special! It's clear to me, seeing it. The land, the rocks, the light... I feel like Mabel Dodge Luhan, or O'Keeffe."

Marc buffalo-stanced into a Mussolini pose and then went straight into a Compton hip-hop impersonation: "Yeah, and I'm like, yo! D.J. Lawrence." *Where did that come from?*

His antics made her giggle, a quicksilver sound, a good thing. He felt heartened as she took his hand and pulled him down the drive. The mildly dilapidated stable came into view. He tried to imagine it through her eyes. Rustic or ramshackle? Inside, they faced two stalls, empty except for loose straw and a couple of stray chickens that ran out clucking.

She swept her gaze around the place with frank approval. "Perfect! Just needs a horse or two," she said, to his relief. She hugged him again, released him, and looked him in the eye. "I'm dying to see Chelsea and Z-boy too. Is this your *stalling* tactic?"

Busted. He slipped his hand down her back to briefly cup and stroke her bottom, warm through her jeans. "Uh, Zane *so* wants to meet you. He took a bath without me making him, and even clipped on a tie."

"And Chelsea?"

"Chelsea, well, she's a strong-willed kiddo, a little mama bear to her brother. She hasn't spoken to me all day," he confessed. "Locked herself in her room. Other than that, she's thrilled."

"Maybe it's too soon."

"Too late to chicken out. You've survived the dogs and the chickens—time for the kids." As if on cue, the loose hens scuttled by, back to roost. "Let's start with Z-boy."

His fingers, nestled against her back, were crossed all the way up to the house.

Marina took an appreciative sniff as she stepped through the front door. "Smells wonderful!"

"Garlic and lots of it. The Italian in me."

"Now, I believe you. You don't look it, but you cook it. Your mom taught you?"

"My grandmother and—" He interrupted himself to call out, "Hey, Zany man, Zane! I have a friend of mine I want to introduce you to."

"You mean girlfriend," Chelsea said, making a glowering appearance.

"There you are! Marina, this is my beautiful Chelsea. Chels, Marina."

"You *are* beautiful," Marina said. "I'm happy to finally meet you."

"Nice to meet you too, I *suppose*." She stared at Marina. "You have pretty teeth."

"Thanks. My dad's a dentist, so it comes with the territory." Marina extended a hand. "Take me to Zane, okay? Maybe he's being shy."

"He's hiding," Chelsea said. "He likes to surprise. It's his thing, a phase."

As they left, Marc checked the pots on the stove and dialed down the music volume, the better to eavesdrop.

"Boo!"

Zane's boy-noise came from the bathroom across from the kids' bedroom, followed by the bang of a bed against the wall in the bedroom—Zane charging and taking a flying leap, aiming for maximum impact. He knew how to make an entrance, that kid.

"You're wearing a tie, you suck-up," Chelsea said, disdainful as an old Italian lady. She and Marina followed Zane into the bedroom. Marc stepped closer, straining his ears.

"Zane, with that tie you look like a Wall Street type. That could be your nickname: Wall Street," Marina said.

"Are you really going to keep a horse in the stable?" Chelsea demanded.

"There's been some talk of that. What do you think?"

"I think you're trying to move in."

Shit. Chelsea's best defense was always a strong offense. Marc froze.

"Would you two like to learn how to take care of a horse? If you did a good job, I wouldn't have to move in. Deal?"

Chelsea's next words poured out in a rush. "My dad really likes you," she admitted. "It's just… divorce, moving back and forth between houses all the time, it gets weird."

"I hear you, girl."

"Then there's the girlfriend thing; it's not just you. There's Corinne—she's French—she lived with us awhile. She wanted to get married, but he broke up with her. He said she was too young. I think he's scared to get married again. Don't get all close to us and leave, 'cause that *sucks*. Capiche?"

Maybe there really *was* an old Italian lady behind those seven-year-old eyes.

The ice broken for better or worse, the voices in the bedroom became hushed just as a pot full of pasta began to boil over, hissing and sizzling.

Marc scrambled back to the stove, turned off the burner, and mopped the sticky foam flooding the cooktop. "Dinner!" he yelled, louder than he intended. "I'm here too, you know!"

Marina, Chelsea, and Zane emerged in an amicable mood.

"Hands washed?" he asked. He hadn't noticed the tension in his neck until that moment, when it melted away.

The kids raced to the bathroom. Marc took the opportunity to give Marina a grateful kiss. "You worked your magic in there, didn't you?"

"They have their own magic. I love them already."

Everyone sat at the table as Marc served with a flourish: chicken cacciatore and chicken scaloppini, rigatoni a la Siciliana, green beans sautéed with garlic, *sarde a beccafico*—fish rolls with currents and pine nuts—and a tossed salad doused in balsamic vinaigrette. He'd prepared a bowl of early cherries for dessert, and they had fizzy Italian soda for fun.

"Grace," Marc said. "Chelsea?"

Chelsea and Zane took Marina's hands, then Marc's. Everyone bowed heads.

"Rub a dub, dub, here comes the grub," Chelsea recited.

"Yay, God!"

Their hands shot into the air, pulling Marina's up in the circle and making her laugh. As Marc watched her help serve the dishes family-style, and as they all settled into the meal, he felt as if they already knew each other from another life.

The food would have met with the approval of his invisible Sicilian chorus, if he did say so himself. Their voices, audible only to him, chattered on in the shadows around the table, an ultrasonic running commentary. What would they say about Marina? Heck, what would *her* people say about him?

Whoa, goombah. He was Ali MacGraw in *Love Story*, staring up the WASPy nostrils of ruddy-faced Whites, Marina's family. Nicole was cool... The parents? He gulped from his water glass, returned to the present. Marina, Chelsea, Zane—so far, so good. *Grazie a Dio.*

Mountain Time

June 18, 1993
Telluride, Colorado

The Telluride Bluegrass Festival was in full swing under the driving downbeat of a solstice sun, extra intense at high altitude. On stage, an acoustic quartet launched into a hillbilly version of Green Day's "Good Riddance," better known as "Time of Your Life." Ten thousand people filled the field, drinking in the music, the parching heat, and a variety of liquid refreshments. Pungent pot smoke wafted here and there, scenting the air, mellowing the mood.

Marc had been attending the festival for years; he was elated to share it with Marina this time, her first time. She was clearly enjoying the music and festival atmosphere, swaying to the rhythms as they spent the morning lounging on a blanket. She looked glorious in a tank top and denim short shorts.

"I want to see more—let's take a walk," Marina announced at the end of a set, jumping to her feet. She arched her back and reached for the sky, her chin upward as she inhaled deeply. Then she let go, let her arms fall, and smiled down at Marc.

"Feeling frisky, sweetheart?" He smiled. They gathered their backpacks and wended their way through the crowd until they came to a fork in the path made by the vendors.

"Right or left?" Marina asked. The choice seemed of paramount importance to her.

"When you come to a fork in the road, take it. Yogi Berra."

"What does that even mean?"

"Means it makes no difference which one we take—we'll get there all the same," he explained.

"Robert Frost is rolling in his grave—he took the road less traveled, remember? 'And that has made all the difference.' So which way do we go? Eeny-meeny-miny-moe." She pointed to the right.

"Well, according to Confucius, wherever you go, there you are. So there."

"So here," she parried, taking his hand.

Within moments they came across the beer gardens, where a familiar face emerged from the crowd. Dale, a young man with an easy smile, was a notorious Santa Fe lounge lizard. He seemed high as a kite.

"Dale, dude!" Marc said. "We're seeing so many people from Santa Fe."

Dale pulled a small plastic bag from under his vest. "Telluride Bluegrass Festival, man! Here, shrooms."

"Hey, thanks. Cool. Let's get you a beer," Marc said.

"I don't drink," Dale responded, eyes merry. "I'm too high to eat." He opened the bag. "That should be enough for you two all day. Have a great time! Dance to the Flecktones, then Shawn Colvin's on. We'll see each other around." He hugged them both and moved off into the throng, a dancing, skipping leprechaun.

"I thought he was smashed every time I saw him." Marc shook his head, then bent over the baggie with Marina. They each took a pinch of dried mushrooms.

"To your health!" he said.

They chewed, studying each other. Marina stuck her tongue out, twisting her lips.

"Ugh, that tastes disgusting!"

Marc turned his eyes skyward, gesturing with the baggie as if swirling an invisible wine glass. "Dominating notes of sweaty basketball shoes broiled in a hot car... undertone bouquet of school cafeteria floor—nope, the mop that was used on it, after a food fight— whiff of dog kennel... tannic finish. Yep." He swallowed. "Truly disgusting. Gotta wash this down with a beer."

They bought two cups overflowing with foam and then, arms around each other, they explored the festival, taking in the sights until they came across an acrobatic mime and clown troupe. One clown was especially macabre, her features painted like a death mask; Marc couldn't help zeroing in on her face. He knew that Marina knew that he had a deep-seated fear of clowns. Mimes too. Irrational, wacky, whatever you wanted to call the fear, clowns had given him the creeps for as long as he could remember.

"Mimes and clowns, the double whammy," he whispered. "You know they freak me out."

Marina's laugh sounded odd, hysterical. "I know." She stumbled against him, gave his shoulder a teasing, affectionate pat. "There, there, sweetheart, it's okay. Don't be afraid."

But he was thrown back in time to when he was five years old and celebrating Easter in Manhattan at Madison Square Garden, an edifice where he happily would have resided. He was there with his parents to see the Ringling Brothers and Barnum and Bailey Circus, the Greatest Show on Earth.

One, two, three, and then suddenly, dozens of maniacal, grotesquely painted mass murderers flew out of a toy car to taunt the crowd mercilessly. Why would anyone think that hideous trick with those fucking clowns was funny at all, especially a little boy?

"Hey, Marina? How you feeling? Feel the shrooms? I do..." Helpless laughter shimmied up from the snake pit in his belly, bubbled and spilled over like the head of his beer. His head lightened. Piss on those damn clowns.

"I've only done mushrooms once before," she said, shaking with uncontrollable giggles. "I'm no expert, but—ninety degrees, sun beating down, crowds—I don't care if Bela Fleck plays banjo like Jimi Hendrix—I want to go up the mountain!"

Marc gave the mime troupe a furtive glance. "Yeah, let's go!"

They rambled through Telluride, a recently revived, beautiful old mining town. It had become a world-class ski destination with 5-star hotels, yet it remained quaint and saloonie. The place was famous for music and film festivals and carried not so much a furs and diamonds vibe as a blue-jeans-and-grunge-flannel feel. Eventually, they found a dirt road leading up the mountain and began to climb, stopping every so often for a kiss or to gesture eccentrically, laughing at mostly nothing.

"Do you think we're peaking?" Marina asked.

"Hope so, but I don't think so."

"Oh, shit, keep an eye on me. Don't leave my side," she blurted before dashing up the road.

Distracted by the movement of her cute rear, Marc belatedly muttered, "What happened to 'don't leave my side'?" He shook his head and took off after her, catching up just as she slowed, panting.

Marina turned to see him and spasmed in hysterics. He took her hand; she swung her arm vigorously back and forth, swiveling her hips in long strides.

"Crazy girl, my beautiful crazy girl." He let his arm swing with hers. Two figures came into view, a young woman and an athletic man of around seventy. Marina let out a whoop.

"Sonya!"

The young woman was attractive and blond, like Marina—the two could have been sisters, Marc thought—and in a mushroom-confused moment, he wondered if he were seeing double, or if Marina had a triplet.

"Marina!"

The women embraced. "We came up for the weekend," Sonya was saying. "He flew in from Connecticut last night."

"We're flying too," Marina said. "Shrooms!"

The older gentleman smiled.

"This is Marc," Marina said. "Marc Hochstaff. Marc, remember I told you about Sonya—she works with me at the opera. *And* she's an amazing singer! You have to hear her."

"Aw, you're my biggest fan, aren't you, honey?" Sonya said. "I'm so happy to run into you here." She turned to Marc. "Pleased to finally meet you. This is my father, Morris."

The older man extended a hand. "Morris Joseph."

"Hey, *Mojo!* Nice to meet you!" Marc heard his own voice as if it came from someone else—the shrooms were doing the talking. Didn't seem to matter; Mojo was smiling cordially.

"The pleasure is mine. Mojo—I've never been called that before. Shall we get together for dinner or lunch before we fly our separate ways?"

"Let's!" Marina said. "Tomorrow? Call us—we're staying at the Sheridan."

"Meanwhile," Morris added, "if you're heading up the mountain, you may enjoy the waterfall and the lake. Quite lovely."

"Gotta go see them!" Marina truly was flying. She gave Sonya another tight hug and sprinted away.

"Sonyasita! Nice to meet you, Moe," Marc said, corralling both of them in an awkward hug. "Gotta follow that girl."

"Yes, I can see that you do," Morris said. "Goodbye, young man. Good luck."

As he and Sonya resumed their walk, Marc overheard him ask, "Mushrooms?"

"Yes, indeed," Sonya said, chuckling with her father.

Marc stumbled off, giddy, on the chase again. Gotta follow that girl. When he caught up with her this time, they wandered into a meadow dotted with yellow, blue, purple, and red wildflowers. A breeze was blowing, and the air was cooler; just ahead, a herd of elk moseyed past. He pointed.

"Elephants."

"Giraffes, silly," Marina replied.

She stopped, slid her backpack off, and he did the same, enjoying the lightness in his shoulders. Light welled up inside his chest, behind his eyes, making him feel weightless, yet full and tight as a birthday balloon on a string. He pulled Marina close for a deep kiss, then removed the blanket from his backpack and spread it over the tall grass. They sank to their knees and leisurely undressed each other, tossing aside items of clothing.

"I could live right here," he said, his head resting on her belly, fingers idling in the little garden of curls just below his chin.

"Right here in this meadow," she said dreamily.

"No, right here between your legs," he said, nuzzling her.

Her belly went taut as she pushed up on her elbows. She tugged gently on his ponytail. "Me too," she said, guiding his body beside hers so she could nestle her face between his thighs.

Later, as they rested, feet in each other's laps and rubbing soles and toes, Marina's eyes brimmed, spilling a few tears. She shook her head and smiled when he asked why she was crying. It seemed the words wouldn't come, or there were no words. Those tears looked like happiness to Marc.

When they had dressed, feeling the lingering effects of the mushrooms, they climbed over a hill to find a steel-blue mountain lake dotted with patches of green and yellow from the minerals of the San Juan Mountains. Marc slipped off his sandals and dipped the toes of one foot into the water. Damn near freezing.

"We're going in!" Marina shouted, starting to undress again.

He was astounded. "It's hard to keep your clothes on today, isn't it?"

"Seems."

Not to be outdone, he stripped and stepped atop a large boulder. "Deep enough here."

"Jump, Tarzan."

Marc did his best Tarzan imitation, beating his chest and yodeling, and leaped into the frigid water. Marina screamed and followed suit. Birthday suit, that is. Pink, white, tan, and goose bumps. Each breath came with a constricted gasp. They splashed and yelled themselves hoarse for as long as they could take before clambering back onto the boulder, shivering, exhilarated, and slapping their wet skin.

"This should straighten us up. My balls are in my chest!" Marc's teeth chattered for percussive emphasis.

"I don't feel very straight," Marina said. "Look, over there." She pointed toward the forest. "A small animal, or person."

"Maybe kids. Hope we gave them a good show."

The bushes below the tall, dark trees near the lakeshore were dense, and some of the leaves were moving. Someone or something was running low to the ground.

"I think I saw eyes—or is it the shrooms?" Marina whispered.

"Lucky kids, catching your bare ass. You nervous?"

"Not at all. For some reason, it's cool." Her teeth rattled.

"Cool? You're freezing, Bubby-cakes. Let's get dressed; it'll be dark soon."

They gathered their clothes with numb fingers and huddled together, sharing the blanket; the sun hung low in the sky as they trekked down the road past the spot where they had met Sonya and her father. Marc stopped Marina, bringing her close to him within the blanket.

"I love you," he said. "Monday night you came to my house late, didn't call. I was worried—the road."

She nodded, and stroked his hair. "Drunk drivers."

"I wanted to yell at you for worrying me. But I saw your face, glowing like today. You told me you'd had your arms up a mare's coochie, helping to deliver a foal! I was so happy and proud. God—I love you."

"You did yell at me—to take a shower!"

He dropped to one knee. "Will you, will you... I hope this isn't the shrooms talking. Will you move in with me?"

"Get up, you asshole. Don't get on one knee to ask someone to shack up! What about your kids, your French ex-girlfriend? Better think this over. I'm *very* high maintenance."

Marc got to his feet, brushing dirt from his knee. "The kids love you. It'll make them happy; you'll see."

"I had a dream that told me to come west and find you." Her voice drifted.

They kissed and embraced, and he felt her taking the measure of his heart as he took hers.

"This was one of the best days of my life," Marina said. "Let's never, ever, do shrooms again."

The Sheridan Hotel was utterly charming in its dramatic postcard setting. Red brick façade, green awnings, historic yet graciously updated, it was the perfect place to end the day. Marc and Marina climbed to their room to share a bath in the claw-foot tub, washing each other's backs and feet with fragrant soap. Marc paid close attention to each of her toes, enjoying her pleasure. Afterwards, he took a shower to rinse. When he stepped from the bathroom, toweling off, he found her lying topless on the bed, holding a string with a crystal pendulum. She looked enchanting in the glow of an antique lamp. He watched her spin the crystal above her forehead. Rainbows whirled from its faceted surfaces.

"What are you doing? Still shrooming?"

"It's for chakras, the energy that runs up and down the middle of your body. It checks your body and spirit for blocks in the system. Come here, let me do you."

"Again?" He gave her a suggestive grin.

"Not that. Let me check your chakras. Lie down, relax," she instructed, kneeling beside him. "So, the gonad chakra is here. It's called the base for us girls."

She dragged the crystal over her pubis. "We move to number two, sacral; three, solar; four, heart; five, throat; six, third eye; and up here, the crown." She touched the chakra points on her own body with the crystal as he watched, appreciating every move.

Leaning over his body, she began at his pubis, holding the pendulum still. It began a slow pattern of clockwise rotation. "Okay, good." She worked her way slowly and precisely up his torso toward his head, clearly engrossed in her experiment. "Wow, Marc, I'm an amateur at this, but you seem really healthy, bottom to top. Would you do me? Take it easy, big boy." She stretched out across the bed.

He rose to his knees, holding the pendulum. "I have no idea what I'm doing."

She reached for a book on the bedside table. "Here. This has diagrams of the chakra locations. Hold the pendulum over each point; it doesn't have to be exact, but keep your hand as steady as you can. The crystal should spin fully clockwise or fully counterclockwise."

"Whatever you say. Odd foreplay." He dangled the crystal over her body. The crystal moved clockwise over her base, but when he held it over the sacral, it didn't spin.

"Try again," Marina said.

He repeated the gesture. "Nothing."

"Okay, just keep going up. Stop fooling around."

He positioned the pendulum over her solar plexus, where it spun counterclockwise. He tried multiple times over her chakra points. "I have better chakras than you—so what does that mean?"

"I don't know, I just started playing with this stuff," she said. "Maybe it means I'm hungry."

"Dinner it is." He lifted the pendulum to his forehead, where his third eye would be. "It's saying something about a steak in our future."

She laughed. "You're going to get the best steak on the menu."

"And you?"

"I'm going for a different kind of high. Remember, I said I'm high maintenance. You'll have to order for me something fussy, in French, which you won't be able to pronounce. And no mushrooms involved."

"Then I'll start by ordering wine," Marc said. "Pinot noir."

When they walked down to the restaurant, in clean jeans and casual shirts, they found the dining room full and bustling, no tables available, so they ordered at the bar instead. The meal was superb, unforgettable, and it seemed impossible to run out of conversation. They remained at the bar long after the other diners had left, savoring everything about the day, relishing dreams of the future.

The Foreboding Apple

One Year Later
June 17, 1994
New York, New York

Marc was feeling it, summer in the city, sweat and humidity gluing his shirt to his shoulders. He stood alone on the crowded sidewalk and laughed aloud, knowing that no one would notice such behavior here in the Big Apple, the city that filled his mind when he thought of the word *home*. This was his city. Back in the day, he felt as if he possessed its keys as he was smoothly ushered to the front of the line at clubs, sporting events, and concerts, burning the candle at both ends and the middle. *Back in the day*. It was a term he now felt old enough to pronounce with minimal irony.

In Santa Fe he slept under fathomless night skies, where the Milky Way rippled like Salome's veils, an experience vastly different from the electric buzz of the city that never sleeps. His former NYC life slipped ever farther behind in his wake, like a waking dream. The city lived on, a river of steel and concrete steaming and teaming with phantasmagorical life forms. You never step into the same river twice, but each dip back into this grand torrent was as revitalizing as a coral reef wall dive, a brisk descent into a whole other world. He plunged forward. Marina would be waiting.

He checked his wristwatch and scanned the scene, no longer viewing it from a sentimental distance but from its seedy guts just below the belt. He strode up Seventh Avenue faster than a tourist, slower than a New Yorker. Madison Square Garden was coming up soon, the Apple's true core for certain sports fans.

By a lucky break, their visit coincided with Game 5 of the NBA 1994 championships tonight at the Garden, Knicks versus the Houston Rockets. Tickets would be in high demand, but his friend Mike still worked for the Garden and with the Knicks as a trainer, so there was hope. Marc wanted to take Marina to the game. She wasn't much of a sports fan but was a good sport. Odds favored an entertaining evening, if only…

He found a graffiti-splattered pay phone and dialed, as throngs of New Yorkers marched past at their trademark superfast pace, bobbing and weaving around meandering sightseers. Haunches rolling, heels striking, chins high, they made a low, human rumble that was punctuated by taxi horns and by the feline sound of diesel engines purring in idle and coughing up hair balls when the traffic light changed. He held the grubby receiver without touching it to his ear, and covered his other ear with a hand.

"Mike, hey, Mike! This is Marc Hochstaff. How are you, buddy?"

"Markie, hey! You still out West?" The words came in that familiar, classic Queens accent.

"Santa Fe, New Mexico, yeah, but at the moment I'm practically around the corner from you." A siren spiraled through the concrete canyon. "What? Yeah, really."

"Let's connect. Kinda frantic around here now—you can imagine—but exciting," Mike said.

"I'm headed uptown to meet my fiancée; we're buying her a wedding dress!"

"Holy shit! Well, congrats. Send me an invite, would ya?"

"Of course! Hey, how's the team feeling to you?"

"You know, we're going to win tonight, but the series is up in the air. Fucking Olajuwon."

"Damn, I'm so psyched!" Marc jogged in place at the pay phone.

"You need a ticket, dontcha, bro?"

"Two. For me and Marina, my fiancée."

"Ay, ay, ay, you got balls, you son of a bitch! You haven't worked with us for, like, years. Hold on."

Marc heard Mike set the phone down. He practiced more anxious jogging in place as he waited, as if he needed to pee.

"Okay." Mike was back on the line. "Consider this a wedding gift—two seats in the media area, right behind Marv. Your nose'll be in his toupee all night." Mike snorted. "Tenth row, center court."

"Great seats! Thank you so much, buddy! I owe you big time."

"You don't owe me *nuthin'*. Love you, bro. And you got lucky; the tickets were sitting on my treatment table. They'll be at Will Call. My love to your fiancée!"

"Thank you!" Marc slung down the receiver and fist-pumped the air. He checked his watch again. Late. He hailed a cab to join Marina at the chic and charming Arcadia on East Sixty-Second Street, where she had lunched with Sonya.

Sonya was living in the Village in Manhattan now, but was about to leave for an eighteen-month conservatory program in Vienna. She would miss the wedding, which really bummed out Marina. After becoming good friends during Sonya's time in Santa Fe, they had hoped she would sing at the ceremony. Her singing career had begun to take off in New York, however, and this visit would be the last chance for the three of them to get together before her extended trip.

Sublime aromas enticed Marc at the restaurant entrance. The interior, decorated with fresh flowers and encircled by a mural of the four seasons, lived up to its rhapsodic New York Times review as magical. He spotted Marina and Sonya lounging in a banquette. Even as he apologized for his tardiness, his words became irrelevant. Haste dissolved, supplanted by relaxed wellbeing.

Sonya greeted him by turning to Marina, announcing, "Here's your handsome fiancé, my dear," as Marina smiled hugely. He was part of Team Fiancés now, a team of two. The notion made him smile hugely back.

"I'm cutting an album," Sonya explained to Marc, and apologized for having to return to her studio. "Finishing it up before Vienna. Here's the demo." She handed him a cassette.

"Fantastic. Can't wait to hear it."

"*You* look fantastic," Sonya said to Marina, getting to her feet and smoothing her skirt. "You'll be a *beautiful* bride." She eyed Marina's barely touched portion of the enormous signature lobster sandwich they had shared. "Such willpower; no wonder you stay so thin. Bye, sweetie!"

They exchanged tearful hugs and kisses.

"I didn't tell her about my stomach issues," Marina explained after Sonya left. "Didn't want to spoil the mood or make her worry. Anyway, I feel great at the moment."

Marc hadn't eaten since breakfast. He plopped into Sonya's vacated seat and reached for the remains of the sandwich. Bacon and lobster, lemon mayonnaise... "You really don't want any more?"

She shook her head, her upswept hair haloing her eager face.

"I know you can't wait to go play dress-up," he said before sinking his teeth into buttery brioche. "Oh, my God. This..." He gestured helplessly.

A glossy-haired waiter sidled over to ask if he wished to order anything. He glanced at Marina.

"I can wait, love. *Mangia.*" She pulled a compact and lipstick from her purse, followed by a pack of Marlboro Lights cigarettes. She placed one cigarette between her lips and lit up, a habit she still indulged lightly. Her smile was radiant, veiled by curls of smoke.

Marc ordered a glass of chardonnay and took another bite of lobster paradise.

They emerged afterward into a dazzling June afternoon, their destination the posh Vera Wang Bridal House, a veritable bridal Mecca on the second floor of the Carlyle Hotel. Marc took Marina by the arm to stroll the tree-lined block over to Madison Avenue. They caught a taxi to Seventy-Sixth Street, and there it was, a gleaming portal to opulence. Genteel awnings flanked by overlarge American flags extended from above the hotel's front entrance. Strategically placed potted topiary shrubs shorn to within an inch of their lives stood below, green border guards separating the public world of the street from the restricted world within.

Marina nearly lost her high-heeled shoes when she leaped from the taxi to the curb. She gathered herself together and turned for the entrance, but stopped almost immediately. Four grim-faced men in dark blue uniforms augmented the spit-and-polish doormen's customary liveried presence, a show of force at odds with the graceful image of a bridal salon. Vera Wang had not designed these outfits. The balmy anticipation of the afternoon chilled, and Marina's posture stiffened.

"What's going on?" she whispered.

At that moment, an open-air bus crammed with tourists pulled up to the curb. A tour leader began an amplified explanation of the reason for this stop, first in Japanese, then English.

"Some people are calling them the Gentlemen Bandits, two men who have terrorized this neighborhood by stalking women and robbing them of their jewelry. Last March they entered the Vera Wang Bridal Salon and *shot* the parents of a young bride shopping for a wedding dress. The victims were seriously injured, and the assailants have not been captured. Some are saying that New York City is experiencing a wave of urban terrorism. Please be careful of your safety and your possessions."

The bus remained in place long enough for a round of shutter-clicks before trundling away, its engine muffling the loudspeaker.

Marina clenched a hand over her platinum engagement ring, her eyes round with alarm, her face drained of color. "Isn't that nice," she uttered weakly.

Marc put his arms around her, feeling her exhale. Wow. Her trip to NYC included all the big items, skyscrapers and random and not-so-random acts of violence. He was reminded that the same month that the bridal salon shooting occurred, the men who had bombed the World Trade Center were convicted. The Gulf War had heightened fears and warnings of terrorist reprisals, and the Big Apple remained a prime target. People were on edge for good reason.

"Bubby-cakes, they'll catch those lowlifes," he said bracingly. "The only thing that's going to get shot today is my credit card. Come on, honey. Maybe they're having a seconds sale—half off for bullet holes."

"Bullet holes!"

"Okay, sorry." He made friendly eye contact with the nearest guard and said with an exaggerated wink, "Pre-wedding jitters. Bride needs a stiff one. But no stiffs, right?"

The guard's scrutiny was quick but thorough. "Bar's in the hotel. You'll need to get buzzed into the salon. Got an appointment?"

Marc nodded. "We'll go straight up." To Marina he said, "We'll get you a glass of water. Or vodka." He gave his name to the guard, who checked via walkie-talkie with a receptionist on the other side of the glass door, and they were buzzed inside.

"A *stiff* one?" Marina said.

"Just got honeymoon on the brain already. And tickets for a show tonight. It's going to be great!"

"Broadway?"

"A little off Broadway. Like eight blocks."

They began to ascend the stairs side by side. Wedding gown, romantic dinner, a show in New York City—a perfect night ahead. Halfway up the stairs, Marina stopped.

"Those poor parents. My God, their daughter, she must hate this city."

Marc stroked her cheek, waited, and watched her silent struggle to pull herself together. They resumed their climb, and a few moments later they entered the salon, a tranquil realm of understated elegance.

The sleek saleswoman who greeted them at the door ushered them toward a pair of armless upholstered chairs. On the table between the chairs sat a silver tray holding two glasses of iced water with lemon, accompanied by linen napkins.

"Got any vodka?" Marc asked. He watched Marina recover her spirits as she gazed around.

"I love New York City! I do!" she said. She was back in the present, completely present, his beautiful resilient bride.

"I like the way you say I do," Marc said. "Say it again."

"I do."

The Bronco and the Garden

Marc had left the Catholic Church behind in his childhood, but not *the Church*: Madison Square Garden, the Temple, the Mosque. From Barnum and Bailey to the Boss, from DeBusschere to Giacomin, Tull to Woody, Lee to Ali, Frazier to Frazer, Madison Square Garden's arena offered charismatic worship services and Holy Communion. For ecstatic or even transcendental experiences there were rock concerts lit by pyrotechnics and Bic-flicks instead of votive candles; its sporting events drew faithful fans prepared to glorify their heroes and damn the fallen.

This year, Michael Jordan was taking a baseball sabbatical, much as if Babe Ruth had taken up synchronized swimming, so the Jordan-less Chicago Bulls had been eliminated early from the NBA playoffs. The Knicks and Houston Rockets were 2-2 in the finals. The Knicks just might win the NBA Championship.

Marc led Marina to a four-seat box, and they plopped down. Sure enough, Marv Albert's beaver pelt perched on his very familiar head just below.

"I think Mike got me these same seats three years ago."

"Really? Great seats. Of course, we could have gotten tickets for *Les Mis*," Marina needled him.

Marc was absorbed in his memories. "It was probably a couple of weeks after Rosana split again, this time for good. I was really down, needed to get the hell out of town. I flew to New York to visit sports friends, hear some music."

"Did you bring any female companionship?"

"No, I traveled alone a lot those days."

"Not anymore," she said, hugging his arm. "What about the kids?"

"Dez and her mom pitched in."

"Darling Dez, I'd be jealous if—"

"Nothing to worry about; I'm not her type. Now you, on the other hand…"

"I, on the other hand, have my hands full with *you*. Veeery full." She stroked his thigh.

He grinned, lifted her chin with a finger. "Yeah, I see you're going to be fascinated by the game tonight. So, listen to this. I'm sitting in this box—this very box for four, which means three empty seats. Three guys come in, all excited. Long hair, flannel, early twenties. Regular season, not like tonight; the Seattle Supersonics playing the Knicks. These guys were Supersonics fans from the Northwest. And they were fans of this player out of Oklahoma, Blaylock, in his first season with the Nets. They didn't get to see the Nets play on that trip, but we had a good time, bought each other beers, yelled, talked music. They knew their stuff. They were into Soundgarden in the eighties, when it was still an obscure band out of Seattle. At the end of the game, we bro-hugged, wished each other well."

"Okay, nice memory, but?" Marina fiddled with a button on his shirt.

"Hang in there. Next day my pal Dave calls. He's coming to the wedding, you know. Says he has second row tickets for Sonic Youth and Neil Young with Crazy Horse, the Don't Spook the Horses tour, out on the island. Nassau Coliseum."

Marc paused as a tastefully dressed, salt-and-pepper-haired gentleman stepped into the front row of their box, accompanied by a glamorous blonde. The man looked old enough to be her father, but that definitely wasn't their relationship.

"Marc," Marina whispered, "he's that TV star. What's his name?"

"Yeah." Marc recognized the actor, whose character was known for a lackadaisical sartorial style. "Relax; it's NYC. He's a big fan."

That was the thing about New York City, and especially about a New York sports audience, that Marc still took for granted: celebrities sprinkled into the hoi polloi. He grinned at Marina's surprise.

"So, anyway," he continued, "I jump on the Long Island Railroad. Dave picks me up. An hour later we're in the second-row center." He remembered the feeling of it, that effortless slide into a New York state of mind. Santa Fe had receded far away.

"And these three guys—the *same three guys* from the Knicks game, just the night before—come and sit right in front of us!"

"No shit!"

"Shit, yeah. A lot of *wow*s, handshakes, more bro-hugs, introductions. One of them gives me this inquisitive look, goes, 'Hey, man, who the hell *are* you? I say, '*Me*? Nobody. But who the hell are *you* guys—nice seats, two nights in a row? *First* row, that is.' He says, 'Neil got us these.' Turns out they have a band, and Neil Young was producing their album!

"Dave asked them the name of their group, and they said, 'Mookie Blaylock.' Dave was like, in his deep voice and *heavy* New York accent, '*Mookie Blaylock?* The basketball player? You can't call the band Mookie Blaylock!' One of 'em says, 'We're getting a new singer, so we may change the name.'

"Anyway, the concert was great; they tried to get us backstage passes, but it didn't work out. We shared well wishes and more bro-hugs, never to see each other again. Not for free, anyway."

Marina's brows shot up, and her eyes narrowed. "You're telling me a shaggy dog story—that's how it ends?"

"Wait. Some months later I'm in a hotel in Las Vegas, getting out of the shower—"

"Towel or no towel? I need the visuals."

"Ha! They're coming, sweetheart. Saturday morning TV is blasting Pearl Jam's 'Even Flow' off their debut album, *Ten*. Ahmad Rashad is narrating a basketball show, playing Pearl Jam. I look at the TV, see Mookie Blaylock, the basketball player, bringing the ball up. Rashad says, 'Pearl Jam, formerly known as Mookie Blaylock—"

She slapped his thigh. "No!"

"Ow! Yes, really. Two nights in a row in the first and second row, I partied with three members of Pearl Jam. I think it was Jeff, Stone, and Mike."

"Quite a tale. And not so shaggy after all." She nuzzled his neck and gave him a gentle nip.

The game was about to begin. His Knicks were going to rock the Garden tonight.

The game was close, although New York was in command, when Marc felt Marina tugging his sleeve. The pressure barely registered at first, since he was busy tracking the players. Then she grabbed his arm and pointed to the screen above the court, where a live display showed a bizarre chase scene. From behind he heard someone say, "That's O. J. in that Bronco! Look at that, that's O. J."

"What?"

Heads turned throughout the crowd, as people switched their attention from the live game to the broadcast video above. Even some of the players on the court became distracted—in an NBA championship game!

Marc watched the helicopter view of the event unfolding; the slow speed of the vehicles made it even odder. "Why the hell are they showing that crap on the big screen?" he asked. "Come on, Pat, pick up the pace!"

Knicks coach Pat Riley seemed to look back at him. Marv Albert turned, his expression endorsing Marc's unsolicited advice. But the car chase continued to air long enough to suck the soul and spirit out of the crowd and risk the game. The players knew the score—they didn't need to check the scoreboard—yet they kept glancing up at the screen where the score posting was definitely secondary to the sullen, obstinate white Bronco lollygagging along the freeway. An edginess, a foreboding, infected the arena.

Marina complained of nausea.

Marc felt out of sorts, somber, the O. J. intrusion an unexpected desecration that he couldn't help taking personally, although he couldn't explain why. But life and basketball went on after all. The Knicks won. They were up 3-2, heavily favored to win the 1994 NBA Championship.

Back at the hotel, every TV channel was airing the O. J. story. The Bronco was now parked and O.J. was under arrest. Marc was still digesting the news coverage, pondering and trying to identify the causes of his resentment, his back tight as he sat at the foot of the bed. At last he gave a heavy sigh.

"Here's the thing." He got to his feet, turned off the TV.

Marina stood in panties and bra in the bathroom, brushing her teeth under the bleaching glow of the overhead light. She wiped her mouth and rinsed, peering at him over the cup's rim.

"Murders and tragedies happen all over the world, every day. How many poor people do you think were murdered in this city today, how many black lives lost—do we hear about them? People who loved and were loved. People who breathed, bled, laughed, cried, tried to make sense of their existence. But the media don't care about them, because they weren't celebrities. How do those fucking talking heads sleep at night? How does anybody?"

He pulled off the bedcovers, leaving only the cool white sheets. They slept, yet not well.

White Wedding

Sunday July 3, 1994
Chatham, Massachusetts

Festive crowds, tourists and locals, milled along the street in downtown Chatham, Cape Cod, near a picturesque white church covered in American flags. No AC/DC T-shirts, no ripped jeans. Most of the people were white to the nth degree of WASPy pedigree and proudly garbed in patriotic red, white and blue for the Fourth of July holiday weekend.

Marc had never seen such a milky flock in his life. He knew that he looked like he'd hatched from the same nest, but the minute he opened his mouth, it was clear he was a bird of a different feather. He didn't mind. The whole scene was a quaint spectacle on a brilliant sunny day. Skin cancer be damned.

Wedding guests were arriving, bringing preppy pastels and Izod alligators to the mix. There was Marina, in her Vera Wang wedding dress, breaking tradition by greeting guests in front of the church. Marc was breaking tradition as well, since the groom wasn't supposed to see the bride before the ceremony. He maneuvered deftly, as if through a school of fish, to the side of the church to enjoy the sight of her. He'd helped to choose the dress—the chance to see her in it like this was irresistible. She looked happy but nervous.

"Ted! Holy shit, do you believe this?" she was saying to a handsome, gray-haired man accompanied by his male partner, both of them meticulously groomed.

"Marina, you are *stunning!* You doing okay? A little stressful, huh?" Ted said.

"I'm good, good. Just want to have it all go well—perfectly, actually. Perfect would be great. Hey, Uncle Jack, Aunt Elaine! So happy you could make it. Excuse me, I have to get to the back of the church—not supposed to be out here. Love you, have fun! See you later. See you, Ted."

"Good luck, gorgeous. Love you!" He shook his head. "So skinny," he said to his partner.

"She's a bride, it's what they do," the other man replied.

Marc felt sweat beginning to permeate his collar; he returned inside to find his wedding party gathered near the altar, dressed in elegant tuxedos.

His father, Jerry, was a big man, pink-faced Irish and German, black hair slicked back. A former Marine, raised by a widowed, Marine-turned-motorcycle-cop—a real tough guy—he looked unexpectedly misty-eyed at Marc's arrival. Marina's Uncle Jack, jovial and paternal, extracted a cigar tube from a pocket and presented it ceremoniously. The solemnity on his florid face declared that he'd been rehearsing this tribute for weeks.

"Cuban, Marc. The best!" he said. "Enjoy in good health."

"Thank you. You'll have to show me how—I'm a cigar virgin," Marc said, going along with the man-to-man rite of passage.

"Virgin, eh? Not for long, boy!" Jack chuckled. "Got a new box in my car."

Marc's co-best men were his father and Zane, who was picking at the tight collar on his dress shirt. They crowded in to see him extract the cigar, sniff it, and admire its decorative paper band. He slid the cigar back into the tube and put it away in a tux pocket, then leaned toward his dad.

"Are Cohibas good?"

"I have no idea. I only smoke Luckys."

Marina managed to extricate herself from well-wishers and get to the dressing room with her mother and bridesmaids. Nicole looked radiant as her maid of honor. Sisters of the womb, they might not always enjoy the most harmonious of relationships, but they loved each other so much, and today never could have happened without Nicole. Marina felt an upsurge of gratitude, accompanied by a trickle of moisture down her back.

The room was close, crowded, and becoming overheated. Bridesmaids were fanning themselves, chattering, adjusting shoes and bra straps, touching up makeup, cooing over Marina and her dress.

Another upsurge hit her, but this time it came from below the heart. Nausea. She backed out the door and through the next door and pushed into the restroom, where she braced herself on the sink to stare into the mirror, taking a deep breath.

"Keep it together, girl," she said aloud. "Big day." She turned, jerked open a stall door, and vomited into the toilet. Oh, God. The gown, fortunately, was not a bouffant organza confection, but tight and draping, and remained unsullied. She caught her breath, turned to rinse and wipe her mouth at the sink, and checked her reflection.

A toilet flushed in another stall. The door squeaked on its hinges, and Aunt Elaine stepped out to wash her hands. Marina tried to compose her features, hoping not to alarm her aunt, but Elaine didn't appear at all alarmed. She displayed a knowing little smile.

"Don't worry, dear; it's our secret. The first trimester is the worst." Aunt Elaine patted her shoulder.

Marina smiled weakly, unable to respond. She put a hand over her belly, where the sharp pain was subsiding. Her cheeks went from blanched to red. She waited for Aunt Elaine to leave, and then pressed a damp paper towel over her forehead and held it there, eyes closed, for a long moment. She had finally gone to see a gastroenterologist. At Dr. Singh's suggestion, she had even undergone an endoscopy, a look into her stomach. Nothing to see, all clear. Antacids were prescribed. Nerves. Damned nerves.

She returned to the dressing room to dig the pill bottle out of her purse, and took one with a gulp of water. Afterwards, she scooped a handful of pastel-colored mints from a bowl by the mirror, popping them into her mouth and chewing. She was about to be married. Marc's glowing image in her mind, his sweet steadiness, steadied her. Everything was going to be okay.

Marc grinned at his father and withdrew a cassette tape from the pocket where he'd stashed the cigar. He strolled to the organ, where a buxom, dark-haired woman sat preparing music for the ceremony.

"Hello, Kate, you're looking sensational! Love the floral arrangement." He eyed the enormous corsage she wore pinned over her left breast. "Here's some pre-wedding-march blues; would you put it through the sound system?"

She nibbled her lip. "Okay. But don't get me in trouble."

Busted. His conspiratorial air must have been written all over his face; he pretended to be offended. "I wouldn't do that to you, Kate. Don't worry."

"Right..." she said, clearly unconvinced.

"Thanks, doll." He moved smoothly away to watch.

Marina and the wedding party gathered in the back of the church as music began to play at background volume over the PA system, and it wasn't Debussy or Vivaldi. Billy Idol's growling, howling, rock-and-roll cruising anthem, "White Wedding," crashed the scene. Marc craned his neck, gleefully anticipating Marina's reaction. She would think this was hysterical!

Throughout the church, wedding guests were looking around, some laughing softly. Marc saw his father. Jerry did not look amused.

Billy Idol's thrumming faded away. The next song began with poignant piano chords, a more appropriate sound. Neil Young's reedy voice pitched in, singing about a change of life. Plaintive, contemplative, yes... Heads nodded. This seemed more like wedding music. Until he wailed that line straight out of a classified ad for a cleaning woman.

Nicole looked stunned, gaping, ready to boil over. She grasped Marina's arm in a show of sisterly outrage and support, and mouthed *asshole* at him. Really? She did it again, slowly, and with great expressiveness. No mistake. *Ass. Hole.*

When the song mercifully ended, "Here Comes the Bride" started up, kicking off the procession, restoring a traditional tone to the ceremony. Flower girls pranced up the aisle sprinkling petals. Zane, the ring bearer as well as co-best man, marched proudly in his suit and bowtie, clutching a satin pillow with the ring held in place by a ribbon.

It was time for Marina, accompanied by her father, to proceed toward the altar. She was an angelic presence, a goddess, her face half hidden by a cloud of white tulle. Marc's vision blurred with unshed tears. He lifted Marina's veil with trembling hands.

Her eyes sparkled. Or sparked. She looked exasperated.

"Asshole," she hissed, for his ears only. "A Man Needs a Maid?"

He gulped. Good thing he'd left out the Allman Brothers' "Whipping Post," a great blues rock anthem. He'd surprised Rosana with it at his first wedding, but—

"Dearly beloved, we have come together," the minister began, looking from Marina to Marc. One shaggy eyebrow perched much higher than the other above his reading glasses.

Marc peeked cautiously at Marina; her eyes still smoldered. Vows were coming up.

"Do you, Marina, take this man, Marc, to love, cherish and hold, in sickness and in health, forsaking all others, as long as you both shall live?"

The words skipped like stones upon a pond, defying the gravity of their declaration. The pause that followed lasted a heartbeat too long.

"I do." Her voice was level and clear. Strong. Beautiful. Unforgettable.

Marc didn't realize he'd been holding his breath. He released an audible and grateful sigh.

"And do you, Marc—"

"I do!" He preempted the minister. "I do!"

A ripple of chuckles twittered through the church, while nose blowing trumpeted from the pews.

The exchange of rings followed, with Marc's hands trembling so badly that he nearly dropped the glittering thing. Marina helped guide him as he slid the platinum band upon her finger. He sought her eyes then, and saw them round and full, as lovely as two pale blue moons.

"I now pronounce you husband and wife. You may *really* kiss the bride." The minister's permission prompted more laughter and applause.

The kiss left no doubt about their commitment. They clasped hands and turned to face the congregation, fists raised overhead, jubilant. "Yes!" they shouted, a Marv Albert moment.

Hugs and kisses broke out like a group fever; even Marc's new mother-in-law, who had been somewhat frosty toward him, thawed, giving him a teary embrace that left sticky smears of coral lipstick on his cheek. Kissing on the lips, a lot of it, involving all kinds of relatives—didn't seem to matter who kissed whom—became a happy epidemic.

"Yay, God!" Zane whooped, tossing the ring pillow high overhead. Marc's heart flew with it.

Hawks

Ten Months Later
May 19, 1995
Santa Fe, New Mexico

A lone hawk drifted over raw and rocky hills as storm clouds massed above. Two, three, four, and finally five hawks joined the first, corkscrewing toward the adobe home hunkered amid piñon trees below. Behind the home sat a modest guesthouse; to the south, a quick stroll down a dirt driveway, stood a stable. The adjacent corral confined a white Arabian and a brown quarter horse, their manes and tails dancing in the quickening gusts.

Light desert rain began to patter. Turquoise *canales* around the roof of the house—gutters and spouts—gathered the falling drops, delivering them to conservation barrels. Steam rose and scented the air, sharp with minerals, as rain dampened rock formations above the dwelling.

The hawks continued their spiral descent. One broke off from the others and landed on the roof just outside large solar windows fronting the second-story bedroom that faced the Ortiz Mountains. The quenching rain ended all too soon, leaving ephemeral puddles.

Sitting on her bed in the loft bedroom, head bent over a box of small, glass medicine bottles, Marina sorted the bottles with shaky hands. One bottle slipped. Her attempt to catch it caused the very thing she meant to avoid—the side of her wrist broke the bottle against the nightstand.

"Shit, damn it!" She tottered to the immaculately tidy bathroom, holding her bleeding wrist. Bright red spots spattered the sand-white carpet.

"Fuck!" She stuck her wrist under the faucet, opened a stream of cold water, and watched blood ooze and vanish, ooze and vanish, swirling down the drain like a silent siren. Her stomach seized with now-familiar pain. She pressed a washcloth against the wound and steadied herself on the sink. Blood smeared the sink handle and tinted the cloth. Tears sprang to her eyes. *Stop. Breathe.* She tore her gaze from the blood to look into the mirror.

"Really? Crying over a little cut?" She raised the stained cloth to her pallid face. A stiff, ironic smile lifted her lips.

After bandaging her wrist, she returned to the bedroom to see several large hawks arrive, their talons scraping the asphalt surface outside the window. Her mood brightened at the sight. She had no words for the wild peace they brought, a feeling akin to riding her beloved horse flat out over broken desert terrain, the pale flags of mane, tail and her own bright hair waving in the wind. Feathers ruffling, the dark birds strutted and stalked. Marina moved toward the glass door to the roof, grateful for the distraction. They would welcome her, she knew.

Hi, guys! Thought you'd never get here!

One of the hawks swiveled its head, made eye contact, and dropped a mighty dump. The rest flapped and joined in. They seemed to be marking their territory like wolves.

A figure lurched into sight on the roof from around the eastern corner of the bedroom. Marc—agitated, clutching a shovel, yelling like a madman. "Hey! Take a dump on someone else's house! Fucking birds, I swear! Shit and more shit!"

Marc felt a twinge in his forearm as he waved the shovel.

The hawks hopped languidly out of his way, a few taking to the air, but not for long. They resettled on the parapet edge of the roof to critique his performance like a flock of Sicilian grannies. Slippery black and white piles surrounded his feet. His ponytail flicked into his eyes, stinging; he turned to see Marina glaring at him through the window. In seconds she was on the roof, no glass between him and the wrath in her eyes.

"What?" he asked.

"What the hell did you do that for?" She punched him in the chest.

He stepped back from a rather formidable left cross. "Ouch! Take it easy!"

She swung again.

He caught her wrist, noticing the bandage and its anatomically significant location. She barely winced.

"Slow down, baby. What happened?"

She ignored his question. "Why did you do that?"

"Look at this mess! I spend hours shoveling and scraping. I'm sick of it."

"They're my friends. I like them. Never do that again." She stood with legs splayed, hands on hips. It was a wonder she could speak, her lips were so tight.

"Come on, it's a Hitchcock shit festival!"

"Never!"

"Jesus, fine! Your friends can stay. Sorry." Ugh, he instantly regretted his tone. Petulance penalty for poor sportsmanship. He lowered his voice. "Are you okay?" He tried to examine her injured wrist.

"Didn't do it on purpose," she muttered, pulling away.

"I know. I asked if you were okay."

"I'm going to take a shower." She turned, stamped into the house through the roof door.

"Okay, we'll do the IV after the shower then, Marina?" he called. "IV post-shower? Okay?"

She paused at the doorway, her lovely features tense and sulky. "Okay. Fine."

He began to scrape at the new deposits of bird crap. A hawk landed directly in front of him. They stared each other down. *Fuck you, bird.* Hawks: 1, Marc: 0. Two more hawks landed, then a third, striding around like they owned the place. Hell, maybe they did.

"Oh, come on. Really?" He tossed the shovel down hard, a crash that might have startled an elephant, but the hawks remained aloof.

"Fine, whatever. She likes you; you can stay. But not *in* the house, got it? Not in the house!" This from a guy who said people who talked to cats were crazy.

Hawks: 4, Marc: 0. Game over.

He stepped from the roof into the bedroom just as Marina dropped her clothes to the floor. He took a moment to contemplate her body; she paused long enough to let him. A simple red scar ran down the center of her abdomen, sternum to pubis. When she noticed his attention on her scar, she turned her back and disappeared into the bathroom.

Remorse grabbed his guts and twisted. *Plain shitty to have lost my temper like that with those fucking birds again*! The sound of shower spray filled the silence, and he walked away.

Winnie, Winterset

Fucking shitty birds. Marc was cursing under his breath as he scrubbed the dishes with a splashing clatter, unable to care that Chelsea and Zane were spectators.

"He's losing it," Chelsea said, as succinct and focused as a sports commentator.

"Losing what?" Zane asked.

"It."

A saucer cracked. "I can hear you," Marc said evenly, without turning his head.

"Sorry, Daddy, but you're acting kinda crazy," Chelsea said, her tone now cautious.

Zane sprang from his hiding place. "Crazy Daddy!"

"Well, I'm sorry you guys caught that discussion on the roof." Little pitchers, big handles, his own dad might have said, followed by a swat to the offending ear. He took a breath, willed himself to cool down. Father, husband, healer, dish-breaker, shit-scraper—

"It's just a little bird shit," Chelsea said.

Scowling at her language, Marc lobbed the word back at her. "You're a little bird shit. Why don't you clean it up?"

He took another deep, deliberate, cleansing breath, and then abandoned the sink, dashing to the living room to collapse on the big couch and invite a tickle wrestling match. "Come on, monkeys, let's see what you got. Who's gonna pin me?"

As they lay panting in a triple scrum afterwards, Chelsea knocked him breathless again.

"Hey, Daddy? Marina will be okay. And I kinda like the birds, too. They're cool, and Marina is cool, so just because *you* aren't cool anymore doesn't mean the rest of us have to suffer—aiiii!"

Marc interrupted with a last tickle. "That'll teach you," he crowed, with the unfair advantage of the non-ticklish.

"No! Birds rule, birds rule!" she shouted gleefully, wriggling away, and Zane joined in the chant. "Birds rule! Birds rule!"

Both children pummeled him, confident that he could absorb their childish brutality with his customary paternal superpowers. He would take all their punches until their will grew tired—the ol' rope-a-dope.

"Got it, birds rule!" he conceded at last, grinning at his headstrong offspring.

"Damn right, birds rule!" Marina's voice rang out from behind them.

Chelsea and Zane abandoned him to greet her with hugs, nearly knocking her off-balance. Marc could see that she was unsteady, but covering it with as much willpower as she could muster. He felt proud of her and of the children, whose youthful wisdom drove them to pretend, for her sake, that they believed she could rough and tumble with them still.

"I love that the birds poop on the roof," declared Zane in a transparent bid for her approval, giving everyone permission to smile.

"Easy for you to say—you're not the one shoveling all that shit," Chelsea said. She gave Marc a sideways glance, tilting her chin, a gesture he recognized as his own. "You're welcome," she said, continuing the mimicry. "Uh... I mean poop. What's the big deal? They both have four letters and mean the same thing."

Marc's face twisted. How the fuck was he going to keep his little girl from turning into a potty mouth? But he was thankful someone was defending him, even sarcastically.

"She has a point," Marina said.

"She always has a point," he said. "Oy."

"The real point is that you guys need to chill out, especially you, Dad. You should get the hell out of town. A beach. A big-ass beach." Triumphant nine-year-old Chelsea clearly relished the power of salty language as she warmed to her argument.

"You guys are my beach," Marina said.

Chelsea was adamant. "We need something drastic around here."

"Okay, let's pack us all up and tour the world," Marina said, grinning.

"Nah, just you two. Chels and I are booked," Zane said.

"Really?" Marina played along.

"Yeah, you need to spark things up a bit." Chelsea tag-teamed her brother with a theatrical wink.

"You don't need a bunch of kids running around." Zane had taken a page from his sister's playbook or had been coached. What a couple of little connivers.

Marc snickered in spite of himself. "Okay, enough horseplay in the house." He shooed the children outside and served two cups of coffee in the kitchen. The caffeine seemed to revive Marina.

"Marc, I want you to put up my Children at Play sign at the blind curve of the driveway. Also, I want to help out with Winnie. I miss him."

"He misses you too."

Winnie, whose formal name was Winterset, was her handsome Arabian. Marina had purchased him with the hope of showing and riding in competitions. She loved Winnie with the ardor of a lifelong horsewoman, causing Marc to joke occasionally about his own standing in the hierarchy of her affections, asking, "Who's number one today, Winnie or me?" Sometimes she would pause so long before saying *you* that the look on his face made her laugh out loud.

"I think he's sick of me," Marc continued. "You're the cowgirl. I'm from the West Side of Manhattan."

"The sign is ready. *I'm* sick of thoughtless people speeding. Someone could die." Her voice rose, fretful. "Just post the hole and cement it in, please? It means a lot to me." She set down her cup and got to her feet. "I'll be with the horses."

Marc finished his coffee and went to gather tools and supplies: a post-hole digger, a shovel, a sack of cement in a wheelbarrow, a bucket of water. He stumbled out to the bend in the driveway, spilling so much water that he ended up making multiple trips to refill the bucket.

The post-hole digger clanged against the rock-hard surface, sending vibrations up his arms and into his shoulders, neck, and jaw. Soon he was perspiring and filthy. He wasn't the handiest guy in the tool shed, but this endeavor was more about persistence and brute strength than handiness. He eventually settled into a rhythm, gripping the long wooden handles, drumming the earth. Chop rock, carry water. Repeat.

Something green glinted in his shovel, an arrowhead of recent vintage: plastic. He slipped it into a pocket, good material for a bedtime story for the kids.

Marina put her favorite mixed tape into her Walkman and headed out to the stables, where Winnie greeted her immediately. She held an apple for him and another for Brown Horse, a placid fellow content to carry Marc or the kids on trail rides. She stroked and addressed each in turn. Winnie's firm muscles rippled under his sleek, white coat; his neck bobbed, and those dark, liquid eyes sparkled with intelligence. He was tall for an Arabian, nearly sixteen hands at the shoulder.

"I missed you too, Winnie. Marc will kill me for this, but I need a ride. Come on, let's saddle up!"

She was accustomed to saddling Winnie herself, but hadn't realized how much strength she had lost since the last time she rode. She staggered under the weight of the saddle. It took longer than usual to get it positioned and buckled properly, yet Winnie waited obediently.

The anticipation of riding spurring everything else from Marina's mind. In the saddle at last, shifting to the familiar rocking of Winnie's stride, she felt as close to her normal self as she had since before the surgery. It was too soon, of course, but time was truly relative these days.

There was Marc, positioning the post. It was in the ground, slanting about thirty degrees, the hole not deep enough yet. He turned at her approach and lifted an arm across his face, squinting and wiping running sweat from his eyes.

"I was wondering if you could stop yourself. Don't you think it's a little soon to be riding?" His tone was light, but his misgivings were visible.

"Yes, but it feels really good. Should we saddle up Brown Horse for you?"

He glanced at the tilting post. "No… give yourself twenty minutes, then get off that horse—you're going to pop a staple."

"Okay, I'll be back in ten." She started to put the headphones on, but paused to say, "Got my riding music cranked up, the tape you made for me with Smashing Pumpkins' 'Zero.'" She patted Winnie on the neck. "Let's go!"

The horse wheeled and away they went. *Run, boy.*

Marc watched with growing concern. Marina wasn't going for a sedate trail ride or a stroll—that was clear. She was going to run that horse hard. Damn. He sighed and returned to ramming the earth.

Eventually, he set the post and shoveled concrete around it, in a hurry now, slopping gray lumps into variegated dirt piles. The sign listed stubbornly. He scavenged scraps of lumber from behind the stable and threw together a makeshift brace of wood and rocks to hold the post in place while the concrete set. That would have to do. He stepped back to admire his handiwork, carelessly wiping bleeding hands on concrete-spattered jeans. What time was it?

The staccato clip of hooves behind him lifted his mood for a moment. But when he turned, Winnie, riderless, trotted past him.

He sagged against the signpost, causing it to tilt again, and this time he didn't care. The sun would set soon. Where was she? What had happened? His heart felt seized, squeezed, emptied out into a hole too deep and cold to contemplate.

The horse tossed its head, restive and mute.

A childhood memory surfaced, strong and insistent, feeding off Marc's worry. Another riderless horse, another woman in distress, and another and another, and another Marc, seven years old, struggling to comprehend. Struggling to act.

One snowy November night, Marc was home with only his great-grandmother, Little Grandma. The house was still and dim, but he was engrossed in watching the lively antics of the *I Love Lucy* show on a grand console black-and-white TV in his father's wood-paneled den. He sat in his pajamas, luxuriously engulfed in the enormous recliner, illuminated by the TV's flickering light. On the TV, Lucy and Ethel were stuffing their faces with chocolates as a factory conveyor belt sped up. "Listen, Ethel, I think we're fighting a losing game!" Lucy exclaimed. Little Grandma's frail voice rose from somewhere outside the room.

"Marco, *vieni qui, subito.*"

He remained fixated on the televised images, laughing at Lucy and Ethel's chaos. Now they had removed their chef hats and were frantically scooping chocolates into them, cheeks stuffed like chipmunks. Lucy was even shoving them into the front of her dress!

Little Grandma called again, breathless. "Marc, Marco, come here."

But he was hopelessly mesmerized.

"Fine, you're doing splendidly," said the stern boss lady, when she marched in to observe. Lucy and Ethel froze, wide-eyed and fat-cheeked. "Speed it up a little!" the boss lady bellowed.

Little Grandma appeared in the doorway, supporting herself against its frame, her brow moist. She was a tiny Italian woman, so short that Marc fully expected to stand taller than her by his eighth birthday.

"I think I am sick…" she said in a thick Italian-American accent.

Marc snapped to attention and shot from the soft leather chair to help Little Grandma into another chair near the doorway. She seemed even smaller than usual.

"My heart, ah, my arm. Rub it there." She was holding her left shoulder, her face contorted, and a pearl of a tear hung in the corner of each eye, which scared Marc more than anything.

He stepped behind the chair, eyes on the perfect bun atop Little Grandma's head, and began tentatively to massage her neck and shoulders. "How's this, Little Grandma?"

"*Grazie, piccolo mio….*"

The pearls dissolved and coursed down her cheeks. New tears bubbled up. The glow from the TV was the only light in the room, but Marc could see that she was abnormally pale. He sensed she was fighting pain, but saw no cuts or bruises. What was wrong with her?

"Let's get you to the sofa, Little Grandma," he said, making a grown-up decision. He didn't want her falling out of the chair, so the sofa seemed safer. He helped her to stand, bowed by the surprising weight of her small frame, and steadied her as she took careful steps.

"Rest here, Little Grandma; Dad will be home soon," he said hopefully, even though he was uncertain about what to do. "Should I call an ambulance?"

"No." She inhaled a shallow breath. "Call Madeleine."

His stomach clenched. Auntie Madeleine was a nurse and would know what to do, but he didn't know her telephone number.

"I think… I am dying…" Little Grandma's voice trailed off.

"Oh, *shit*. Relax, Little Grandma. I'll be right back!"

He tore from the den and raced to his bedroom, pulled a ball of socks from his dresser, tugged them on with shaking hands. He slammed open the sliding door on his closet, grabbed his rubber boots, and thrust his feet into them. His wool peacoat was in the hall closet by the front door. He buttoned it over his pajamas and added a balaclava, a green and red knitted thing that covered his entire head, leaving holes for his eyes, nose, and mouth. A fleece-lined hat with earflaps fit snuggly on top, and mittens finished his getup. The long mirror on the inside door of the closet showed a small Siberian bank robber. He clumped back to the den.

"Little Grandma, I'm going to run over to Zizzi Madeleine's. I'll be fast. Stay calm; I'll be back soon."

Little Grandma remained propped on the sofa. Her eyelids fluttered; her chest rose and fell. She managed a slight nod. Lucy and Ethel were gone, replaced by a cigarette commercial.

Marc ran to the kitchen, scraped a chair to the high cabinet, climbed to stand on its seat, and reached for the big metal flashlight. When he pressed the button, faint, rust-colored light flared. "Yes!" He jumped down with a resounding thump on the linoleum and raced to the front door.

Swirling and disorienting curtains of densely falling snow obscured the shadowy street. Concrete steps leading from the front door to the sidewalk were slick. He grasped the handrail, lurched down. Snow was accumulating in drifts, blown by erratic gusts of wind. The snowflakes were like the wind's fingerprints, visible traces of invisible hands slapping his lips and nose with stinging force, poking at his eyes. He was alone in a blizzard. The flashlight beam caught snowflakes instead of illuminating the gloom, so he turned it off.

Auntie Madeleine's house was several blocks away. He alternately trudged and ran, slipping constantly, his legs wet with snow, his back damp with cold sweat. *Please help, Zizzi Madeleine*, he silently begged. *Little Grandma needs…*

His aunt's house looked empty when he arrived. He banged on the door, calling her name, his voice loud enough in the muffled street that surely someone would hear. But no one answered. His pounding became more insistent and desperate. His throat tightened. His chin began to tremble.

At last, a pair of headlights shone down the block through the maddening snow dance. The approaching car was traveling very slowly. Marc considered running out to flag down the driver until he recognized with relief Zizzi Madeleine's Mercedes. He loved that car. It pulled to the curb in front of the house, and Zizzi Madeleine, a tall, dark-haired woman in chic winter coat and boots, emerged from the driver's seat.

Marc tottered to her, calling her name, half-sobbing.

"Is that you, Marco?" his aunt asked, peering at the balaclava.

"Zizzi Madeleine! I think Little Grandma is dying! Please hurry!"

"Get in," she said abruptly, sliding back into the car. He clambered into the front passenger seat and they were off, fishtailing into the storm.

Zizzi Madeleine gripped the steering wheel with fancy-gloved hands. The windshield wipers swished back and forth at top speed, but the short trip felt agonizingly long. Marc wished she would drive faster. He glanced up at her profile. Madeleine wasn't really his aunt, his zizzi; she was his mother's cousin, but they were like sisters. Madeleine was distinctive, glamorous like a movie star. She wore her black hair up, and blood-colored lipstick on her wide mouth. Her dark eyes were focused on the slushy road. But when she turned them to Marc, he felt as if they could see right into him. He fiddled with the little ashtray in the car door's armrest. After yelling his lungs out, his throat was dry and he had nothing to say.

Finally, they were home, and there was his father's Lincoln in the driveway. Marc's spirits rose at the sight of the big car. Dad always drove Lincolns. He said the Italians bought Cadillacs because Caddy trunks were bigger. Marc didn't understand why that made his mother and aunts roll their eyes. Dad also refused to buy a foreign vehicle, declaring such a purchase not only unpatriotic but damn near traitorous. The sight of Madeleine's Mercedes would pucker his mouth, but that was all. She had a way of capturing attention and obedience that made people defer to her, even his father.

Where is he? Marc peered through the windshield. The Lincoln was empty, but light brimmed from the house.

Zizzi Madeleine strode to the front door without a backwards look, Marc trailing behind. Now that he was home, he felt nervous, sick to his stomach. What was going to happen? He found the narrow hallway crowded with grownups, though there were only his mother and aunt. His father came out of the den, cradling the limp, unconscious body of Little Grandma in his arms.

"Marc, wait there," said his father, catching sight of him. "Madeleine, call an ambulance."

"Jerry, she wouldn't like that," Madeleine objected with cool authority. "She's ninety-one. Sicilians don't do hospitals. Lay her on your bed."

Marc's father stopped. The conflict played out on his face—the urge to call for an ambulance countered by Italian determination to keep death a private family matter. The fact that Madeleine worked in a hospital didn't affect her attitude one iota when it came to culture and tradition.

Without another word, Marc's father took Little Grandma into the master bedroom. Everyone followed, watching as he placed her carefully on the double bed. He, Zizzi Madeleine, and Marc's mother hovered around her, murmuring, loosening her clothing, putting an ear to her chest, tenderly dabbing her brow with a damp cloth.

Marc watched from the hallway, thawing in his balaclava. Zizzi Madeleine must have sensed his presence, for she turned, looked at him calmly, and closed the door. He continued to stand stock still as snow melted from his coat and boots, forming puddles.

Dr. DiPietro made a house call that night. The prognosis was grim—probable heart attack. Little Grandma was dying. The family decided that she would die peacefully in Marc's parents' bed, and so she did, in the early hours of November 22, 1963.

Little Grandma's body was laid out on the double bed in queenly fashion, surrounded by piles of white lilies and gladioli, red roses and chrysanthemums, pink carnations and the Virgin Mary's tears.

Six women, Marc's aunts and cousins, sat in the room conversing quietly in New York Italian accents, their faces drawn with grief, wrinkled handkerchiefs clutched in their hands. Marc wandered between the women's tableau centered on dead Little Grandma in the bedroom, and the men's gathering around the television in the den, the focal point of another drama of death.

"She looks peaceful, *cara* Nicolina," said Auntie Zevazine.

"I don't think she suffered at all," said Cousin Carolina.

"So sad, the president. Oh, my God, Little Grandma, the president, so sad. What the *hell* is going to happen next?" said Cousin Lucia, hands waving, bracelets rattling.

Just yesterday afternoon, the man who had killed the president had himself been shot and killed. The women were divided over whether that was a good thing or not. Meanwhile, the men's momentary distraction, the Washington Redskins' win over the Philadelphia Eagles last night, was also a source of argument. Should Pete Rozelle have let the games go forward? Was football a holy sacrament?

Uncle Gamanuch poked his head into the doorway. "JFK's on TV," he announced. The Kennedys would be on TV all week.

"Poor Jackie, and those beautiful children," said Auntie Francesca. "Poor Nonna, ay, ay…" Her voice broke on a ragged sob.

Auntie Fortunata and Carolina moved to comfort her.

Marc rubbed his eyes, itching from three days and nights of tears and sleeplessness. Barely twelve hours after Little Grandma's death, the calamity of the president's assassination had been a tidal wave sweeping all other deaths along with it.

Marc stared at the figure of Little Grandma on the bed, wanting to record everything about this moment in his eyes as if they were cameras. Her stillness. Her hair! He had always seen Little Grandma's silver hair pinned in a bun on the top of her head. Someone had lovingly washed, combed, and fanned it out into an extraordinary display. Her crowning glory reached her ankles.

"That little bun made all that hair!" he whispered, awestruck.

His mother, in tears, guided him gently from the room before returning to sit with the weeping women. Marc went back to the den that was fogged blue with smoke from Lucky Strikes, Camels, and Winstons. Five men intently watched the TV. Today they weren't arguing about which cigarette brand was best.

"Dad?"

"Shush. Come here," his father said, his voice as firm and gentle as Marc's mother's hand.

He climbed into his father's lap; they watched the funeral procession without speaking. The flag-draped coffin rested on a large-wheeled cart led by many white horses, their hooves clattering like rain. Jackie and the kids. John John's salute. A dark, riderless horse guided by a serviceman. And drums, their military cadence insistent and ominous.

The sight of the riderless horse filled Marc with dread. The animal was glossy and lively, but its simple saddle carried the empty presence of a man who was gone. Tall, shiny boots stood facing backwards in the stirrups. Marc shivered, barely aware of the comfort of his father's arms.

Little Grandma and the president. His mother grieving; she had loved this president and voted for him, nearly triggering a divorce. Marc's ears had stung when his father yelled that she had canceled his vote. A terrible fight had followed, unforgettable, fierce, frightening. Marc had never heard anything like that fight in his house before, and the echoes never really left its walls. His mother's vote had mattered in some deeply mysterious, grownup way. Now her president was gone.

All who loved that man—his children, his wife, Marc's mother, millions of people watching TV at this moment—would not get him back. Little Grandma gone, too, his beautiful Little Grandma. It was almost too much to bear. He was supposed to be taller than her next year.

The riderless horse tossed its head and beat the pavement with its iron shoes. Its light, four-legged rhythm rang in counterpoint to the pattern of the drums. The drums grew louder, strong and powerful, and it seemed they would never stop. Marc felt overcome by an impulse to follow them.

"Winnie, you son of a *bitch!*"

Marina's shrill yell struck Marc's attention like the bite of a bull snake, alarming and painful, but not deadly, thank God. Relief flowed through his veins. She was stalking up the road, rigid with anger. When she got close enough, she grabbed Winnie by the mane and smacked him on the muzzle. The startled horse shook his head and snorted.

"What the hell was that?" she shrieked. "He threw me, nearly killed me!"

"Are you all right?" Marc scrambled closer to check her out. Her chest was heaving, and she was dusty but not bloodied. There didn't seem to be anything broken. "Did you hit your head? Did you—"

She backed away, agitated. "I'm fine." She gave Winnie another smack, screaming, "Don't ever do that again!"

Marc felt bloodless now, in shock. "Wow, you're a real horse whisperer, you are."

Fucking unthinkable, losing her mind with her beloved horse. That scared him as much as her being thrown. Marina, who right up until the surgery had devoted spare hours volunteering at an equestrian center for disabled kids, had struck her horse. The volunteer work lifted her spirits, and the equine therapy community adored her. Something worse than losing her ride had happened out on the desert today.

"I'm going to take Winnie back to the stable," she said sullenly, the fight gone out of her.

He left the post-hole digger lying at the side of the road. "I'll help you."

"No, finish the sign. It's important. I want to be alone. Shit, can't even ride anymore." Her voice cracked. She slowly walked Winnie back to the stable, her shoulders slumping in defeat, her legs unsteady.

The sign was done. A little crooked, but done. Marc picked up the post-hole digger and loaded the wheelbarrow. His neck ached with a dull throb, barely noticeable compared to the fiery hole in his heart.

He lifted his face to the cooling sky, where pink, orange, lavender, marine blue, and silver clouds blazed above the darkening hills. Another outrageously beautiful Santa Fe sunset over the Garden of the Gods.

Yes and No

May 22, 1995
Santa Fe, New Mexico

After a typical packed Monday at the gym, Marc fed the family and animals and helped get the kids to bed, sparing no time to think about himself, which was probably a good thing. Marina went up to the loft early as she frequently did these days, but wasn't asleep when Marc entered the bedroom. He found her propped against the pillows in a simple, sexy nightgown, a book in her hands. He stripped off his shirt, his body warming at the sight of her.

"What's up?" she said, as if nothing were up.

"I don't know, baby. You tell me."

"Well, okay. When's the last time we made love? A month ago? That's not like you, stud boy."

Wow, she had to shoot straight to the heart—or worse, the— "I'm sorry, but for God's sake, I... It's hard." He left the obvious joke hanging.

"I don't turn you on anymore, with all of this?" Her eyes nailed him to the floor.

"Not true." He meant it.

"Then what is it?" Before he could respond, her book bounced across the bed. "I'm sick, not *dead.*"

"I hate it when you talk like that." His throat tightened. "What do you want me to do? I'm doing the best I can here." He hated hearing *himself* talk like that.

She pushed down the bedcovers and stepped before him, reaching for his waist. He caught a glimpse of bruises blooming on her thigh and hip from being thrown by Winnie.

"I'm sorry," he said, dangerously helpless in the moment.

"No, I'm sorry. I'm sorry for all of this."

"Don't say you're sorry." He enclosed her in a tentative embrace, moved his lips to hers, tangled his fingers in her hair over the nape of her neck.

Her hand, with its bandaged wrist, stroked his bare torso, shoulder, upper arm. He felt the hunger in her touch, the play of haste and pressure in her fingertips. She walked her fingers down his belly, then settled her hand on the mound of his denim-covered crotch.

"Anything happening down here?" she asked.

Hell yeah, he fervently hoped. He released her and flopped to the bed on his back, arms open. "Why don't you come find out for yourself."

She inserted a cassette into the stereo, and "I Touch Myself," by the Divinyls, began to play. Then she faced him, bright-eyed and singing along. The short nightgown accentuated her breasts, concealed her scar, and exposed her legs. She began to dance, her hand sliding down the silky fabric to her thighs and between them. In the next moment, she opened a bedside cabinet to pull out a pair of pink fur-lined handcuffs, twirling them around with a mischievous grin. Holy shit, this was something new.

He raised himself on his elbows, the better to enjoy the show; he'd really missed this playful side of her. A sudden ache pounded his sternum, reminding him of the knuckles she'd driven against him in her defense of the hawks. The sheer nakedness of her spirit seized his breath. A one-two punch—a cocktail of love and sorrow, hope and dread, shaken not stirred, desperate but not helpless—chilled him from the inside out.

As she leaned to kiss him, bringing her chest to his, her legs over his, he tried to match her passion, but numbness overcame him, leaving his body sprawled like a dead man. Nope, he wasn't going to rise to the occasion. Her kisses trailed off. Her arms loosened. She rolled to her back beside him and sighed.

"I'm sorry." His words sounded as inadequate as he felt.

"It's okay, baby."

"No, this is lame." He was sliding fast into a blue funk.

She turned off the music.

"You know what I think?" she said. "It's the meds they put you on. I researched that drug in the PDR, and the side effects are many times—" She gestured with her index finger, pointing straight up, then slowly curling it down, like a finger-puppet show. A finger-penis show. "I love how they throw around *side* effects. They're *effects!*"

She adopted an authoritative British accent. "They're *side* effects, like they are waaaay over there." Then she switched to a baby voice to add, "Tiny, little, fairy side effects." She squeaked, pointing to the side of the room.

Tactful of her to turn her frustration into a gift for him, an excuse, but it only made him feel worse. "Maybe you're right," he said, "but I can't stop taking them. I've got a lot on me."

"*You* have a lot on you?"

"Come on, don't do that. You know, I just... I need the pills right now."

"Okay, fine! Fuck me on *your* timetable. *You* have all the time in the world!" She hurled the handcuffs to the floor and sprang from the bed, all sympathy furled tightly back inside her. She flounced into the bathroom and slammed the door.

Marc lay flattened on the bed. He stared up at the roughhewn vigas of the ceiling, rubbed his eyes, tried to breathe again. There was one more chance to feel like a man tonight, to feel like himself. He pulled his T-shirt back on.

"I'm going downstairs to watch the game," he said through the bathroom door, aiming to beat a retreat to a less urgent life-and-death game, the seventh by the New York Knicks in the NBA playoff against the Indiana Pacers.

"Have. Fun." Marina shot the words at him.

Marv Albert, Voice of the Knicks, yammered his famous stream of commentary from the living room television as the game clock ticked down. Marc hunched in a leather armchair, cursing the Pacers' Reggie Miller, a dead-eyed shooter. Like every true-blue Knicks fan, Marc bled orange and blue. More than a fan, he cherished his memories of working for the team after grad school at NYU. Fantastic luck, being able to do that.

"Come on, Patrick!" he bellowed. The playoff game was hot, a passionate substitute for the fizzled game of passion upstairs. *Keep it up, guys, somebody has to.* "Come on, get it in there!"

Albert continued his rapid-fire delivery: "Jess Kersey in a conversation with Derek Harper, who will throw in, Haywoode Workman giving him the room right here, and now gets the delay of game call. Larry Brown able to check over the Knick alignment. It looks like the same kind of setup, they'll look for John Starks running out to the top, as Starks trucks to the corner, inbounds to Ewing, down to three, down to two, Ewing *no*, a hit and it's all over."

"*No!*" Marv Albert was known for *Yes!* Marc hated Marv's *no*s.

"The Indiana Pacers defeat New York Knicks 97 to 95 to take the series in seven, and they advance to the Eastern Conference Final to face the Orlando Magic. Patrick Ewing had the shot, but it went in and out. And now many questions concerning the New York Knicks."

At least *something* went in and out. Marc bounded to his feet, snarling. "Yeah, no shit! You're seven foot—dunk the fucking ball!"

This was not the resolution he'd been looking for, up- or downstairs. He was losing the *game*. He glared in enraged disbelief at the television, unable to make sense of the words being spoken, unable, maybe unwilling, to rein in his anger. He lurched over to a group of small bronze horses displayed upon the mantle, and without hesitation, he grabbed a rearing horse and fired it at the illuminated screen. *Boom*! Glass scattered everywhere, flying like deadly shrapnel around the room. Marv was silenced.

Marina screamed from upstairs. A moment later she stood pale-faced in a white bathrobe, peering over the edge of the loft. "What the hell are you doing? Jesus, baby, you scared me to d— Are you hurt?" She began to descend the curving staircase.

Marc stood stupefied, a trickle of blood dripping into his eye from a cut on his forehead.

"A little upset. Knicks blew it; I overreacted. Sorry, won't happen again." He felt like a raging, monumental schmuck. Not a drink in months—not that that would have been an excuse. But the pills were supposed to help him keep it together.

"You overreacted?" She halted on the stairs. "Go back to Dr. Jefferson! Tell him to get you off those damn pills. *Talk* to the man. That's what he's there for."

"We've been through this. I don't want to talk to him. I don't want to talk about *this* with Jefferson." Meek, apologetic, he stepped toward her, his slippers crunching on glass.

"Stop! You can't keep doing this. I can't take it. I love you, Marc. I love you so much, and I am so…"

She reached the last step of the staircase as he arrived at its foot. She remained on the step, eye to eye with him.

"Don't say it," he said, his voice breaking.

"I am so *sorry* this has happened."

"It isn't your fault, Marina."

"Listen. You know the first thing that went through my mind when they told me? I thought that everyone I loved was going to hate me. Even now, when I see you so torn up, I feel it's my fault."

"Why would you think that?"

She shrugged, put a palm over his heart.

"I just had a moment, but I'm good. I'm okay." He wiped blood from his eye. "I'll get this mess cleaned up."

"Go to Dr. Jefferson."

Nothing left to say. The silence was broken by a wail from Zane.

"Damn, I'll take care of him. Don't come down—you'll cut yourself. I'll call Jefferson in the morning, I promise."

"Yes."

The only *yes* he was going to get that night. She turned to climb the stairs.

Marc picked his way cautiously through debris into the kitchen and around to Chelsea and Zane's bedroom. Thick adobe walls had helped to muffle the crash, but not enough for the kids to sleep through it. He found Chelsea on Zane's bed, comforting him. A nightlight on the wall glowed dim and cozy.

"Hey, big man, what's the matter?"

"I got scared." Zane's voice was small.

"What scared you?"

"Thunder."

"That wasn't thunder, Z-boy. I, um, had a technical problem with the TV. But good news, guys, Daddy's buying the family a new TV tomorrow." Good news, right, for the favored TV salesman.

"Yay!" Zane said, a little cheerier. He bought the lie, or pretended to.

"What were you and Marina fighting about?" Chelsea asked, not buying it.

"We weren't fighting. Sometimes we have serious discussions, but it's okay. It's fine, sweetie." He knew how bogus that *fine* sounded the moment it fell from his mouth.

"Was it about the cancer?" Chelsea would not be deterred.

"Chels—" Marc warned with a nod toward Zane.

She followed his glance. "He needs to know, right? We can't tell him she went on vacation."

Could he feel any lower tonight? A lesson in manhood from his sick wife, now another one from his little girl. These gals were made of pure grit; his own seemed to have crumbled and washed away. He swallowed hard.

"Chels, honey… take care of your brother."

Marc kissed the tops of their heads and closed the door behind him. Stopped in the kitchen, grabbed the avocado-green rotary phone from the wall, trailed its long, curly cord as he rooted for the telephone book in a cabinet. He flipped through the yellow pages and dialed furiously, then listened until the call was picked up on the other end.

"Good evening, Delta Airlines," said a female agent's voice in a pleasant chirp. "How may I help you?"

RX

May 23, 1995
Santa Fe, New Mexico

Dr. Jeffrey Jefferson's waiting room, clearly outfitted by an obsessive enthusiast of unbridled Southwestern style, could have doubled as a tourist shop. Georgia O'Keeffe and Miguel Martinez prints hung on the walls; katsina figures, exquisite pottery, and crude wooden howling coyotes decked in bandanas sat prominently on shelves; tchotchkes galore covered every available surface.

A sad-eyed black and white Koshari clown caught Marc's attention, not in a good way. He was convinced it followed him with its painted eyes; he would turn it to face the wall when he entered the waiting room, and it was always turned back by the time he left his appointment with Dr. Jefferson, even when the waiting room appeared empty. Today he didn't touch it, but he did shield himself from its disturbing gaze with a golf magazine.

He'd been lucky to get in to see the doc at such short notice. At the recommendation of his friend, Dr. Richard Frank, the appointments had become a semi-regular thing since Marina's exploratory surgery. Richard—Marc sometimes called him Ricardo, indulging a New York impulse to nickname—was chief medical officer at the local hospital, a good friend to have in any case, a great friend to have in these circumstances.

Jeffrey Jefferson, who went by J.J. with his friends, was a good doc and a reasonable guy, despite his over the top style. Originally from back East like Marc, he didn't fool anyone about his origins with his Southwestern getup. His accent was all New York, gravelly and intense.

"Hey, Marc, come on in, dude."

Dr. Jefferson leaned into the waiting room, a man of modest physical stature, but one whose presence stood large. He sported a leather coat, a belt with an enormous silver buckle worthy of a World Wrestling Federation entertainer, an equally eye-catching bolo tie, lavishly tooled cowboy boots, and turquoise and silver bracelets. He even wore a cowboy hat indoors.

Marc followed him into the office, as Southwestern kitschy as the waiting room.

Dr. Jefferson settled into an overstuffed chair and gestured across a coffee table toward a garish couch. "Have a seat. How've you been?"

"Fine, Dr. Jefferson." His tone affected boredom.

"We're behind closed doors, Marc. Call me J.J. Like the new couch?"

"Lovely. It's you!" he responded automatically with the sarcastic tone of a New Yorker. The patterns hurt his eyes, but there was no point in saying so. He settled back uncomfortably.

"So?" said the doc. So many questions in that one little word.

"Ah, shit, Doc... J.J. My wife is sick, my former wife is a continual pain in the ass, and—oh, yeah—my dick doesn't work. I'm just peachy."

"Is that all?" Dr. Jefferson crossed a jean-clad knee, one pointy boot aimed at Marc.

"I threw a horse through the TV last night," Marc added, unemotionally. "A sculpture of a horse. Little thing, big mess."

"Saw the game. Ewing? Walt Fraser was my guy," Dr. Jefferson said, equally impassive. "The sculpture—a Star York piece, by any chance? Love her stuff."

"Yeah," Marc said, distracted. "Bronze. Birthday gift for my wife. Scared the kids. The crash, I mean. Called in a favor at the Candyman this morning to get a new TV, monster size, big as a Volkswagen, supposed to be delivered this afternoon. I've given them probably ten thousand dollars of business, what with stereos, drum kits, music—"

"What did you do then, after the blowup last night?"

"Bought plane tickets. The Yucatán. Me and Marina."

"Sounds great."

"Thought it might help."

"It might, but it's not going to change anything. You know that."

"I don't know. We really need it, anyway. The kids are making me."

"I think a vacation is just what the doctor ordered, or ought to order."

"Marina wants me to stop the antidepressants."

"How do you feel about that?"

Classic psych question. *How do I feel? How do I answer that?* "That's the problem. How do I feel? What I *don't* want to feel hurts like hell anyway. Scares me to think of how much more it could hurt. What I *do* want to feel—shit, it's so messed up, but—I think I should keep taking them." Marc hesitated, defeated.

"The sexual effects can have a lot to do with the meds. That's common. They also could be due to the massive stress you've been under."

"Yeah. I didn't think about the side effects' effect. I take time off for Marina, and my patients find someone else to crack their backs. My appointment book has been a bit thin lately. My patients, my wife, my kids... I need to be able to get up every day, keep everything going, keep myself going. Feels like I'm crawling, just... crawling."

"How are the kids?"

"Zane doesn't really understand. Chelsea seems okay, overly strong for her years. Growing up fast. Marina is..."

"Yes?"

"Marina." Marc's face spasmed.

"Do you feel alone in this?"

Dr. Jefferson's persistent matter-of-fact questions rescued and slew him at the same time, painful but medically necessary interventions. The acid taste of pre-vomit soured his mouth. He looked at his hands. "Chels holds it together for Zane's sake; they still have their mother, and the pills keep me..."

"From throwing artwork at the TV? Pills may help you stay out of the red zone, but—"

"But meanwhile I have a life, a family to provide for, and my wife has cancer. End of story. I thought we were talking about my dick."

"You want to talk about your dick?"

Marc heaved a shuddering sigh.

"It's going to take time."

The doctor's voice was gentle, but Marc choked on impatience and frustration. "I don't *have* any fucking time." The words fell wet into his hands.

Dr. Jefferson passed a decorative tin tissue box from the coffee table. They sat holding the agonizing moment between them in silence.

Eventually Dr. Jefferson said, "Well, this trip will get you away, get you guys on a beach, Marina in a bikini. And you want to make love, so that's a good sign." He waited. "Am I wrong?"

"No." Another hugely loaded little word.

They fist-bumped across the table.

Dr. Jefferson scribbled on a pad. "We'll taper off and discontinue the meds. Not all of us psychs are pill pushers. Let's see how you feel. You'll let me know." He looked up. "Have a great trip; please give my best to Marina."

He handed Marc the paper. On it were instructions for the meds, followed by *Rx for fun, love and wonder.*

Moonflute

It was a long day, with the Jefferson appointment and an afternoon of Marc's own patients. Skidding into his driveway, Marc swerved out of the way of a delivery truck churning up dust, heading back to town. Thanks, Candyman. Thin appointment book, thin wallet, but the show must go on. The new TV had better be top of the line.

He saw an old blue Subaru station wagon covered in bumper stickers parked ahead of him. Whirled Peas. I Brake for Jackalopes. Water is Life. Meat is Murder. Hug a Tree. Hug a Cactus. If You're Not Outraged You're Not Paying Attention. I'm Already Against the Next War. My Other Car is a Broom. Well-Behaved Women Seldom Make History. Free Leonard Peltier. Support Organic Farms. Love Your Mother Earth. Save the Frogs. Save the Tiger. Save the Planet.

Behind the Subaru, what Marc called the Birkenstockmobile, sat a junior-size basketball. Marc grimaced as he stepped out of his car, picked up the ball, then tossed it into a nearby bin. "Yes!" A portable child's basketball hoop lay tumbled across his path with a rope tied around it, drag marks in the gravel. He righted the hoop and moved it out of the way of the vehicles.

Inside, the colossal new TV was blasting cartoons in the living room. An elaborate fort made of cushions, small tables, sheets, and clothesline had transformed the room into an obstacle course.

"Marina? Chelsea?"

Zane bounded in from the kitchen, his face stained red from the nose down. In one hand, a red Popsicle tilted toward the floor, trailing bright drips. Chelsea came behind him with an overflowing bowl of popcorn.

"Where's Marina, baby?" Marc asked.

"Upstairs with Moonflute."

"Ol' Moontoot. Christ, she might as well move in. Who's watching Zane?"

"I am!" Chelsea said.

"Okay, and who is watching you?"

"Also me! Oops." A cascade of popcorn hit the floor. "Don't worry, I'll clean it up." A second cascade fell as she bent to gather the fallen puffs.

"And your couch castle too, or you're moving in there. Zane, buddy, you've got a Popsicle bloodbath going on—keep it in the kitchen, please. Come on."

He took a step toward Zane, intending to steer him toward the sink, and tripped over a low-slung clothesline attached to a chair leg. The chair jerked, banging his shin. "Shit." He caught himself, tweaking his neck in the process.

"Sorry, Daddy!" Zane said.

Marc rubbed his neck, then his leg. "No harm done, but let's not push our luck, bud." He propelled Zane toward the kitchen and untied the clothesline, causing sheets to fall across the room.

"Chels, get going with this before someone breaks a neck. I'm supposed to heal necks, not break them."

"You okay, Daddy? Want some popcorn?"

"No thanks, kiddo. Hey, turn down the Looney Tunes, would you?" *Plenty of loony tunes around here already.* He followed Zane.

As he scrubbed Zane's grubby little fingers, he wondered what woo-woo weirdness Moonflute had brought in her big ol' hippie bag of tricks this time. Who'd have thought—least of all Marc—that woo-woo would come to roost in his house. He had joked about "alternative" counter-culture therapy since coming to Santa Fe from New York, where his own brand of therapy, including stretching exercises instead of hydrocodone, was considered suspiciously alternative. Yeah, opiate street drugs were the devil's work, but freeze-dried heroin shit was soooo appropriate—

"Ow!" Zane said. His hands were still red, but well-scrubbed. "Not so hard, Daddy."

Marc turned off the faucet, dropped the scrub brush. "Sorry, dude. Let's inspect." He turned Zane's hands palms up, then down. "Looking good; go help your sister."

Zane wiped his hands on his pants and took off.

Marc headed toward the stairs, but stopped to remove his shoes, the periwinkle carpet soft under his feet. He felt a rascally urge to sneak up on 'em.

Marina was a vision of loveliness in a sky-blue dress, sitting on the floor of the loft bedroom. Her eyes were closed and her face reflected an inner striving for peace. She was holding what looked like an arrow across her lap, and remained very still, except for the rising and falling of her chest.

Moonflute, a tousle-haired woman whose every freckle seemed to crackle with energy, sat on the floor before her, erect and intently focused on Marina. A pheasant feather dangled from a beaded leather thong in her hair. Both women were chanting; the sounds, or words, were foreign to Marc's ears. Moonflute cocked her head to acknowledge his presence.

"Turn outward your thoughts and free your heart," Moonflute said. "Breathe… Breathe."

"Or try holding your breath. That's what I do," Marc said, unable to stop himself.

Marina's eyelids sprang open.

"If you want to be negative, afraid I can't let you in the room," Moonflute decreed.

"I'm absolutely positive, M.F., that this is my room," he volleyed back. It was a running joke, at least on his part, what he meant by calling her M.F., though she always refused to take the bait.

"I know," Moonflute said. "I tasted your salt the minute you stepped in here."

"Hear that, Marina? She just came on to me."

"Good. Maybe she'll have more luck with you than I have."

"Well, before I limp out of here on one ball, M.F., you know I love you, but can you give us some privacy?"

"She's not going anywhere," Marina declared.

"You, breathe," Moonflute admonished. "Marc, why don't you join us?"

Her gracious tone caught him by surprise.

"Than-*Q*," he replied with a deliberate nod.

Marina shot him a pissy look.

"Ignore him and breathe," Moonflute interjected. "Thoughts turned outward."

"What does that even mean?" he asked. "And what's up with the spear—chicken sacrifices next? I'll fire up the barbecue—"

"It's a prayer arrow," Marina said severely.

"A way for her to collect herself before she dreams," Moonflute added, speaking as if to a two-year-old. "Then she'll dream what she collects."

"I get it; you're spooky and New Age. I can handle that. But now you're just making stuff up."

"You need something?" Marina was definitely not in a joking mood.

"Yeah, I need to talk to you."

"Talk."

"Without Moontoot, please."

Marina crossed her arms. "Whatever you need to say, you can say it in front of her."

Moon's superior grin utterly got his goat. "Fine. I bought two tickets to Cancún, leaving in two weeks." He gestured dropping the mic and walking away, but couldn't resist a glimpse back. Marina's mouth was an open O.

"What? No! I'm sorry, no. For how long?" If she'd looked aggravated before, she looked distressed now.

"Ten days. Ta-da!" He spun and bowed like a magician.

Panic squeezed her voice. "Ten days? I can't—I want to be here, with my horses—with Moon—we talked about this!"

"We did," Marc said. *Gotta sell the hell out of the trip now.* "I thought this was the best way. Beach, surf. Dr. Jefferson thought it was a great idea."

"Well, I don't! I told you I wanted my husband back in bed, not to go and spend way too much on a vacation and take me away from the things I love. Moon, help me out here."

"Oh, yes, M.F., please weigh in on this. That's exactly what we need." He heard the bitterness in his tone and didn't care. What the fuck.

Downstairs, a crash was followed by a shriek of laughter from Zane.

"I didn't do it!" Chelsea shouted.

Marc looked from Moonflute to Marina, held up his palm in a stop-action gesture, and stuck out a finger. "*Aspetta.*" He jogged down the stairs to check on the children.

Marina waited for Marc to move out of earshot. "Can you believe that? I mean, I love him for it, but it's crazy."

Moonflute stared at her as if she were a creature from another planet. "Crazy? Honey, what the hell is the matter with you?"

Marina's jaw dropped. "What?"

"Your sexy husband just told you he's taking you to the Yucatán. Now, I wasn't going to take his side with him standing here—I would never do that to another goddess. But you have to go on this trip, Marina, my love."

Marina gulped. "I—the timing seems wrong."

"Timing? You are smack in the middle of this profound moment in your life, and can't see it. Don't get stuck." Moon's wagging finger pressed firmly against Marina's sternum. "So, *I'm* telling you—*go*. Do you know the spirits that live in those waters and underwater caves—those *cenotes*—and on those shores? What if you collected shells from the sands of Tulum? What would your dreams show you then? And when you complete your arrow, you can release it to the water. Then your dreams will be forever on the waves."

Marina tried to digest this new counsel; she felt foggy, uncertain. "Sometimes I don't know what the fuck you're talking about."

Moon reached for her hands and clasped them, never releasing Marina's gaze. "Yes, you do. You really do!" She burst into a belly laugh.

Marina's doubt burned away in a bonfire of mutual hilarity.

Marc re-entered the room to find both women wiping their eyes and quaking with residual giggles. *Now what the—*

Childlike, Marina sprang into his arms. His knees buckled. He grabbed the dresser for a semi-controlled fall to the floor, where she straddled him and kissed him, her hair brushing his nose.

"Yes, yes! We'll go!"

"Okay, who *are* you?" Hell, maybe Moonflute had magical powers after all.

Apparently, the appreciation was mutual.

"I gotta hand it to you Marc, you're a romantic at heart," said the what? Sorceress?

"Why, thank you, that means a lot coming from... What do they call you people now?" he asked.

"Counselor, guide, therapist, friend—all of the above. And for the next hour, babysitter. I'll leave you two lovebirds alone."

Moonflute stepped over his legs to descend the stairs. "Chelsea, Zane, hey, why don't you take me to see your baby chicks," she called.

"You're a sweet man." Marina's voice was husky in his ear.

Desire and relief mingled in his chest as he exhaled tension. "We're together in this," he said. "Together."

The Kindness of Strangers

June 10, 1995
Albuquerque, New Mexico

The newly renamed Albuquerque International Sunport was minor league compared to Kennedy and LaGuardia, the New York airports Marc had grown up with. It would take two planes to reach their destination on Mexico's Yucatán Peninsula.

The check-in line was short. Marc hauled a suitcase and a cooler while Marina carried two small bags and a purse. Not a lot of stuff but awkward to handle, and she refused his suggestion to use a wheelchair. She dropped the bags to the floor and began to shuffle them forward with her feet. One of the bags bumped into the man ahead of her, a stout, older Navajo wearing a wide, lavender bandana around his forehead. He cast her a quizzical glance.

"Sorry," Marina said. "I hate these airport lines."

The man scanned the sparsely populated airport. Before he could respond, he was called to an open counter.

"You're up next, babycakes," Marc said, watching the cracks in her mood grow. *Please keep it together, babe.* She was notorious for travel anxiety; packing and the drive to the airport were the most fraught activities. To her credit, once the plane's wheels separated from the tarmac and the plane accelerated into liftoff—when other white-knuckled flyers would show their stress—she would loosen up, caress his arm, shift into vacation mode. She plopped her bags between the counters.

"Good morning," said the check-in agent, a solid-looking woman with a pleasant smile and hair pulled into a ballerina bun. "Where are you kids headed today?"

"The Yucatán," Marina said.

"Oh, Cancún, lucky you! Can I have your ID, license, or passport?"

Marina presented her documents and moved toward the security line. Marc didn't want to let her out of his sight.

"Sir, you're next."

His nose was itching—he had forgotten to take his allergy medicine in the rush of getting out the door. He set his suitcase between the counters, unsure what to do with the cooler containing Marina's remedies and medical equipment. A handful of decals decorated it, souvenirs of concerts—a Grateful Dead logo of a skull with a fat lightning bolt for a brain, a bright green marijuana leaf—

The agent peered around the cooler, frowning. "What do you have in there, sir?"

"The kids."

Her expression remained stern. Marc looked to Marina for comedic support, but her back was to him in the security line.

"Okay, take a look." He started to lift the top from the cooler, and a ghostly mist, accompanied by an herbal aroma, wafted out. He slammed it shut. "Sorry, not the kids. Organ transplant."

The agent's nose twitched. She beckoned another agent to consult with her, a crisp, unsmiling woman in an identical ballerina bun who repeated the question, "What do you have in there, sir?" Eyes narrowed, mouths grim, they scrutinized him like he was bringing a radioactive zombie swamp creature aboard Air Force One.

If anybody needed a funny-bone transplant, it was this pair of Tight Buns.

"Just a bunch of alternative remedies, concoctions, IV equipment, and dry ice," he said, hoping to get the interrogation over with. He started to reopen the cooler.

His nose itched more intensely now; there was no chance to stop it. The sneeze was explosive. Both Tight Buns sprang energetically out of the way—*nicely synchronized, ladies*—and their movement was followed by another rib-cracking sneeze. And another, all over the cooler. So, drippy nose and no tissue. Marina, who carried tissues in her purse, was gone. His face felt like an umbrella blown inside out, busted by the wind.

"Sorry! Not contagious or deadly, just allergies."

Grumbling grew behind him. The line of passengers had doubled in length in the past few moments, and he had doubled the number of agents whose time and attention were unavailable to them.

"Sir!" Tight Bun Two seemed to be the senior agent. She banged the cooler lid shut. "Please take *this* over to the security checkpoint to your right," she ordered, gesturing.

Where was Marina? She must have passed through already. Marc lugged the cooler over to a long table, where the security officer stood at attention. The officer was a pink-cheeked, very young man, hopefully cooler with the cooler.

Marc donned his game face. "Dude, what do you charge for a cavity search here?"

Blank stare.

Talk about a tough crowd, I tell ya. Shit, I'm bombing. Do. Not. Say. That. Out. Loud. Marc was starting to sweat, pulling on his collar, jutting his chin out. Hell, this kid—*no wonder he wears a mustache, trying to look older than twenty*—probably never heard of Dangerfield, or any of the Borscht Belt comedians, for that matter. Too far west of the Mississippi, too deep in the heart of mañana-land for Catskills humor.

Marc opened the cooler again, mouth-breathing to avoid more sneezes. "Dry ice." Took out the cold pack, set it aside, pulled out bundles of herbs. "Alternative remedies, *curanderismo* stuff, you know." Maybe this bumpkin was familiar with local folkways. "So, where're you from?"

The kid was digging for illicit treasure, a joint tucked away to smoke in the sky-high lavatory. That might have been Marc's choice back in the day, but that was then, this was now. Out came an enema bag from under the roots and berries, held tentatively aloft with its tube hanging down.

"Balmorhea, Texas, sir," he said.

"Ball-more-rrhea..." Marc repeated, fighting the urge to pun. "Hey, got a tissue?" He was saved by a nose: his own, dripping.

The bag came down, thank God, and a gloved hand passed him a tissue before returning to the search, carefully extracting brown glass bottles, small tubes, ampules, IV needles, a bottle of pills.

"What are these, sir?" The voice held a note of triumph.

Geez, if getting stuff *outta* the States into Mexico was tough, he could only imagine the ordeal at Customs getting back *in*. "I have a prescription for those," Marc said, deflating Junior G-Man.

Arms encircled his waist from behind, but almost immediately dropped. Marc heard a sharp intake of breath and turned to face Marina's music. "I'm not taking them."

"Then why do you *have* them?" Her voice was arctic.

He had no snappy comeback. She stalked toward the gate.

"The cooler will have to go with checked baggage, sir; it's too big for the overhead bin. You are done, sir."

Marc, his vacation mood sunk, considered the display laid out on the table. "Yeah. Looks like." He shoved everything back into the cooler in a jumble, re-duct-taped it shut, and pinched a handful of tissues.

Marina was halfway down the fuselage in an aisle seat, a brewing tempest reflected all over her face. The middle seat was empty, the window seat occupied by the Navajo man from the check-in line. Marc squeezed between the two of them.

"How 'bout them Indians?" he said to the man, his go-to sports greeting. His breath caught; damn, too late to reel it back in. Their noses inches apart, the man regarded him for a moment, stony-eyed.

"Cleveland," Marc added.

Another painful moment of silence passed before the man spoke, slowly and thoughtfully. "My money's on the Braves."

"Seriously?" Marc said. "Atlanta, huh? Got a weak start, but the season's young."

"Had some shake-ups; they'll come around."

"Who's your football team?" Marc asked, cheered by the prospect of guy-to-guy sports rap.

"Washington Racial Slurs," said the man with a hint of a smile. "Redskins."

Before Marc could respond, Marina's storm broke.

"Goddammit, you are a complete *asshole*."

Marc's expansive mood shrank. The damn pills. "I wasn't going to take them. I forgot they were in there."

"Was I unclear on the fact that the one thing I need in my life right now is a fucking orgasm?"

"Can you calm down, please?" He kept his voice low, chagrined to see his fellow seatmate's entire set of teeth. Marina was winding up to pitch a royal fit.

"This was a mistake; we're not supposed to go. The plane's too full. I want to get off! I miss the kids, and you're a liar. You told me you got rid of those pills!"

A slightly plump flight attendant appeared at their row, her black hair in a shiny braid coiled at the nape of her neck. "Is everything all right?"

"Yes, fine," Marc responded mechanically. *Fine* no longer meant anything but *shitty*.

"Dandy," Marina added, not attempting to hide her sarcasm. "We're going to Cancún, but while everyone else is having sex, my husband will be doped up and drooling on the crossword puzzle."

That elicited a handful of barely stifled snickers around them.

Marc's humiliation maxed out. "Okay, stop it! I mean it. I am trying my best here."

"Good for you."

"Why are you doing this?" he asked.

She didn't answer. Her face crumpled, and the tears fell.

"Shit." he whispered, looking up at the flight attendant, who had remained in place.

The attendant knelt in the aisle, took Marina's hand. "Breathe, *hita*."

Marina raised her eyes. As Marc watched, she seemed to find her lost self in the eyes of a compassionate stranger.

"Right… Breathe. Thank you."

"I can tell you two really need this trip. Let me give you some advice."

"Please," Marc said.

"Go as yourselves, as the loving, spiritual beings you are. Take your bodies with you, but let your *spirits* move you." She studied Marina's face again, and spoke with strange emphasis. "You are here to fly. We all will be in the air soon."

Marina nodded, mesmerized.

The woman released her hand and stood before proceeding up the aisle.

Marc exhaled. "More good and weird advice."

"She's right." Marina sighed deeply and leaned her head against his shoulder. "I'm sorry. I had a moment there."

He felt the power of the sigh, felt her body relax, and the tightness in his chest washed away. "It's all right. But for a second I was looking forward to getting arrested."

She kissed his cheek. "From now on, I'm just me and you're just you, spiritual beings. This is going to be a great trip." Within moments, she was asleep.

He checked her breathing. When he had assured himself that she was all right, he peered out the window, and caught the Navajo man's eye.

"Cancún, huh?" the man said.

"Yeah."

"I was there six months ago. Had lots of orgasms. You're going to love it."

Part 2
Música

Welcome to Paradise

"Sweetheart, we're landing." Marc felt Marina stir to consciousness against his shoulder, and then peer out the window at the tilting views of sea and sky. The water was a brilliant Technicolor turquoise separated by strips of white sand from the jungle-covered contours of ancient, unexcavated cities.

It was remarkable to see how extensive those cities had been, how sophisticated the civilization they represented. There was, of course, the little matter of human sacrifices, but contemporary civilizations hadn't kicked that custom either. He studied the green bumps, struck anew by the aerial views, just as he was every time he flew into Cancún. The signature hills stood out clearly, looking like breasts or ass cheeks, three in a row.

He handed Marina his earphones. "Listen." He'd cued up "Welcome to Paradise," by Green Day. Marina smiled, awake now, and gripped his hand.

A pelican landed with a splat on the salty docks below, jarring a fish loose from its beak pouch. The fish flopped around vigorously, scattering silver scales as the clumsy seabird tried to re-catch its meal.

Cancún International made the Sunport in Albuquerque seem palatial. Small and low-slung, the airport, like the buried cities just beyond its terminals, appeared to be on the verge of suffocation by the surrounding jungle. Inside, stone surfaces and the sharp, slightly nauseating smell of cleaning fluid fought the good fight, but mold had the upper hand. Marc realized, as he noted the scents, that the allergies plaguing him had remained behind in New Mexico. He took a grateful lungful of air and draped the strap of one of Marina's carry-on bags around his neck, leaving her with one bag and a purse.

He dragged the suitcase and pushed the cooler along in the slow-moving Customs line. Flashing red and green lights randomly determined which passengers would pass easily through Customs and which would get stuck with a bag search. Yes, green. He dipped his knee, a quick genuflection to the Customs gods. No more enema displays for the day.

The van from the airport was half empty and had functional air conditioning, helping to maintain Marina's positive but fragile mood for the first hour, as they headed south toward Playa del Carmen on a two-lane paved road. But counteracting the air conditioning were the *topes*, colossal, Mexican speed bumps shaped like concrete parking blocks on mega-steroids, miniature Mexican ruins.

Just as Marc experienced the sight of Cancún's ruins with a pleasurable jolt, he also experienced the ubiquitous *topes* with a different kind of jolt. A series of jolts. Because for whatever reason, he was blind and an amnesiac when it came to those teeth-cracking, spine-compressing, axle-wrecking, ruin-shaped road obstacles. If their purpose was to slow traffic, they certainly did that, particularly when Americans came across them unexpectedly. Which Marc did every single time he drove in Mexico, once causing a tire blowout and a $400 repair job on a rental car. Only when he noticed a sign to the right of one of the bumps, with an image of what looked like a plateau, did he understand. Chichen Itzá in the middle of the road.

Today he could see that the stop-and-go was taking a piece out of Marina, but she wasn't complaining, probably relieved that the van driver was paying attention and not ramming into the mini-mountains.

The other reason for slow-downs was a different kind of roadblock: military blockades. They were evidence of the burgeoning drug trade, mostly cocaine these days, passing from Colombia through Mexico and into the U.S. Twice, the van driver came to a full stop, ordered by men armed with machine guns. He remained quiet and docile, and Marc knew enough to keep his own mouth shut.

The armed men were small and serious, swallowed by their green fatigues and boots. Marc considered the villages he had traveled through, the poverty and the rags these men had traded for their uniforms, and it was easy to understand the appeal of their dangerous employment. They had little to lose. He and Marina hugged each other silently after the jungle consumed each blockade behind them.

The road threaded its way in and out of dense vegetation along the coast, offering tantalizing views of the sea. Marc felt a reflexive rush at the sight, reminded of the thrill of diving. On previous trips to

Cancún and Cozumel, he'd explored deep beneath those glittering waves, discovering enchanted reef gardens and their diverse inhabitants, many named for creatures of the air—eagle rays, parrot fish, butterfly and angelfish, hawksbill turtles—as well as nurse sharks and hammerheads, sensuous, green moray eels, and enormous groupers, all unafraid of the humans in their midst.

The Palancar Reef and its psychedelically colored coral structures and marine life rivaled any manmade wonder Marc had ever experienced. Parrot fish, with their bony beaks perfect for scraping algae from coral, were responsible for much of the fine white sand on Caribbean beaches—the charming painted creatures were living processors of the coral rock, shitting clouds of sand as they fed. Just as astonishing, they were gender-benders, shifting fluidly from female to male as they grew and changed color, even several times, experiencing multiple identities if not multiple lives.

How did a fish consider its life, its experiences, its beginnings and ends? To a parrotfish, was each iteration of itself truly a new life? Did its memories move from one life to the next?

Marc recalled the rhythm of his flippers beating in sync with the current of life all around him, and Marina, her hair and limbs flickering in the same flow. They were fragile, Marina and the coral reef and the fish. Vulnerable. Endangered. *Damned humans.* Too much fishing, too much whatever it was.

He stroked Marina's hair, catching her by surprise. She looked sleepy again, about to nod off against his chest, when the paved road turned to washboard dirt and gravel. For the next half hour south, past Playa del Carmen and toward Tulum, they bumped along, much slower now.

Arriving at Retiro del Pirata, a charming resort of grass-and-wood bungalows hugging the beach, Marc was pleased to see that Marina looked pleased. The place appeared rustic and simple but not about roughing it. Guests in bathing suits and casual attire, some holding hands, strolled paths connecting the bungalows.

After checking in, he directed the van driver to motor ahead to their bungalow with the bags, while he and Marina made their way on foot, following wooden arrow signs.

"Home away from home," he announced when they stopped before their lodging. The cooler and bags sat piled next to the door, which stood slightly ajar. He rapped with his knuckles before pushing it open and peeping inside. "Hello?"

A short, stocky man was sweeping the floor and singing to himself. At Marc's greeting he turned, unhurried. He was dark, soft-bellied, maybe in his fifties, with very Mayan-looking features and eyes like green olives. He broke out a welcoming smile, his big white teeth like plates.

"Ah, come in. I am finishing the cleaning. *A sus órdenes, señores. Me llamo Esperanzo.*"

Marc picked up the cooler and entered, Marina right behind him. The room was both sparsely furnished and lushly decorated with vases of fresh grasses and fragrant flowers. A low bed rested against the far wall; a desk and table were accompanied by a few chairs. A thin layer of sand covered the stone floor.

"This is clean?" Marina said, a little edge to her voice.

"*Muchas gracias,* Esperanzo," Marc said, ignoring her remark, slipping Esperanzo a fifty-dollar bill. "You're my guy, okay? If I need something." He enjoyed the tipping process, New York style.

"You come to me, *señor!*" said Esperanzo with alacrity.

"*Gracias.*"

"*De nada. Bienvenidos!* I hope you and your lovely wife have a delightful time here on the Yucatán. *Es muy especial.*"

"It's… charming," Marina said, recovering her manners. "The room is..."

"Not much, *señora, sí,*" said Esperanzo easily, unembarrassed. "But the bed is very comfortable. We mean to keep it *sencillo* here, *en el* Retiro del Pirata. *Pero la comida*, the food, *es muy especial*—I am sure you will enjoy it! Five-star food, for five-star people," he said with pride.

She smiled politely and sank onto the bed. "You're right, it is comfortable." Her smile was now genuine.

"I will let you be alone. If you are in need, just ask." Esperanzo finished sweeping.

"*Ci, vediamo,*" Marc said. "Thank you." He began to eject the medical arsenal from the cooler onto the table as their attendant waved and left the bungalow.

"'*Ci, vediamo?*' That's Italian, isn't it, not Spanish?" Marina said. "How do you say, 'this room is dirty,' in Spanish?"

"It's not dirty."

"It's not clean." She brushed sand from the bed, transferred there by her toes.

"I like it. It's a little sandy, exactly what we came here for—sand and lots of it." He was determined to counter any mood slippage.

"What was the man's name?"

"Esperanzo. Means hope." Marc took the last brown bottle from the cooler.

"How do you know that?"

"I read." He started organizing the bottles, studying their labels.

"What?" She raised her voice above the booming surf.

"I said I read." He looked up from the bottle in his hand.

"God, the waves are so *loud*," she continued, fretful.

"Yes, so much louder than the desert." He set the bottle down and walked over to sit beside her. He'd just started to slide his arm around her shoulder when she flinched. "Whoa, you okay?"

"A little anxious, I suppose. Tired."

He jumped to his feet, aiming to please, as usual. "Mr. Aggressively Insecure at your service." He offered a sweeping bow, hoping for a grin. "You know what that means: you get some rest. Are you hungry? I need to find ice for the cooler, so I'll bring you back something."

"Sure, grab some beers for that cooler."

"Yeah, man, beers instead of all that stuff." He gestured at the medical provisions.

"I thought that *stuff* was the nectar of the gods, the one possible path to beating this thing." Her voice quaked.

"Well, there's nectar here. And…" He began reading from the bottles. "Shark cartilage, herbal Hoxsey tonic, beaucoup burdock root, IVs, vitamins C and B12. This one, Ukrain—not the country, that's the name of the drug—is from Austria. We've also got wheat grass, flax oil, and organic coffee, complete with enema paraphernalia."

"Sounds like a Frank Zappa tune," Marina said.

He grabbed the opportunity and ran with it, doing a Zappa impression complete with air guitar and rolling eyes. "Alternative enema bandit! I wonder if Frank used any of this shit—I mean stuff. Nectar of the gods."

"Right?"

"Okay, how about a swim?" he asked, swept by the moment of levity straight into the past, when such a suggestion would have made sense.

Marina's face went green. "I'm tired. Actually, more than tired." She bolted for the bathroom. Seconds later, Marc heard the sounds of violent vomiting.

Shit. "Let me hold your hair, sweetheart. I'm sorry."

When the waves of nausea subsided at last, they remained collapsed on the bathroom floor, speechless, immersed in the roaring breakers. Marina's head was bowed over her upraised knees. Marc encircled her with his own raised knees and arms, his hands supporting her damp forehead. She eventually raised her head.

"Water. I need water. Bottled."

An hour later, Marina lay in bed trying to ignore the IV needle stuck deep in her thin left arm and to focus instead on the book in her hands—*The Book of the Dead*, as a matter of fact—light vacation reading. *Holy shit, what was I thinking?* She gave herself a mental kick in the ass and glanced at Marc fussing around with the holistic medicine bottles. She reread a paragraph for the third time, maybe fourth, and though it was in English, it might have been Tibetan. Or Egyptian hieroglyphics. Or Martian, for that matter. And what language was Marc speaking?

"Bio supplements. Butatuta frutaloops. Eye of Newt… One of Newt's eyes." He caught her watching him. "Gingrich. How many eyes does that guy need, anyway? He doesn't use them." He set aside a small notebook open to a scrawled list. "Deepak Chopra. He's deep, that dude. You packed his book with the dive mask?"

He was trying hard to entertain her, she could see that, but at the moment, it was overwhelming. The treatments, the nausea, the fear, the pain, the hoping. Was there anything really for hope to hang on to?

"God, Marc, it's so much."

He made a stupid face, holding his crotch.

Really? Of course, he'd go there, but she couldn't, not right now.

"I'm talking about all *that*. I can't believe it all goes inside of me."

His hand flew from groin to mouth, stifling the obvious wisecrack.

"My poor stomach… Maybe I should have gone through the intensive chemotherapy."

There, she had voiced it. The doubt, the question that had been tormenting her, out in the open. What was the right path, really? How could they know?

"If you want, we'll see the oncologist again as soon as we get back. You liked him, right? You said he was open."

"He was, but the hood and sickle were scary," she said bluntly. She watched him search for new words of comfort. "Have you noticed that I've been worse since the last endoscopy?"

"Yes."

"You haven't said anything."

His lips disappeared, curling into his mouth. "I was hoping you wouldn't notice," he confessed.

"Maybe that's why we haven't been able to talk to each other. I'm getting worse, but neither of us wants to admit it."

Her words hung in the air like gulls on an updraft, her body left behind, drawn into the bed and toward the sand below. The bed sagged as Marc added his weight to it. Ballast. He slid a finger under her chin, tilting it toward him.

"I haven't given up on Newt's eyes yet, and neither should you," he said.

"I love you."

"And I love you. So how about that other thing?" he asked.

"What other thing?"

"I think you referred to it so eloquently on the plane as a 'fucking orgasm.'"

"Oh, that. You're off the hook for now. I'm sorry." She wished she could even imagine an orgasm at the moment, but she felt completely spent.

"You don't have to apologize to me. Ever. I'm sorry for the dirty room and the loud waves and…"

Don't say you're sorry for the cancer. "I like the waves. They're soothing. And it's not really dirty, I'm just such a manic—a manic coming clean." She forced a smile. "Or should I say *anal*?" It sure had been awhile since… "We'll get back to my orgasm, don't worry."

He grinned. "Want me to ask Esperanzo in here to work on that? He seemed up for anything, and I did give him fifty."

"Hey, Esperanzo, we were thinking—you, us, a bottle of wine, some needles and syringes." She joined in the bawdy game.

"He's a little short for me, actually," Marc said.

"Plus, you like them blond. And French."

"And female. But we'll throw in another fifty for a French falsetto."

Marc glowed in triumph when she howled with helpless laughter, rolling back on the bed. It sure had been awhile for that too.

The Hammock

Muscles taut, Marc felt at home in his body after a morning swim. He stood in the bungalow doorway, a towel draped around his neck, his trunks dripping, and wiped sand from his feet.

"Hey, sweetheart, good morning," he called out.

Marina lowered the music on her cassette player. "You were *gone* when I woke up."

"Sorry, babe. Couldn't sleep anymore. The waves. I thought if you can't beat 'em, join 'em."

"We've been here for fifteen hours, and so far, all I've seen are the ceiling and toilet."

"Did you get sick again?" He wiped his chest with the towel, suddenly clammy.

"Yes, I got sick again. I've been nauseated all morning."

"Oh, honey, I'm sorry. Are you okay?" He stepped cautiously closer, wanting to hug her—would she hug back, or push away? Her movements were jerky, her voice tight.

She banged a drawer shut. "I'm sick and I get sick and I'm really sick of you asking me if I'm okay. 'Are you okay?' 'Are you okay?' 'Are you all right?' *No*, I'm not all right. But at least you got in a swim."

"I didn't want to wake you."

Marc watched her yank clothes out of a bag. She didn't respond, just kept meticulously refolding.

He sat down to watch. "Did you sleep okay? Can I ask that?" Puddles formed at his feet.

She stared at the water dripping from him. "I had some weird dreams."

"Yeah? Did you dream something you've collected?" A suck-up move, but he was making it. He motioned to her prayer arrow.

When she looked up, her mouth was oddly twisted. "Not unless you've been sneaking around with your French ex-girlfriend behind my back."

"What?"

"I dreamed of Corinne. Your French ex-girlfriend."

"That's because we were joking about her last night."

"I don't know. It was very vivid. Moonflute says I've already begun to cross over and I'll know things now." She returned to folding beachwear.

Cross over. Had he been standing, the impact of those words would have knocked *him* over. He stared at his wet feet, feeling as if an abyss had opened beneath them, a tumble of sand, terrifying, endless. He sucked a ragged breath, glad for the noisy cover of the surf.

"Moontoots is looney-toots," he said at last, with careless bravado. He stood to put his arms around her waist, not caring that his wet swim trunks dampened her shorts. With her cheekbone cool against his salty neck, she returned the hug. He clasped one of her hands and brought it to the front of his trunks in a desperate impulse to shift his own mood, if not hers. Desire, laughter, something to keep them both from falling. Play. Silliness. Give it a shot.

"You wish you had a penis," he said. The giggle she stifled into his chest was a soothing balm.

"Please, I got into enough trouble in my life without one of those." Her eyes glistened, and her hand remained on his crotch.

"You're feeling a little better!"

"Guess I am. Let's go into Playa del Carmen, buy a hammock, and T-shirts for Zane. I need to get outside. Cabin fever." She withdrew her hand.

He kissed her forehead and both eyelids. "Whatever you want, bubby-cakes. I'll rinse and change and be ready in a minute. And you"—he took her hand and put it back upon his trunks— "hold that thought."

Playa del Carmen's shopping district was thronged with an international crowd, tourists from Europe, Asia, the States, and all over the world. Ferries bustled back and forth between Playa and Cozumel, their pleasure-seeking cargo on the lookout for bargains, baubles, and designer-label boutiques. Under the hot sun, glass storefronts and vivid awnings beckoned. Pop tunes, tangos, rancheras, and well-worn rock standards vied for shoppers' attention like raucous canned barkers. The modern hotels offered everything from comfort to unabashed luxury.

As was common with Mexican seaside resorts, the district of the lotus-eaters was reached overland by traveling for miles through starkly contrasting and desperately impoverished barrios. Marc connected across the gaping divide without fear or condescension, through simple conversations and curiosity. He didn't ignore the poverty; it was a major part of the country, of the lives of those who lived there. The grandeur and complexity of humanity living within these circumstances was what kept drawing him to Mexico, an attraction he found hard to explain. But Marina was overwhelmed by the economic divide. The drive through Playa's slums and shantytowns made her anxious, and left a shadow on her mood as she ambled arm in arm with Marc. He carried a large, shocking pink hammock over his shoulder.

"Why do you do that?" she asked, stopping him.

"Do what?"

"Haggle. That fine gentleman offered a perfectly fair price for a hammock, and you started with the haggling thing. I don't see you doing that with a six-pack of beer. You're a racist."

"What? Let's not get carried away."

But she was on a rant. "He has a lovely handmade product, and you, Mr. Cool-Ass liberal that you think you are, treat him differently just because you can." She planted herself before him, oblivious to the human flow she was interrupting. He was very nearly pushed into her by a distracted shopper.

"You're not kidding," he said.

"No."

"Okay, I surrender. My great haggling career is over. Better?" He leaned in to kiss her and stem the argument. She looked uncertain. No chance to find out what she would have decided, though, because a familiar, French-accented voice cut through the multilingual hubbub.

"Marc! Marina!"

He whipped around. "Oh, my God."

Marina's lips became a thin line. "Holy shit. Corinne."

"Marc!"

Corinne was closer now, forging gracefully and insistently through the crowd, and then—sunburnt and happy and gorgeous and French— she was right in front of them, depositing two large shopping bags on the pavement of the car-free street to throw her arms around each of them in turn.

"Hi!" she said, drawing out the single word with singsong effusiveness. "I have been thinking of you. I was to call you when I go to Miami, on my way back to Paris. Marina, how are you?"

Marina's covert glare at Marc might have been a laser ray gun aimed between his pupils, its message as clear as if he could read her mind: *"If you tell your French ex-girlfriend I have cancer, you'll die first."*

"She's *great,*" he said.

"Oh, I'm *so* glad!" Corinne embraced him again, hanging on a few seconds too long. "Cherie, what a happy accident! You both look wonderful, and very much in love!"

"We are," Marina snapped.

"Well, I'm leaving for the airport in ten minutes. I wish we had more time," Corinne said, sounding sincerely regretful.

"Me too," Marina said, her brow relaxing.

"Please, stay in touch. I'll call from Paris or St. Tropez soon."

"It's great to see you, but—wow, how weird." Marc shook his head.

Corinne stared intently into his eyes. He had forgotten how green they were.

"These things can happen when people are connected and care about each other," she said. "Please send my love to the children. Bye-bye."

She pulled him close for a last squeeze and emphatic air kisses at both cheeks, then did the same with Marina, before picking up her bags to dissolve into the crowds of Playa del Carmen.

Marc gawked at Marina. "You're... you're a witch."

"I'm not a witch." She contemplated the direction Corinne had taken. "She's really a gracious woman. I married the man she once loved. If I didn't need another reason to hold onto my life, here's one: I'll become friends with her, just to drive you nuts!"

Marina giggled at his obvious astonishment, then became pensive.

"Marc, you need to start looking forward. Sometimes the past is too easy, too available. Don't take the path of least resistance. Be as bold as I know you are. Light a new path—be your own light."

Marc's brain felt scrambled. "What are you talking about?"

Without answering, she scurried to a nearby vendor's stall. "Hey, let's buy that wild Major Spaceman T-shirt for Zane. He digs the space stuff!"

After a stunned pause, he followed. "You're unbelievable! My ex-girlfriend, whom you dreamed about last night, pops out of nowhere—and all you can think about is buying a T-shirt for Zane."

"I adore Zane and Chels; I love being their stepmother, and they love me back. They've been such a blessing in my life." Her face was inches from his now, intent, filled with fire. "Take them, Marc, always take them with you. Show them as much of the world as possible."

"Whoa, there, you're talking like—"

"I just want to see them grow. Let's get this one for Zane." She held up a deep blue shirt with its beloved spaceman character.

"Okay, whatever you want." His scrambled brains were definitely, thoroughly cooked, his heart wrenched in too many directions at once—Marina and the children, the future—what future? Time and space, love and loss—he blinked in bewilderment at Major Spaceman, saw himself as if in a mirror, floating in inky, endless space. But Major Spaceman was grinning through his bubble helmet, perfectly at home in all that emptiness. An image of acceptance.

"And pay him the asking price," Marina instructed.

Marc tore his attention from the T-shirt to Marina's face. Her smile was small, yet brave. He smiled back at her, Major Spaceman–style, and handed her a wad of bills. Enough for a hefty tip.

Dive

Marc was sound asleep, his chest moving with the regularity of the surf outside. The bungalow was shuttered and dim, but Marina, surprised to find herself awake and without that wretched, familiar morning sickness, raised herself on an elbow to watch him.

It was comforting, intimate, and heartbreaking to see him so, his eyes closed yet his own shutters flung open, his spirit on display even as his body lay unaware. He looked vulnerable and strong. She studied his smooth brow, the curves of his cheekbone and jaw, tuned for smiling, the sculpted nose and chin. The nose had been broken and put back together; so had the collarbone, from high school football. His skin was burnt and freckled, the coppery hair strewn across his pillow sun-bleached. He would scoff, she knew, if he caught her—it wasn't his thing, paying attention to his looks. He stirred, snored faintly. She restrained herself from touching him.

She slipped out of bed and into her poppy-red bikini. Brushed her teeth with customary thoroughness. Medicines and concoctions? Not yet—let sleeping stomachs lie. A colorful, tightly woven bag for collecting shells, the Walkman for music, and she was out the door, closing it with care.

Sunlight splintered upon the water. The sand beneath her feet was not yet hot; a light breeze tickled her legs. Alanis Morissette's lyrical tribute to courage, "You Learn," had her shuffling to the rhythm. Nearly alone on the beach, she didn't care if anyone noticed her enjoying her private party. There were shells to seek, bits of this sparkling seashore for her prayer arrow.

She moved closer to the thunderous waves, an avid gleaner poking through the traces left behind. There—a nearly intact shell, a hole in its side revealing its inner spiral. She picked it up, blew off fine bits of sand, dropped it into her bag.

She turned to check how far she had wandered from the bungalow and noticed three small figures, saw that they noticed her too. One was a topless woman, an unexpected sight on this beach, as the resort wasn't clothing-optional or nudist. They looked perfectly at home in their bodies, smiling and waving. Marina returned their greetings with a sense of kinship.

The next foaming wave crept over her feet, drawing her attention, covering her toes in glitter and depositing a pink, green, and gold conch shell, sleek and decorated with bits of seaweed. She bent to pick it up, but nearly dropped it when it moved in her hands. The shell wasn't an artifact; it was a living home.

Growing up around waves and tide pools, Marina knew crabs, clams, starfish and jellyfish, lobsters and barnacles. She'd gathered shells since she could walk, but this was the first time she'd found herself eye to eye with a conch. The utterly alien black-and-yellow-mottled creature poking from its familiar exterior—actually waving at her with its stalk-eyes—repulsed and fascinated her. Between the eyes, something like a long snout extended from a golden flexible body, ending in a claw shape. She had the sense that she ought to be afraid of its strangeness, but wasn't. She returned the creature to the water and watched it scuttle away. She would find more shells, but nothing like the one just released.

The diving center beckoned, its boats moored and waiting. Morning had barely begun, but they were open for business. The man at the desk, bare-chested and very brown, wore hot-pink swim trunks. She imagined he put on a shirt only for weddings and funerals.

"Diving will be good today," he said. "*Hace muy buen día*. It is a beautiful day, yes."

"Yes," she said. "It is."

Heading back to the bungalow, she found the beach still empty of people except for the same three she had come across earlier. They strolled together as before, until one of the men stepped into the water and dove, smooth and low. A leisurely moment later, a shining silver dolphin burst from the surface just where the swimming man might have emerged for a breath... had he emerged.

Marina shielded her eyes and stared. The dolphin rose and plunged again, a luminous vision of grace, a celestial magician's sleight of hand. Her heart leapt, enraptured by the sight. Magic it was, yes, as glorious as the daily marvel of sunrise.

The remaining man and woman continued to smile, unconcerned. Marina felt herself magnetically drawn to them. They waited at her approach, exchanging shy glances. They were smaller than she had realized, not much taller than Zane, though they weren't children. She accompanied them along the wavering border of firm wet sand between dry earth and sea, her hands in theirs, her mind emptied of all but a gentle hum of reverie.

When she stopped to turn from the waves, the woman clasped her hand a moment longer, looked up into Marina's face and uttered a single word: *naia*. The serene strangers embraced her and kissed her cheeks before running into the water.

She watched, saw them enveloped by a rolling wave which crested and tumbled into itself. As it ebbed, three dolphins arced in unison from the trough left behind and then disappeared under the water once again.

Marina hugged herself, feeling her fingers pressed to her ribs as if they belonged to other hands. The dream, illusion, dolphin magic, whatever it was, pressed just as firmly upon her mind. She nodded at the scuttering surf, at the mystery of water in endless rhythmic motion. "Thank you," she murmured. "Thank you."

Marc was still sleeping. Marina settled herself quietly on the floor, cross-legged, with her prayer arrow and materials around her. A while later, the bed creaked and he sat up, bleary-eyed.

"Good morning, sleepyhead," she greeted him. "You've shifted into vacation mode. I haven't seen you sleep this late in ages."

He stretched, yawned. "Morning! Guess I needed that." He swung his legs over the side of the bed and reached for a shirt. Before he put it on, he shielded his face with his forearm and said, "Don't throw anything, but how are you feeling?"

She tied off a thread, knotted it. "Good, actually. Traveling was rough, but I feel at peace here, now. I wish the kids had come."

"Children never know that parents love them, more than they love us, until they're parents themselves, right?" he said.

"We would have had beautiful children, you and I." Her eyes were downcast, her hands momentarily stilled in her lap.

"Marina..."

"Just talking." The first shell she had found that morning, the one with the hole in it, was now tied to the prayer arrow. She rolled it delicately between her fingers.

"You're really making something there, aren't you?" No longer using the topic as a suck-up move, he was sincerely impressed.

"I collected shells at the beach this morning. The water was so inviting, I decided something when I saw it. You're diving today."

"Okay, I'll get us some breakfast, and we'll go." He pulled on his shirt.

"No, I said *you* are diving."

"Without you?"

"Too soon after surgery; you know I can't. But I want you to dive." She set down the prayer arrow and stood. "I'll stay and finish my arrow, and write my mom and dad. I'll take all of my remedies and supplements and feel great when you get back. We'll go to dinner, okay? You must tell me everything about the dive. Embellish and exaggerate as usual."

He hesitated. "Okay... If you lie in the sun, make sure you put sunscreen liberally on your scar. You wear it proudly." He traced it with one finger, leaned to kiss it, tucked a lock of hair behind her ear, and embraced her.

"You'll miss your boat." She pulled back and returned to work in silence as he prepared for the dive without his usual enthusiastic hustle. When he was ready, he opened the front door, but didn't leave.

"My favorite part of diving is following you," he said.

"So that's why you were always behind me! Marc, we all leave. You'll come back; I'll be waiting and loving. We might *all* come back—that would be nice." She gave him an encouraging grin. "Bye, baby!"

He blew her a kiss and drew the door behind him.

After an hour of meditation and stretching, Marina felt ready to eat breakfast and make good on her promise to take her remedies and supplements. The covered tray Marc had ordered for her was sitting on a bench outside the front door. She lifted the cover, found fresh sliced fruit, muffins and juice, coffee. She carried it to a table on the beachfront porch, fetched her pen and notepad. The hammock awaited.

Dear Mom and Dad. She nibbled a muffin flavored with cardamom, mango, and lime. *I'm writing to you from the Mexican Caribbean. I have no guilt about doing* nada. *I am in a fabulous hammock Marc bought me, which he strung across our porch that sits right on the beach. My body is burned and I wore a bikini today and yesterday.*

Her pen stopped. She pushed the floorboards with her toes, rocking the hammock, considering which direction to take with her next words. How to communicate with her parents authentically and meaningfully from a distance, Mexico to Massachusetts, Marina to John and Patricia White. Up and down, back and forth. Was falling into patterns of behavior as easy as this mindless rocking? Could she recognize and escape the patterns, the family dynamics, or was escape a momentary myopic illusion?

Marina closed her eyes, envisioning her parents' faces. Mom with her tight smile, and eyes that spilled no secrets; she liked her wine, oftentimes a nightly bottle rather than the nightly glass she admitted to. Dad, a wiry athlete, loved scuba diving, a passion Marina felt lucky to have shared with him; his more personal passions he kept to himself. Her parents slept in separate bedrooms and seemed to be riding out their marriage with no crisis of rupture, but with something more subtly alarming, passive resignation. It was hard to read much past the surface. They were stiff upper lip almost-WASPS—WASPs without the *P*, Unitarian Universalists, defined more by their reserved temperaments than by external affiliations.

Marina was made of different stuff, more expressive—wayward, she had been called for as long as she could remember—and that difference had driven years of conflicts, button-pushing, hair-dyeing, and a host of moderate rebellions against their pragmatic-leaning conservatism. They were who they were, and she was who she was. The storms had died down recently, the opaque gulf lashing between Marina and her parents subsiding under the pressure of her dire diagnosis.

Sitting on the blue and white dive boat, Marc took in the congenial crowd of divers and divemasters plowing their way between the island of Cozumel and the Yucatán shores. They would be making a drift dive at the Palancar Reef, following the strong, northbound currents aimed at Cancun. He reached into his bag for the decongestant he routinely took to clear his head before a dive, and swallowed it with a gulp from his water bottle.

It promised to be a great dive day. He looked forward to being underwater, but the most recent dives he'd made had been with Marina; her absence left him forlorn. He'd fight the blues for her sake. If she couldn't dive, she needed his dive to be excellent.

Engines cut, the boat settled and the water relaxed into endless chop. Divers divided into groups of six and eight, each led by a divemaster. Equipment was checked, instructions issued.

Soon, it was Marc's turn to enter the water. He stood in scuba gear on the bow of the boat; then he jumped feet first, holding his mask. The reef dropped away in a dizzying, hundred-foot cliff through water that alternately buoyed and sucked at the divers, pulling them into powerful currents. Marc respected the currents as skydivers respected winds—as forces to work with, to dance and play with, not to bargain with or to take for granted.

I put sunblock on my scar, which is healing perfectly, so I have a white streak with a scar down the middle of my belly, Marina wrote. *Funny, since skin cancer, at this point, seems insignificant.*

Reef garden, spectacular colors. Marc took in the sights as visuals, experiences, far apart from words. He paddled his finned feet, moving easily through schools of undulating fish of electric violet, cobalt blue, acid yellow, silver and bronze, orange and lime green. Many of them hovered gape-mouthed, facing him, scooping up current-delivered edibles like patrons at a moving banquet. A queen angelfish sauntered across his path, and a hawkfish darted from the coral, its face speckled with cinnabar spots like a pox. An elegant black and white drum fish peered languidly from its resting place, reminding him of a Vera Wang mannequin.

He was getting back into the groove of diving. Other divers were off in their own worlds, no one near him except for three, small Mayan-looking divers wearing flimsy, tattered shorts. No masks, no tanks. And twenty-five feet underwater, at least. They were beautiful and smiling—how do you smile underwater? A cloud of bubbles momentarily obscured his sight, and they were gone. In their place, a six-foot nurse shark cruised by. He observed its sinuous movement with wary respect. It wouldn't bother him, as long as he didn't bother it. He continued to descend. A dolphin flickered into view farther down, followed by two more. They sped ahead, powerful, efficient swimmers.

The moisture in my skin and hair feels luscious. This place is different from our usual getaway spots—casual, with limited amenities, except for the ocean, beach, weather, sand, palm trees, flowers, fish, and so on...

Marina speared a thin slice of peach-colored melon, took a bite. Sweet. The second bite was just as sweet.

Seventy-five feet down, Marc became acutely aware of the pressure above and around him. He waved his arms through the bubbles, his cool slipping away. Something was rising in his chest, his throat—he struggled with his mask, panicking now.

Two swimmers appeared at his side, a man and a woman—the Mayans. What were they doing all the way down there, still without tanks? The woman positioned herself before him, her long hair like slow-dancing black seaweed behind curtains of bubbles. He felt a nudge between his thighs—a dolphin's snout. The dolphin turned to look right up into his eyes. *Fuck, I'm crazy! Drowning!*

He thrashed his legs and flippers, trying to propel himself from one deep blue toward the other far above the surface—to the sky, to Marina—but to no avail. The swimmers grasped him by the arms and legs, surprisingly strong, decelerating his frantic thrust, keeping his ascent within the realm of his bubbles. *Slow down.* I don't want to stay down. *Slow down.*

He knew why—decompression sickness, serious business if you rise too fast—but panic followed its own rules. The dolphin remained with him, a calming, buoyant presence, until he was halfway to the surface, when it and the pressure of hands on his limbs melted away.

He accelerated again. Another twenty feet and two divers from the boat joined him, gesturing *take it easy*. With fifteen feet of water separating him from the surface, he was forced to make a safety stop, three torturous minutes held in place by the kindness and strength of

strangers. *Wait. Stop. You don't want to get sick,* they communicated
to him wordlessly. *Breathe.*

*It is so perfect for just being and healing. I'm making a prayer
arrow for a traditional healing ritual associated with the Yucatán. I
brought the stick from home, a piñon branch. You take some twine,
preferably cotton, and wind it around, saying a prayer each time, the
same prayer. You can adorn it with meaningful objects such as shells,
feathers, or beads. This morning I got up at six a.m. and took a sunrise
walk to scoop up shells for the arrow. I met this couple. They didn't
speak English or Spanish and were quiet, except they giggled a lot.
The woman took my hand and said one word: Naia. I think it was her
name. They each held one of my hands as we walked. Gentle. Big
green eyes, long noses, smiling and comforting. They kissed and
hugged me, waved as they ran into the sea. Gone, like that.*
Marina hesitated, sighed, a single tear welling in each eye.
Brushing them away, she pressed pen to paper.
Today, away from appointments, formulas, opinions, I'm just being
*and I feel different. Such love for Marc, a bigger awareness of his
essence, seeing through the ego and fears straight to his heart.*

Marc burst to the surface. "Marina!" He hauled himself onto the
boat with the help of another diver, ripped off his mask and sucked air.

*Please write to me and share whatever you have to offer. I love you
with all my heart. Thanks, your loving Marina.*
She carefully folded the pages into an envelope, then licked the
fragile postage stamps that would send her letter on its way.
"Let my words be birds," she said aloud. "With strong wings... for
strong winds." The sea drowned her voice with a resounding outburst
against the shore, that faded into a whisper. She reclined in the
hammock, the pressure of its pink, woven strands caressing and
supporting her body.

The helpful diver on the boat removed his own mask before
leaning over Marc to check his pupils, his breathing, his color.
"Hey, man, you okay? Have a drink of water; you don't look so
good."

The tattoo of a triangle with four rows of four lines radiating around it decorated his forearm. Marc recognized it as a combination of symbols—the triangle for AA paired with Zia Pueblo's sun sign. Maybe he was a fellow New Mexican, this dude.

Meanwhile, the rescue divers had climbed aboard and the others had gathered to look on. When it was clear that Marc was out of danger, they backed away to give him space. He stood to regain his balance and the remains of his dignity, and reached for his sports bag and a bottle of water. The little plastic bottle of antidepressants fell out, began to roll away.

The tattooed diver retrieved the bottle, scanned the label. "Dude, you don't really take this shit, do you?"

"Not lately."

"Freeze-dried booze, man." The diver shook his head.

Marc took the bottle, pausing only a fraction of a second before he jump-shot it toward the trash bin six feet away. He could hear Marv Albert's yell: "*Yes!* Patrick Ewing hits from the corner!" Marc felt it, could see it. Madison Square Garden, Ewing shooting for the Knicks to win the game, the crowd going wild, roaring *yes* at the top of their lungs.

Marc pumped his fist. "Yes!"

The sun was still high as he ran up the path toward the bungalow later that afternoon. He stopped at the sight of Marina in the hammock, reassuring himself that she was merely sleeping. The scar upon her abdomen rose and fell softly. He touched it, waking her.

"Hi, baby. How was your dive?" she asked, her tone musical, like sleepy baby talk. She stifled a yawn. "What happened?"

"The dive was good." But his face was wet long after the seawater had dried.

"Are you crying?" She wiped his glistening cheek.

"Lost it under there. Wasn't in any danger, but I came completely unglued," he said, unable to protect her from his terror.

"Marc!"

"I'm fine now, really. I felt weak, closed... alone. But mostly, deeply, profoundly, lost in a world without you. Pressure on all sides, you nowhere in front of me." His body was sinking, folding into a contorted pose as he spoke.

Cupping his chin, she locked eyes with him. "Is this your first realization of my death, love?"

Death. The word fell between them like a bone on sand.

"Maybe the first realization of my own death. We have no control. Being here with you now, looking into your pale blue eyes, I know love is my only guide. What will I do when your eyes can't remind me?"

"You have such a zest for life, Marc. You'll do just great. Besides, my pale blue eyes are unforgettable." She scooted over, helped him join her in the hammock. "Close your own eyes, and you'll see them. You'll travel, make love, and be the most loving father a child ever had. You're not done having children."

She put her lips to his neck, kissed her way to his mouth, holding his face in her hands. "Now, you owe me a dive story. Embellish, please. Lie to me, baby. Entertain me!"

Beginning to regroup, Marc exhaled. He played with Marina's fingers.

"Okay, well, besides freaking out, at about twenty-five feet I saw these Mayans swimming like dolphins without masks or tanks. I guess they were dive assistants making sure the tourists didn't get caught in the Palancar currents. Two guys and a girl smiling—how do you smile underwater? And—hell, I must have been hallucinating—but when I was deeper, so much deeper, totally losing my shit, I think they helped me." He shook his head.

"They held onto me, didn't let me rise too fast. And there was a dolphin. Crazy, just crazy… Then they disappeared, and two divers from the boat tag-teamed me the rest of the way up. When I asked about the Mayans, everybody seemed to figure I was just hysterical."

"I believe you, love. They helped me today, too, when I was walking on the beach. They held my hands, made me feel safe, like I truly belong to something bigger than myself, something beyond my body and senses, the smallness of my individual identity. There is a kind of magic here, an opening. I am so glad we came." Marina's smile was perfectly sincere. "Tell me more about your dive."

Marc found himself able to smile back, lightening up a little. "There was a gargantuan nurse shark, and three beautiful dolphins swimming together. This big-mouthed doctor from New Jersey got bit feeding a big-mouthed grouper. I followed one of the divemasters into a cave filled with silverfish. We swam right through them, thousands of them."

Marina reached for the zipper on his wetsuit, gave it a tug.

"The fish ran along my body."

She slipped the wetsuit down one of his shoulders.

"And there, in the crystal warm water…"

She pulled the wetsuit low around his waist.

"They kissed me."

She hugged him hard, kissed him with a surge of warmth, her mouth salty and sweet.

In the bungalow moments later, his wetsuit and her bikini, along with half the bedding, lay on the sandy floor. Sheila Hylton's sensual version of "Bed's Too Big Without You" played softly.

"I've missed this so much, my love, oh, my love," Marina murmured. She licked the hollow under his arm, traced his ribs and hips with her fingers. He moved with her, two swimmers joined in glorious, free-dive communion, carried together by the forces of their own invisible currents.

Soaring clouds in golden skies, a whoosh of wind, an eagle drifting by. Hawks swooped and dove, countless numbers of them, Marina in their midst, healthy and radiant in a flowing amber gown, moving effortlessly, laughing out loud, hair whipping free. She banked towards a regal hawk to introduce herself.

"Hi, there. I'm Marina! My name is Marina!"

The hawk turned its fiery eye upon her and spoke with Marc's voice. "Marina… Marina…"

She rolled her head, eyes closed, focused inward on the limitless sky, the dance of sinew and feather upon thermals and downdrafts.

"Marina, baby…" Marc's tender words, his tender voice, coaxed her back.

The dream washed away in a sighing tide. Marina became aware of waves rising and falling outside. She sat up, blinking.

"That was a really nice one."

Low light bathed the room with that exquisite transition of sunset to dusk. The room was unfamiliar until Marc's solid warmth drew her back to him. He sat on the edge of the bed, studying her face.

"Sorry, love," he said. "You asked me to wake you in an hour. It's been two. This long nap, is it a good thing?"

"Oh, yes." She stretched her neck. "Wonderful to be able to nap and dream; I don't feel sick. Good healthy rest, that's all," she reassured him, rubbing his shoulder. "I finished my prayer arrow today."

Marc picked up the prayer arrow from beside the bed, examined it, dumbstruck by what she had accomplished. Her ritual object was more than the sum of its diverse parts; it was truly a work of art—colorful, creative, painstakingly crafted, even musical, an instrument for the wind to play. The arrow's attachments jingled, pinged, and clicked as he moved it about. Among them, he noticed the toy arrowhead he had dug up while planting the Children at Play sign.

"I added the last pieces I brought from the desert, joined with the shells and glass I found here." Glowing with pleasure at his admiration, Marina ran a finger over a fragment of green beach glass bound to the arrow by cleverly knotted yarn. Once sharp, it was now translucent and soft-edged, transformed by pulsing sand and waves. "To think that this glass was made from sand."

"A glass bottle. Once full of Dos Equis, probably."

"Sand, liquefied by fire, transformed to a bottle of spirits," Marina continued, her words trancelike. "Never an empty vessel. It carried a message to the waves, ashes to ashes, sand to sand." She contemplated the glass as if reading its story.

"Not just sand to sand," Marc said. "Being part of a bottle wasn't its main purpose. It belongs to an *artwork*. You changed every molecule in it by doing that."

He lifted her arrow to catch the sunset's final flare streaming through the window. Glass and mother-of-pearl shimmered among feathers, wood, stone, and bone. He laid the arrow on the bed, lifted Marina's hands to his lips, and kissed each fingertip. "You've changed me too."

She stroked his temples, his hair, completely present once again. "We've changed each other. We're parts of each other now, and always will be. Always."

Wait

One Week Earlier
Albuquerque, New Mexico

Dr. Gram's waiting room, a small space decorated in shades of chocolate, dark to milk, was more sober than Dr. Jefferson's. The few magazines fanned neatly across side tables were dedicated to fine food and exotic travel. Marina picked one up, leafed through it without reading.

"What do you think he's going to say?" she asked.

Marc sat forward in his chair, his hands clasped. "Well, you—we—decided not to do a damn thing they suggested. They said radiation, we said burn. They said chemo, we said poison. If I were Gram, I'd fire us."

She joined him in nervous chuckles. "He's a good guy. Sees everything."

They trusted Dr. Gram, even liked him. From their first surgical consultation with him, he had been forthright about Marina's situation, yet respectful and encouraging of her choices, a reassuring combination. The suggestion that he might discharge her—fire her—as a patient, was a comfortable joke. But the waiting room wait was never comfortable. She had prepared for her appointment this time without donning her usual fashion-forward dress-for-the-city attire, choosing casual sweatpants and a hoodie instead. She stretched her legs, bounced the heels of her gym shoes restlessly on the carpet, her fists jammed in the hoodie's pockets. A water cooler hummed. Bright sunshine slanted through the blinds, casting striped shadows onto the floor. Air conditioning kept the room much cooler than the summer day outside.

A short, black-haired nurse beckoned from the front desk.

"We need to get your weight and vitals, dear. You can come too," she said to Marc, who had already stood. Marina asked him to fetch a cup of water from the cooler as she fumbled with her handbag before following the nurse. Moments later, they were back in their seats, her hand in his. Her spirits and energy looked up as she smiled at him.

Dr. Gram, heavyset and handsome, with unruly curls, opened the waiting room door and stepped in. He wore the traditional white coat, but dropped professional decorum to greet them both with familiar affection and to hug Marina.

"Marina, hi, you look great!" He turned to give Marc a strong handshake. "You look better, too. Come in."

Sitting in silence in Dr. Gram's office as he peered at Marina's medical chart, Marina crossed her legs and became as still as a statue, while Marc tried unsuccessfully not to squirm in his chair. At last, Dr. Gram looked up, removed his glasses.

"Two months already. The nurse says you gained ten and a half pounds. Wow, that's really good."

Really good, Marc thought. Wait, *what*? Ten and a half pounds? He cranked his neck to stare at her.

"Yeah, I got my breasts back," she responded quickly, flicking a glance at Marc and pushing her hands in her hoodie pockets. "And we're going to Mexico, the beach!"

Dr. Gram returned his gaze to the chart. "So, no radiation or chemo, right? I have no idea why you're doing so well. Whatever it is, keep it up." He paused. "Marina, there's really no reason to continue to see me anymore. For surgical purposes, I mean. But I'd like to stay in touch. Let's make an appointment for six weeks from now. Continue with all the alternative remedies. Stranger things have happened."

He stood and leaned across his desk to give her an affectionate goodbye, and Marc another handshake, looking him straight in the eye.

"Keep your chin up, my boy. I'm proud of you. Proud of both of you."

As Marc followed Marina out into the stark hallway, he caught her removing two small hand weights from her hoodie pockets, and slipping them back into her handbag. He held his tongue.

The Arrow

Nurse sharks cruised through night-darkened waters in a languid school, quietly hunting and scooping up their prey. Marc held fast to the dorsal fin of one of the largest, moving his own fins in rhythm, following its direction. The reef was near, but out of sight. He looked to his left and right, seeking Marina. There she was—limbs translucent and pale, red bikini a florescent flash—but she was partnered with a swifter shark and was gone, carried away into indigo depths. He wanted to let go of his shark and swim after her, but couldn't.

Marc abruptly awoke, drenched in the saltwater of his own sweat and gripping a corner of his pillow, only releasing it as the disturbing dream released him. Marina was sleeping on her side, her back to him. He brought his knees up behind hers to spoon, felt her snuggle sleepily against him. She was naked and warm, a safe harbor.

In the morning he found her already out of bed, sitting on a small, round rug in a meditative pose. She wore just her red bikini bottom. Her eyes closed, her hands lay palms up in her lap with the prayer arrow balanced across them, its red, blue, and green twine vibrant with primal energy.

Raven, hawk, dove, gull, and bluebird feathers, fragments of a cholla cactus skeleton, sun-bleached shells, sea glass, quartz from the Cerrillos Hills, a turquoise and silver pendant, the delicate bone of a bird's wing—all of the arrow's adornments expressed the beauty and complexity of the artist who had bound them together. Marc dismissed the dream, enthralled by the vision of the woman in front of him. The bed grated against the stone floor as he shifted his weight to rise.

Her eyes opened with a smile. "Hi, I'm ready. I want to do a simple ceremony," she said.

"Can we do your IV first?"

"Okay. Then I need you to indulge me."

He prepared the IV, the magic potion, nectar of the gods. She took it without flinching, her expression distant, her mind somewhere that he couldn't follow. He watched without questioning, waiting until the IV was finished to ask if she wanted breakfast.

"Later. I want to get to the beach." She pulled her bikini top on, tied it, picked up the prayer arrow, and walked out to the porch and down the few stairs to the sand.

They stood together at surf's edge, before the living sea. Marina held the prayer arrow in both hands while Marc flexed, stretching his legs and torso as if preparing for a sporting competition.

"Okay, this is your party, baby," he said. "What do we do?"

She addressed the arrow. "Every time I wound this thread around you, I prayed. Not just for myself, but for all of us. Men, women, humanity; animals, family, plants, God, infinity. And for you, my husband."

She turned to Marc. "I want to live, but while I fight, I prepare not to. Let my prayer fly into this wondrous sea."

She waved the musical arrow and the sea breeze played upon it, a nameless tune of earth, sea, and sky. After a moment, she presented it to Marc. "Okay, Tarzan, do your thing. Swim the arrow out into the deep water, and let it go."

"That's it? Wait—you're not coming with me?"

"No."

"What do you mean? Why not?" He tried to erase anxiety from his tone. "You've lived your whole life on Cape Cod, probably lost your virginity with sand between your toes."

"I did," she acknowledged.

"You're always the first one in the water, and now, in the most exquisite body of water on earth—"

"It's not the water, it's the sharks. I think it has to do with the shark cartilage I'm taking."

His jaw dropped. "The sharks know, and they're plotting revenge, like Jaws VI?"

"I can't explain it, can't explain everything. Yes, all of a sudden, okay!"

"Okay. It's okay, baby."

"So, go. Let it go."

He reluctantly withdrew his attention from the blue depths of her eyes to the infinite reach of the sea, the ever-distant boundary between sea and sky.

"Watch out for those sharks!" she added, dead serious. "Go, you big, gorgeous man!"

After taking his first steps into the waves, Marc gathered himself and dove, pointing the arrow before him like a prow. Waves slapped and stung his face. Twisting to look for her, he saw that she remained planted on the shore, calling out, barely audible, "Farther, farther!"

She was fading from sight, separated by time and space, but the arrow reminded him that they were together in this endeavor. He passed it from hand to hand every few strokes, at last settling into a tranquil patch of water beyond the surf. Marina was now a tiny figure in the distance. He took a last look at the arrow, engraving it to memory, before hurling it as far as he could toward the open sea. It landed with a plop, rocking and floating.

"There."

This was what she wanted, what she had asked for.

The swim back to shore would be easier empty-handed, but loss weighed heavy on his limbs. He shielded his eyes, squinting toward Marina on the beach, and the ache in his arms became a hunger to hold her. He swam with urgent strokes.

The prayer arrow danced and spun upon the membrane of the sea, a glistening ornament linking water and sky, until a thin brown hand broke the surface from below, to slowly pull it under.

Afternoon slipped toward evening as Marc lay peacefully in the hammock, rocked by breezes and his own heartbeat.

The floorboards of the little porch creaked.

"Have you seen my journal?" Marina stood before him, her eyes lightning bright with an awareness that seemed to have been intensifying over the past few days.

"I think it's by the bed. It's usually your constant companion."

"Yeah, I've been taking a break, living instead of writing. But I need to write something down before I forget."

"Tell me."

Crouched on the step, she faced the sea. "Moonflute told me in my journey work with her that I have a hawk guiding me. She says I'm an old soul. I had another dream last night, Marc."

Her voice was calm. "There are cosmic agendas bigger than you and me. I don't know why I got cancer, and now, that question doesn't matter anymore." She turned her head, caught him studying her profile.

His raw and tender pain, suddenly exposed, reflected in her eyes. She gave a soft sob. A tear coursed down her cheek.

He reached for the tear with the side of his finger, gently smoothed it from her face, swallowed hard.

"And I'm gonna live to be ninety, with no teeth, chasing nurses when my kids can't stand me anymore," he joked. Light tone, heavy lifting. His heart throbbed with the effort. He kissed her forehead; the familiar scent of her skin and hair weakened his composure.

"I hope so!" She shuddered, sighed, and matched him tone for tone, her lightness a prodigious display of strength. "Take care of your teeth, though, okay?" She inhaled a deep breath. "There's something else."

Marc sank deeper into the hammock, pushing his toes against the weathered planks of the porch. Rocking again, he sought to dampen the surge of anxiety between his ribs.

"It's something that Moon said, about the Michael entity," Marina continued. "The entity that speaks through channelers."

"I don't like where this is going." He rocked the hammock faster. "Aren't entities and channelers usually more dramatically named, like Great Googly Moogly?"

She took his hands, stopped his restless movements.

He braced himself for more of what they had come to call Santa Feisms and what he privately called woo-woo shit. "Okay, bring it on, baby. You have my full attention. I should arrange a channeling with the Michael entity." He played with her wedding ring. "This is tough." *I will never say woo-woo again.*

"Well, you're tough. If what Moon says is true, I could even communicate with you—in a sense, anyway. I don't know exactly how, but you'll see me. I'll make sure you know it's real. So, when you're ready, see the channeler."

Her grip on his hands remained firm until he said, "Okay."

"Go to Telluride too." She turned his palms up, her fingertips balanced atop them. "We fell in love there. The mountains are young; they have enormous energy. It's hard to explain, but you have to go. Please."

His brow jumped before he could stop it—his wife had lost her mind, fallen deep into woo-woo doo-doo. But even as the thought arose, he knew it was a cop-out. She was still her clear-eyed self, more intensely herself than ever, in fact, seeing things he couldn't see. Seeing into him and through him. This was her launch pad, this place, this peninsula. What did that make him—ground control? That sounded helpful, even important, but above all, ironic. Her flight was out of his hands. His fingers slipped nerveless from hers.

"Just two girls talking; take it easy, hon," she said mildly, reading his face.

"You ask, I'll do it. I completely understand. I'll do it. Telluride." He silently swore to himself to get a grip, then pulled her into the hammock beside him and rested his ear lightly against her chest, listening to her heart flutter like a bird.

The beach spread out before them, an enormous stage flanked by hushed palms, lit and decorated by a fire-streaked sky. The Caribbean performed its ceaseless drumming dance. Surfers enraptured by the waves clung to fleeting crests, while children played in the sand, their voices thin, joyous, fretful, or victorious, as they dodged trickster wavelets, all of them—he most of all—defying the impending darkness.

Rubbers

The last night in Mexico was hot and clear, the thunder of waves a now-familiar orchestral accompaniment as Marc and Marina took their seats at the Retiro restaurant's outdoor café. They had dressed for the occasion—to the nines—his shirt pressed, Marina in a little black number with bare shoulders and lace shawl. Her heels were open-toed and delicate, high enough to keep his steadying hand upon her waist as they took the footpath to the restaurant.

Marina leaned on the table, her eyes lit by candlelight, stars, and love. "I dreamed of you again last night. You were smoking a big, fat cigar, a Cuban. You were tight, fit, and very handsome."

"It must have been a dream." His face flushed under the sunburn.

"You were at a café, drinking," she continued.

"Drinking?"

"Coffee. You were smoking and writing, calm and focused like I've never seen you before. Perfect."

"Perfect? I like this dream. Go on."

"A tattoo of a hawk, like the hawks back home, shadowed your arm. I was so proud of you. That was it, just me watching over you."

She sipped from her water glass, glanced into the main dining room. The plainly decorated restaurant exhaled divine aromas of grilled seafood and tropical fruits into the open-air dining patio. Ceramic planters brimmed with greenery and garden fragrances. A strolling musical trio, playing a romantic Mexican ballad, approached the table.

Marc asked the nearest musician, "Can you play any Soundgarden?" At the man's apologetic smile and headshake, Marc slipped him a generous tip and gestured for the group to play for another couple across the patio. He beamed at Marina.

"Can't we stay at this table together forever, with you telling me how handsome and perfect I am?" he asked, only half in jest.

She reached across the table's white cloth to stroke the back of his hand.

Esperanzo, in crisp black attire, arrived to take their order. "My friends! Marina, you look truly *iluminada*, full of light tonight. You leave us tomorrow?"

"Yes, time to go home," she replied, sounding regretful. "We have lots to do, don't we, Marc?"

"Apparently," he said, unsure of what she meant.

"I hope you will keep the peace you have found here. Take it home in your heart and soul. When life gets hard, remember this place," Esperanzo said, looking intently at Marina. "Remember the sand and water."

Her eyes widened for a fraction of a second. "I will. Esperanzo, thank you so much."

He turned to Marc. "Come back to see us; bring the children. I would love to meet them."

"*Gracias.* You're my guy."

"*Sí, señor.* Now, I hope you have brought your appetites tonight." Esperanzo grinned, rubbing his stomach, and recited the menu specials, taking their order when he was through. Behind him, a petite young woman approached bearing a water pitcher. "My daughter, Naia," he said, with affectionate pride.

The familiar features, the bashful smile—

"*Dolphin girl,*" Marc whispered to Marina, jolted. "I think?" It was hard to be sure, as she was dressed for restaurant service.

Marina nodded, her eyes shimmering, and Marc understood her expression without another word. Naia, dolphin girl or not, was like the sea, the hawks, the immeasurable night sky, the dreams that had brought him and Marina to this place in their lives. There was no need to question; accept the mystery.

"Thank you," Marina said to the silent girl. Naia nodded back, her charming acknowledgement completing the keen current of awareness Marc felt coursing around the table.

Esperanzo bowed, hands together as if in prayer, before departing into the dining room with his daughter.

"Do you get the feeling he knows us a little too well?" Marina asked.

"What do you mean?"

She tilted her head. "He didn't invite me back, only you and the kids."

"Don't be silly," Marc said, a little too quickly. "He meant you also."

"I'm not being silly." She remained serene.

"Well, these are spooky, mystical times. Nothing surprises me anymore." He kept his manner light, but surprised himself, realizing that he actually meant it. "Hey, here's the wine."

Esperanzo placed an expensive bottle of Italian Chianti upon the table, opened it, and served half a glass to Marc for his approval. Marc swirled the glass and made a lengthy show of tasting and considering, before giving Esperanzo the nod to pour.

When Esperanzo had left, Marina picked up her glass, contemplating the ruby wine. "We haven't had a drink in ages," she said. "Are you scared?"

"Thoughtful." He lifted his glass.

She gave it a gentle clink. "To your health," they said simultaneously, before sipping.

Marina set her glass back down and put her hands together on the table. "I want you to say the Lord's Prayer with me. You know it, don't you?"

Marc strove to wipe skepticism from his eyes. "Um, sure I know it. Good Catholic boy. But—"

"Our Father who art in heaven, hallowed be thy name," Marina began softly.

Marc chimed in, the words automatic. "Thy kingdom come, thy will be done, on earth as it is in heaven. Give us this day our daily bread, and forgive us our trespasses…" He watched the crown of her bent head. When she came to the last lines, *and lead us not into temptation, but deliver us from evil*, their words diverged.

"… deliver us from *fear*," she pronounced firmly, lifting her head. "That's my new version. *Deliver us from fear*. Please say it with me every day."

"I like your version." He recalled how his words *no fear* had comforted his dying cousin Leo, and how he had shared that story with Marina their first night together at El Farol. He raised his glass. "*Deliver us from fear*. You have my promise."

"I want you to make me another promise. Stay close with my family, especially Nicole. She's as close to me as you could ever get. You could marry her."

He nearly knocked his glass over, stunned by her words. "Marina!"

"Why? You always say how much you love her." She spoke as if the leap of logic were obvious.

"I do, but—"

"Or Diane."

"Diane? Is this really our conversation tonight, your suggestions for whom I should marry?" He leveled his chin. "Marina, I'm married."

"You're almost widowed." She sipped again from her wineglass. "Don't worry; my list of women you can marry is a lot shorter than the list of those you can't."

"Oh, God, you're serious. I'm biting my tongue, but go ahead."

She dug into her purse to pull out a folded piece of paper, and began to read aloud, as if reciting an invitation list for a party or a wedding. "The *Can't Marry* group: Rosana."

"She's a *definite* can't—" Marc chimed in.

"Oh, yes, a definite *can't*. But she *is* the mother of your children, so always be kind to her."

"Wow, you're incredible…"

"For the kids."

"I understand, and I hear you. And I love you so much," he said, his voice wobbling.

Esperanzo was back, pushing a wheeled cart. Their meal sizzled and steamed upon it, lobster, shrimp, grilled vegetables, salad.

"*Provecho, provechito,*" he said, serving them with dexterity.

"What a spread!" Marc inhaled, glad for the distraction.

"Looks fabulous," Marina said, refilling their wine glasses.

Marc was savoring his first buttery bite of lobster when she resumed her discourse.

"Anyway, the rest of the *Can't Marry* group: Corinne, Anna, Rose, Janis, Pamela…"

A bit of lobster flew from Marc's mouth, ejected in surprise. "How long is this list?" he asked.

She took a delicate bite, chewed, dabbed butter from her lip. "Mmm, this is delicious."

He waited, slack-jawed.

"Thirteen."

"Lucky number. Can't we do this later?" As wonderful as the meal was, his stomach was reacting to the list, and the list was winning.

"Here, keep it and read it," she said, extending the paper. It wavered, warmed by the heat and smoke from the candle.

He reluctantly took it from her, slid it into his jacket pocket, and tried desperately to return his attention to the creamy flesh of the lobster on his plate.

"I want to be cremated," she continued.

He set his fork down.

"And have most of the ashes buried on the hill behind our home near my prayer circle, next to the medicine wheel."

"Don't you think you're still too healthy to be talking about this?" he managed to ask. The blood had drained from his face and a chill swept down his back, despite the sultry evening. He was not ready for this. What made her think he was ready for this?

He stared at her. How the hell was *she* ready for it?

The woman sitting across the table from him, his dear Marina, all the lovely warmth and life and flesh and spirit of her, the breath and pulse and ardent heart of her, now seemed made of spun steel, fiercely tough under the web of her lace shawl. Still his beautiful Marina, she was even more beautiful, transfigured by the crucible of illness.

Her next words came hard, metallic, and precise. "Why not talk about it? That's what's wrong with our civilization; we never talk about death. It's my death— I should be able to talk about it— I won't be able to, afterwards. And I know you. You'll beat yourself up, wishing we had spoken about our fears and uncertainties."

"All right. I'm just having trouble being as clear as you are. I admire this newfound state of grace, and acceptance, but—it's hard for me to see through such sadness. I know, yes, love, I know… this is going to kill you."

Waves rolled in and then slipped back up the beach, filling the silence at the table with growls and whispers.

"I don't think I've said that out loud before." Marc's voice shook. "I'm a healer to strangers. My heart is—it's ripped open by my failure to heal you." His restraint utterly fractured, tears fell to the table and his shoulders shook. He rubbed his eyes and pushed against his mouth to keep the anguish from flooding out uncontrollably.

"Marc, you've been supporting me, researching the cancer, spending tens of thousands of dollars on me. You're going to have to heal. I promise to help, from wherever I am, near or far away. It will get better."

He drew a wrenching breath and wiped his eyes with the napkin from his lap. The pieces of his heart were scattered, but he aimed high. "We can still fight, still be diligent in our quest for a healthy illness."

"Healthy illness? Like jumbo shrimp?" Marina performed an ironic victory wave with a shrimp, before nipping it in half.

"I'd like to try that clinic in Tijuana, get more aggressive with the alternative treatments," he suggested. "What do you think?"

"If you go with me."

"Every step, and to the ends of the earth."

"Watch your step. The end is near, my love," she said with utmost tenderness.

The waves pounded, drawing and redrawing the ends of the earth just out of sight in the Caribbean night. Marc cleared his throat and focused on the black water, unable to speak.

Marina, however, spoke on. "I want some ashes spread at North Beach, Cape Cod, where I grew up. You can talk to my dad about that."

"Cape Cod. Okay."

"Promise me something else."

"Anything," he croaked, barely able to squeeze the word from his constricted windpipe.

"Rubbers."

"Rubbers?" He wasn't sure he had heard her correctly. "*Rubbers?*"

"You have to use them. I know you hate them, but you're going to need the closeness of a woman when I'm gone and—"

"First off, not as soon as you might think!" He pointed an agitated finger at her, stared at it theatrically, as if surprised by its independent behavior, and slowly curled it down. "Second, of course I'll use condoms, Jesus. And third, it's getting hard to talk and eat and bite my tongue at the same time. Can we wrap this up?"

"Just promise." She looked suddenly exhausted, the luster in her eyes fading. "Love, please take me home to bed."

"Belly okay?" He started to get to his feet.

"Yeah, just bushed. The wine, the lobster, the cancer."

He waved to Esperanzo as he helped Marina out of her chair. When they reached the restaurant's exit, there was Naia, with her shy smile and luminous green eyes. Marina reached out to caress the angle of her jaw. "You're my hero angel. Thank you." The girl returned the gesture, delicate and solemn. Wordless.

They made their way back to the bungalow very slowly, stopping to take off Marina's shoes, Marc carrying them in one hand as he supported her against his shoulder. Barefoot, she was steadier. She wrapped an arm around him and remained quiet until they were inside again, where the lights were low and welcoming. He brushed sand from her feet and helped her to undress, to slide into bed, and she let him.

"Are you coming?" she asked sleepily.

"I'll be right there. Gonna grab a quick smoke."

"Okay. I love you." She closed her eyes.

Marc paced to the porch, where he stood unmoving, not breathing. He pulled a short cigar from a case in his suit jacket and lit it with trembling fingers, watched it burn bright orange as the smoke drifted swiftly away. Tried to hold himself together, failed. The roar of the surf drowned his wail.

Sand and Water

The last of the lengthening days of the year, the day before solstice, had arrived. As the Yucatán sun approached its zenith, it shone with climactic energy, scattering firework sparkles across the noisy waves below, drawing steam and sweat into the vault of the azure sky.

Marc's feet burned in his flip-flops as he returned to the bungalow from the resort office, where he had gone to check out and to reconfirm their reservation for the van to the airport.

It took a moment for his eyes to adjust inside the shady room. He found Marina wearing her big sun hat, a sleeveless blouse, and shorts, methodically folding clothes and packing her bag. He began tossing medical supplies and remedies haphazardly into the cooler.

"You're acting frantic again," she remarked, the very image of cool, calm, and collected, as she went about her business.

"We're going to miss the plane—do we have all the gifts?" he asked. Damp circles bloomed under the sleeves of his sky-blue guayabera, a Yucatán-style wedding shirt Marina had found for him, its pockets perfect for protecting cigars.

"If we miss the plane, we miss it," she replied.

"Come on, we really have to hurry," he said, his urgency spurred by her lack of it.

She carefully tucked a sundress into her bag. "I plan to be on time, but I'm not in a hurry."

Before he could argue, Esperanzo appeared at the open door. Even though he could see inside, he knocked politely. "The car is here." He carried the bags to the idling vehicle as Marc waited in the shadowy doorway, eyes on Marina.

Marina pulled a glass jar from the cooler, took it to the bathroom sink, emptied its brown fluid, and rinsed it thoroughly. She walked out to the porch and down to the foaming surf. Marc trailed behind and watched her scoop sand and seawater into the jar. She filled it to the brim, screwed the lid shut, and held it aloft. White sunlight both reflected from the glass and passed through it, glinting upon swirling grains of sand. Galaxies of them. Marina lowered her arms, then paused to contemplate the sea and sky before stepping purposefully back to the bungalow.

"What's that?" Marc asked.

"My new remedy—sand and water, particles and waves. Light. I'll keep it close to our bed to remind us."

Her smile lanced through Marc like a shaft of sunlight through storm clouds, and was just as fleeting, gone with the turn of her head. She strode to the waiting van, where Esperanzo had thoughtfully ensured that the air conditioning was turned up high.

Marc took a final view of the watercolor horizon. Three dolphins were jumping in unison, as if waving from the waves; he acknowledged them with a tilt of his chin, picked up the cooler, and followed Marina to the now-freezing van.

Part 3
Melody

Summer Lightning

Santa Fe proudly displayed her splendor in late July, and a picnic in the mountains was Marina's plan for the day. Marc was eager to oblige. The kids were visiting their mom for the weekend before heading off to summer camp, in keeping with Marina's wish to maintain routines as much as possible. She had hugged them goodbye with honest, cheery assurance that they would all be together at home again after camp ended. Her efforts to preserve normalcy in their lives, or at least the illusion of it, were belied by her own evident changes. Her appetite and energy had fallen off noticeably; fresh mountain air would feel good and might help her to eat.

Marc felt her studying him as she sat at the kitchen table while he prepared lunch, more food than either of them could put away in the best of times. Organic tomatoes from Dez's garden, with basil leaves, olive oil, and soft slices of mozzarella layered and arranged to please the eye as well as the palate; roasted red peppers and potatoes, seasoned with garlic and oregano; fresh trout, a gift from a grateful fisherman patient, bathed in lemon and capers; pasta salad, fruit salad, iced tea with mint.

Aromatic steam rose from the stove as Marc, his face beaded with sweat, choreographed ingredients into their culinary roles. The knife in his hand reverberated at machine gun speed against the wooden cutting board, sharp as a flamenco dancer's heels.

Marina plucked green grapes from their stems, adding them to the bowl of strawberries and blueberries.

"Here, taste, please," Marc said, offering a spoonful of pasta salad.

A bite, neat, with those dentist-father teeth.

"More celery?" he asked. "Cilantro?"

She chewed and swallowed. "No, nothing more. Just the way it is. Here." She slid a grape into his mouth.

"Now that's an interesting combination, grapes with the pasta salad." It had tasted fine before, but the fruit, with its sweet, juicy crunch, made the salad more than fine. He began to slice a handful of grapes in half, adding them to the pasta. "I don't know that Grandma Delfina would approve, but sometimes you just gotta go with your gut, or in this case, your tongue." He set down the knife, leaned forward to kiss Marina.

Her fingers stroked the back of his neck. "I'm going with your sweet tongue."

He assisted her out of her chair, and they embraced in the sultry kitchen. "You calling me a sweet talker?"

"I love you like crazy, you dear, crazy, sweet-talking man." She pressed her face against his chest.

"Okay, enough syrup already; we've got savories to keep an eye on—don't let me burn the potatoes." He gave them a quick stir in the cast-iron frying pan.

She returned to her chair. "This is going to be the best picnic. Remember Telluride?"

"How could I forget? You, naked, the lake—"

"And *you* naked, big boy. It was breathtaking."

"It still is. You still are." The spoon dangled from his hand as he studied her. Her eyes seemed to have grown larger, her T-shirt and cut-off shorts roomier, her legs coltishly thin. He scooped another spoonful of pasta salad, brought it to her mouth. "*Mangia, amor.*"

"*Grazie, amor.*"

Summer afternoons in the Sangre de Cristos often brought thunderstorms, but today was clear, dry, and hot, ninety degrees in town. The twisting road leading to the ski basin carried a procession of vehicles, so many people with the same idea: head for higher ground to escape the heat. Aspen Vista's parking area was nearly full, and the trail itself was thronged with hikers, dog walkers, and picnickers. Marc hoisted the heavy basket, and took Marina's elbow to help her walk to a nearby scenic spot that he hoped would be unoccupied.

They were in luck. Their venue was vacant and quiet, hidden by a copse of blue spruces. Beyond those, a sweep of aspens descended the steep incline, their leaves rustling in the breeze like programs fanned by an audience awaiting the first notes of a concert. Marc spread a blanket upon the leaf litter and set up the picnic, while Marina stretched out in the dappled shade, smiling under her sunglasses and hat. The stroll had drained her strength but not her mood.

"Cheers!" Marc offered a glass of iced tea for a toast. "To our very own *Luncheon in the Grass*."

Removing her sunglasses, Marina said, "No fair. That would mean *your* clothes stay on and mine don't."

"*Touché*. Was it Monet or Manet? I get those French painters mixed up."

"Manet. I remember seeing that painting in Paris with Nicole one summer when we were in college. We had such a good time. We drank too much wine, kissed a Frenchman or two, or was it three?"

"The grief you gave me about Corinne, and now I hear this? Three or maybe four Frenchmen kissing my wife? What's the story here?"

"Oh, Mr. Aggressively Insecure! No orgies with Frenchmen, I promise. French pastries, definitely. Eclairs, palmiers, little cups of bitter coffee..." She gazed off into the aspens. "Make sure that Chelsea and Zane get to Paris when they're older, but still young. Take them to France and Italy. Show them Rome the way you know it. Show them the old country."

"Here's a taste of Italy."

He forked up a slice of mozzarella dripping with olive oil and delivered it to her mouth. "I solemnly swear that Chelsea and Zane will learn the difference between Roman and Sicilian pizza and will become insufferable pizza snobs. And if I have anything to do with it"—he tipped his nose heavenward and made the sign of the cross upon his chest— "so sorry, Nonna Delfina, but here goes—I hope they prefer Roman, with a thinner crust." He paused, acting as if he expected a lightning bolt to strike him dead for heresy.

"Not snobs," Marina said. "Just— There's so much for them to taste and experience. They're so lucky to have you for their father. Cheers."

She raised her glass and leaned back in an odalisque's pose. "Now, let's explore this feast. I think I'd like a peeled grape."

"At your service, my lady." After selecting a grape from the fruit salad, Marc made a show of peeling it before slipping it into her mouth.

Barely an hour later, they were descending the narrow, mountain road as fast as Marc could manage, his vehicle's brakes burning at the sharp turns.

"Aaagh!"

The tires veered toward the guardrail-free precipice at Marina's cry, and Marc saw her grab her right ribcage as if she'd been knifed. Hands tight, he jerked on the steering wheel to bring the tires back into the lane. Marina slumped against the side of the SUV, gasping, hunching forward when the spasms came, ugly travesties of labor pains, searing and relentless.

Shit, shit. shit pulsed silently between Marc's teeth, a mantra for a safe descent down the mountain. He became an actor portraying a charade of calm.

"Stomach… in my mouth… Pressure." Marina's face contorted. Her hands clutched her belly.

"Going to the hospital right now, sweetheart. Grease job and an oil change. Quick."

"Better be." She was blanched and sweating, her voice ragged.

The drive proved a torment of curves, a breathtaking 180-degree turn from the pleasures of the picnic. At the emergency entrance to St. Vincent's Hospital, Marc leaped out to grab a wheelchair, and ran it recklessly to the car. He flung open the passenger door and unbuckled Marina's seatbelt. He cradled her in his arms.

"We're here, love. Let's get you in."

"I'm not staying, you understand?" She was wrung out. "No matter what happens, get me home. Do we understand each other, Marc? No matter what."

"We understand each other perfectly, love," he said, fighting to keep his voice from cracking. He helped her into the wheelchair and maneuvered her carefully toward the glass doors, which slid apart in unwelcome welcome.

A young couple with a newborn in a pink cap was about to exit, the mother and child in a wheelchair, the new father's brow shiny with sweat and pride as he walked behind them. "Let's get you home, girls," he was saying.

Marina sank low in the wheelchair, her head lolling helplessly. Marc's fingers shook as he stroked her temple; he sensed her gathering all the strength left in her, all the force of the last moments of labor, to lift her head and whisper good luck to the new mother. He and the new father exchanged nods. Silent stories poured between them in an instant—blessings, hope, anguish. Then they separated, wheeling their loves away, steering their presents and futures in very different directions.

"Marc?"

"Yes, baby?"

"Sunrise, sunset."

He knelt before her in the hospital lobby and gently straightened her body. "I'll get you home fast."

Kestrel

Marina was still in the hospital three days later. Pain management, palliative care, and a feeding tube were trial and error procedures undertaken to get things right. *Right* being a relative term; she needed pain relief but was adamant that she wanted to remain alert, not zoned out. She also wanted visitors, but didn't want them to see her suffering. Balance was elusive.

Marc managed to check in at work a couple of hours each day, getting coverage from his reliable staff and a greenhorn PT eager for experience. He came and went quickly, businesslike, brushing off expressions of pity with his best professional mask. Most of the time he sat with Marina; he also watched over her treatments and naps, and ran interference with docs, nurses, orderlies, and visitors. He was just leaving her room to grab a late lunch in the hospital cafeteria, when a white-coated doc stepped from an adjacent room. The friendly, familiar face registered surprise.

"Marc, hello," said Dr. Kestrel in his British accent. "What are you doing here?"

"I— My wife is ill." He gestured toward Marina's room. She had just fallen into a fragile sleep. "You?"

"One of my patients," Dr. Kestrel said, shaking his head, his face drooping with fatigue.

"Get a cup of coffee with me, Niles? I'm heading downstairs to see what's left of lunch."

"Sure."

After Marina's hospital admission, Marc had fetched the picnic basket from his car and brought it to the nurses' station so his feast wouldn't go to waste. You can't tip nurses and doctors, but you sure as hell can feed them. Each day he brought flowers to Marina and food to the nurses' station, but had little interest in anything for himself and kept forgetting to eat. Marina had heard his stomach gurgle loudly as he was adjusting her blanket today, and insisted that he go eat something. He promised. He and Niles took the stairs without speaking. They picked an out of the way table in the mostly deserted cafeteria.

Niles Kestrel was an odd duck, a Brit who thrived in the American Southwest. A straight, married man with children, and a doctor whose medical practice was devoted to HIV/AIDS patients. He had switched from general medicine at a time when victims of HIV/AIDS, mostly gay men, had few medical advocates and resources. Fear of the illness, among the broader public, had intensified stigmatization and isolation. When Niles first began to treat these patients, he was horrified by their suffering and vowed to concentrate all his efforts on their care. Marc had known him for years as a general physician with an elegant, yet approachable public persona, and as a man with an earthy and irreverent sense of humor in private.

"Cheers," Niles said, toasting with a Styrofoam cup of watery black coffee.

"Cheers." Marc's cup wavered.

"I'm sorry, I didn't even know you were married. A bit out of the loop lately," Niles said. "What's your wife's name?"

"Marina. Married last year, Cape Cod. Where she grew up."

"Congratulations. Tell me why she's on that ward," Niles inquired with delicate concern. "My sickest patients are up there."

Marc rubbed the bridge of his nose. "Severe gastric cancer. Inoperable. We've tried different things."

Niles sighed. "I'm so sorry, Marc." He paused, a compassionate silence. "It's going to look very similar to end stage HIV."

Marc's sandwich, turkey on spongy white bread, lay inert upon a paper plate. Thinking of Marina with her feeding tube, unable to eat, he suddenly couldn't imagine putting that thing in his mouth.

"Have you talked about hospice?" Niles asked.

"The 'H' word. She's not ready to think about that yet. I'm not either, I guess."

"Too final? Too depressing? I can't say I know what you're going through, but I have had—I have—many patients who receive hospice care, and for the most part they seem to find it helpful. It isn't about giving up, or giving in. It's about living with dignity, with as little pain as we can manage. Sometimes patients rally and don't need it anymore, for a while at least. Sometimes they remain in hospice care much longer than anyone expected. Think about it. Call me."

"Thanks, Niles. I'll do that," Marc said, without conviction. He felt as flat as the inedible sandwich. He pushed back his chair. "Gotta check in at the clinic, see what's left of my practice. I'll call you. She might come home day after tomorrow."

Niles scrawled a phone number onto a napkin. "Call this agency, ask for Roberta—Bobbie. She'll connect you with home help." He finished the nasty coffee with a gulp. "And eat something. Marina can't, but you must. Get some real food, something with scorching green chile, not this bland crap. Plaza Café."

They shared another bro-hug. Marc had hugged a lot of men lately; the bros seemed dissatisfied with a mere handshake. Not a good sign.

Priorities

August 14, 1995
Santa Fe, New Mexico

Marc's eyes were closed. He reached for Marina, but the bed was empty. His eyes opened in a flash. His heart pounded, ears strained.

The shower was running, then off. She stood wrapped in a white towel, brushing her teeth vigorously in the bathroom doorway. The tube in her nose, taped to her cheek, dangled, swinging with the rhythm of the toothbrush. She was contemplating him with steadfast composure.

"Love…" he said groggily. He had woken countless times in the night to watch her sleep.

She disappeared into the bathroom for a moment. Re-emerged to stop at the stereo, push a button. Jeff Buckley's "Last Goodbye" began to play, unsparing and intimate. She returned to bed still wrapped in the towel and damp from the shower, a small brown bottle in her hand.

"Love," she said, sliding out of the towel as she straddled him, taking him by surprise. She dripped oil from the bottle onto her palms, and began to smooth them over his chest like tides arcing and receding.

His body woke vibrating under the warm, insistent pressure of her movements. Marina's last ride, businesslike and efficient, ended with a light and lovely orgasm as Marc's throat and shoulders rose in shattering paroxysm.

"Kiss me," she murmured, her head bowed, her thin arms folding.

The clamped end of the feeding tube hit him in the forehead, then dragged like a loose rein across his nose. He flinched, and looked up at her.

She was there but not there, already somewhere else. After pushing the tube away to give him a lingering kiss, she climbed from his body and donned her robe.

He watched her draw a scrap of paper from the robe's breast pocket, examine it, then put it away again before she descended to the kitchen to take charge of the day.

Marc found the paper ten days later. A to-do list. *Feeding tube out* was second on the list.

Shells

A week had passed since the feeding tube was yanked.

Marina sat at the kitchen table, sipping ice water through a straw, draped in a pale, turquoise silk kimono. Marc stood at the sink, filling ice cube trays. Half of a freshly quartered lemon sat on the cutting board.

One of the lemon quarters flavored Marina's water; she held another in her hand, about to suck on it, when the shift happened without warning and she began to slip, a slow-motion topple from her chair, just as Marc turned. Her eyes were wide and glassy.

Marc caught her in his arms, all the diminished weight of her, without a word. He had no words.

He carried her up the seashell spiral of stairs to the sleigh bed she loved, whose every creak and whisper evoked memories. Lovemaking—languorous, energetic, exploratory, athletic, graceful… Pillow talk, intimacies Marc had never known with anyone else. Giggles and silliness, fears and tears… Children, dreams, music, and love. Always love. And sleep.

She slept now, the deep sleep of coma.

Marina's last meal had been the picnic in the mountains, a source of unspoken anguish for Marc; had he fed her to death? Their pell-mell descent to the emergency room resulted in the feeding tube, then hospice care. He'd agreed that it would be her decision when the time came to have the tube removed. She lived with it for nearly a month, until it became clear that the feeding tube was feeding the tumors.

Now, their bedroom became a place of vigil. Family, friends, countless volunteers, all helped to carry on with the business of living, while helping with the business of dying, swelling the household as if the house itself were filling its belly for the one who no longer could fill her own.

Suitcases and makeshift beds made the spacious living room look like an airport lounge during a massive storm delay.

Someone was always sleeping. Someone was always cooking, showering, doing dishes and laundry, sharing news of the day and of the night. Hands touched. Bodies pressed against each other in consoling embraces. So many people ate, drank, slept, and worked in the house that the septic tank overflowed. John and Patricia White paid the pumping company.

The last days were filled with the unstoppable minutiae of ordinary existence—footsteps on the stairs, telephones ringing, dogs barking, the teakettle whistling, muffled sniffles and chuckles. Voices. Solicitous, sorrowful, anxious, courageous, self-conscious, humorous, bossy voices. An ocean of human sound around the clock, a tidal flow of love and mourning, ever moving. Missing were the voices of Chelsea and Zane, as Rosana had insisted on taking them away when the coma vigil began.

Marc's and Marina's parents, and her twin, Nicole, devoted themselves to the vigil; they were gathered bedside at the moment of Marina's passing. Marc was the only one in the room who didn't see her take her last breath, but heard it, a long sigh. He lifted his head from *The Book of the Dead* at the soft words of Nicole saying, "Goodbye, Marina."

Marina's eyes were open to the light-filled room, their aqua color like arctic ice, sightless now. Marc closed them.

Twice.

The still-warm lids flexed like butterfly wings. The glow beneath them melted away.

Marc descended to the living-room-turned-waiting-room on numb legs, arms limp at his sides, as though his body had died with hers, even though his continued to breathe. His face told the news.

Ever-present Moonflute presided over bathing and dressing Marina's body. She asked Marc if he wanted to see Marina afterwards, and he said no. Her shell was empty.

Moonflute then came to him with a comb and a pair of scissors in hand, reminding him of a vow. He nodded, and dropped into a kitchen chair wearing the white shirt he had worn when Marina first came to dinner. Moonflute combed his hair into a smooth ponytail held with an elastic band. With decisive snips, she severed it.

Marc asked for the jar of sand and water; Moonflute brought it to him. He stepped outside to climb the stony hill above the house to Marina's sacred space, to absorb her cherished views of the Cerrillos Hills, the parade of clouds above, the stable with her beloved horses below, the home she had imbued with her devoted presence. He placed the jar in the center of her circle and sat, spilling his tears into the dry sand. The sky was empty of birds.

Only when rising thunderheads over the Sangres grew tinged with apricot, peach, and plum, did he become aware of time having passed. Strange for him. His time sense was so uncannily accurate that Marina had liked to say he told the clocks what time it was. Today he had gone somewhere out of time, wasn't sure where he was anymore. He stood and stretched, stiff from sitting on the hard ground.

The house was still crowded when he went back inside, but Marina's body had been wheeled away, along with his ponytail. Moonflute told him that she had placed the ponytail on Marina's breast.

There were invitations to sleep elsewhere, in other beds, under other roofs.

"No, thank you," he said. "I need everyone to leave." His face felt like a mask.

The low-key words had the effect of a push broom. Knowing that it was time for the house to be empty, the flock respected his wish. Belongings were gathered, stuffed into vehicles. Hotels were called. Indian Market had come and gone the previous weekend, packing Santa Fe with thousands of visitors, but now there were rooms to be had. After quick goodbyes that dragged on forever, the last vehicle finally turned its headlights into the blinding night and drove slowly past the Children at Play sign.

Marc waved from the doorway, Met and Jet at his feet. Winnie whinnied in the stable, his call much louder than usual. Crickets trilled the song of the stars.

The house blazed with light and bore traces of an event just ended—a party, even—but it was only an interlude. There was a funeral to prepare for. He turned off the lamps and climbed the stairs—slowly, so very slowly—to sleep alone in the bed he had shared with Marina, the bed she had died in that very day. Their bed of life and death. He thought of the night Little Grandma had died in his parents' bed, the twenty-second of November, 1963. Only days later, his parents had lain down to sleep in that bed, Little Grandma's death bed.

Marc stepped into the loft bedroom, expecting to find minor disarray. Instead, the sleigh bed was freshly made with the blue-green sheets Marina had chosen when they married. She had told him the color was called celadon, named for an ancient ceramic glaze, and that it reminded her of his eyes.

She had asked to die in those sheets, and so she had.

But she had also left instructions with Moonflute to wash them after she was gone, and remake the bed with them for Marc. The same sheets. He hadn't known about that before, but he understood her plan for him now as he contemplated the sheets, neatly turned down over the sand-white comforter, where several seashells had been arranged. The largest, a conch, rested between the pillows.

The sheets gleamed like the sea early on a cloudless day. They had hung to dry in the breeze of a desert afternoon and been shaken free of pollen and dust. Loving hands had tossed and waved them, held them open to the sky to gather sunlight and scented wind hymns from the mountains, from ponderosas, spruces, aspens, mosses, wildflowers, and even very distant butterflies. The bed exuded a fresh scent of renewal, not of death, Marina's love all around him in the crisp language of the bedding. But the familiar human scent of her, his Marina, was gone, a loss that left him bereft. He strove to hold fast to her intention.

He collected the seashells into a small pile where Marina's heart would have rested and then slipped between the sheets. He stared across the room at an O'Keeffe print on the wall, a wedding gift from Sonya. In it, a white, spiraled seashell appeared to sleep in the embrace of blood-red hills. He turned off the last light.

Marina, where are you? Marc wanted desperately to run his fingers through her hair, to stroke her forehead. The night pressed at him, choked him, a thick, black, sea of hopelessness. The new moon was barely a day old and invisible. *Where are you? I can't see.* He reached for the shells and found the conch. He traced its rough surface and smooth inner lip, held it to his ear, and drifted to sleep.

Sand & Water

Santa Fe New Mexican
Wednesday, August 30, 1995

Deaths

   CERRILLOS – Marina White Hochstaff, 34, died at her home in
Cerrillos on Sunday from gastric cancer. Wife of Marc Hochstaff,
loving stepmother to Chelsea and Zane, she is also survived by her
parents, John and Patricia White, and twin sister, Nicole White, all of
Chatham, Mass. Hochstaff was born in Camp Lejeune, Jacksonville,
N.C., in 1960. She was a resident of Chatham, Mass. from 1962 until
she moved to Santa Fe in 1993. She graduated from Emma Willard
School in Troy, N.Y., where she excelled as a competitive equestrian.
She received an associate degree from Cape Cod Community College
in Barnstable, Mass. and a bachelor's degree in early childhood
education from Bridgewater State University in Bridgewater, Mass.
She was a beloved volunteer with Horse Feathers Equine Therapy
Center of Santa Fe, and will be deeply missed by its clients and their
families. Her family requests that donations be made to Horse
Feathers' therapeutic program for disabled children and to Santa Fe
Hospice. Services will be private.

End of Innocence

September 3, 1995
Santa Fe, New Mexico

The end of summer was a reminder of why so many artists had been drawn to Northern New Mexico. Cinematic cloud dramas filled the sky, casting shadow plays upon the red and green hills around Marc's home. Today the clouds went off to play elsewhere, however, leaving a blistering, record-breaking hot day for Marina's memorial ceremony. It wouldn't be rained out but umbrellas opened anyway, as parasols.

Streams of mourners and well-wishers arrived in a continuous, sedate caravan along the rutted road throughout the morning. Marina's Children at Play sign played its part. Nicole and Moonflute helped to manage the event, distributing water bottles and tissues, directing mourners to Marina's medicine wheel, a distinctive cluster of rocks above the house, but Marc was the master of ceremonies.

As the crowd swelled, he noticed the arrival of a hawk, circling high in the searing sky. Then another, and another, and more, until nearly a dozen swooped through the air, crisscrossing over the heads of the humans.

Music accompanied the hawks and mourners, as Sonya's ethereal voice rose from a PA system. Marina hadn't told Sonya of the severity of her illness, afraid that her friend would have sacrificed completion of the conservatory program to come be with her had she known. Marc hadn't been able to reach Sonya in Austria to give her the news of Marina's passing, but her music at the funeral made Sonya's kind and loving presence real.

The service was a celebration of life. Tears and laughter, stories, some shared for the first time, were passed around and around.

Marc, accompanied closely by Zane and Chelsea, handed out cigars. Cubans, of course. His buddies and colleagues were there—Dr.

Jefferson, Dr. Richard Frank, Dr. Kestrel, Armando, and Dez, Ruby and Kata, Nikos from Evangelo's. So many who loved Marina, who loved him, came.

There were dozens of Marc's patients and former patients, including Herb, who arrived with his lady friend on his monster Harley; Marc's and Marina's families; friends from the Santa Fe Opera and Horse Feathers, from as far as Chatham and from as nearby as down the road; neighbors from Chelsea and Zane's school.

Mourners even made the trip from France—Corinne brought her fiancé, flying across an ocean plus half a continent. And Esperanzo— Marc did a double take when he spotted his friendly face in the crowd. Who had notified him? Had he swum across the desert?

Marc felt as though he were watching a puppet version of himself soothing the mourners, trying to help everyone else feel better, as his real self and his real grief withdrew into hiding. *Be strong. Ease their heartache by suppressing your own. Marina was strong for so long, do it for her. Perform.*

He looked out at the gathering and smiled. "To quote Elvis—Elvis Costello, that is—'What's so funny 'bout peace, love and understanding.'" The PA system segued into the Costello version of the song by that name, one of Marc's favorite covers when playing at Evangelo's. Rocking guitar chords, rocking drums, Nick Lowe's heartfelt lyrics. Marina's medicine wheel reverberated with the bracing music. Elvis's delivery was righteous and urgent, his summons an irresistible challenge. Where were the strong?

"We are the strong!" Marc shouted in answer to the song.

"You bet your ass. Well said, brother." Herb's familiar raspy voice shouted back.

Marc raised his arms high, hands outstretched. "We love you, Marina!"

"We love you, Marina!" responded the assembly, in a crescendo of love.

Several guests commented on the flocking hawks; some grew nervous and beat an early retreat to the house. The rest made their way down the hill in a slow procession.

Marc finally descended, the last to leave. Goodbye, Marina, we love you. *I love you.*

Mourners gathered in the spacious living room around tables laden with potluck comfort food, everything from green chile enchilada casseroles, to bowls of watermelon and cherries.

Marc wandered through the house, searching for Esperanzo. He had questions. But no one he asked had seen the gentle man, so he was left to acknowledge and thank Esperanzo quietly in his mind for making the journey.

Moonflute collared him in the kitchen. She had brought an enormous bowl of a grainy, vegan concoction and insisted that Marc taste it, despite his lack of appetite. He politely took a plateful, ate a bite in front of her, then played the cigar card.

"Gonna grab a smoke while I eat." He took a cigar from his shirt pocket, left the kitchen, dish in hand, and settled into the pink Playa del Carmen hammock on the patio. Met and Jet's food bowls were out there. Two dogs, innocently happy enough to chow down on horseshit, enjoyed their first vegan meal.

Marc rocked gently in silence, smoking his Cohiba and playing an exquisitely painful game of devil's advocate with himself, a game that he had succeeded in pushing out of his mind until now.

Had he done everything in his power to prevent Marina's death? Were their choices appropriate? Could she have been saved by burning and poison—radiation and chemo? The corrosive uncertainty scorched the depths of his soul, a self-inflicted burn and poison treatment.

He blew a billow of smoke and closed his stinging eyes, picturing Marina in New York shopping for her wedding dress. Reliving the sweet joy of those moments was now unbearably poignant.

He replayed the most memorable words of the most intimate conversation he'd had with his father-in-law. John White had looked him in the eye and said, with a calm betrayed by the slight tremble and upward pitch in his voice, "We have to respect her decision."

We did that, Marina. We did. But was it the right thing to do?

The desolate heart-to-heart with Dr. Singh at the Gecko Bar a few days after the exploratory surgery had seemed, at the time, to answer that question, but *what if?*

He forced his thoughts back to the day of the operation, five months ago. Marina, full of life and hope, had hid her nervousness well. After the frustration of months of illness without a diagnosis, the surgery had looked like an opportunity to take care of business, a positive step. Would it have been better not to know?

Who could answer the devil's advocate?

Around and around he circled the same ground, the same arguments and questions, hours after all the mourners had left, ending up each time back on that Tuesday morning in April, at UNM Hospital, where the surgery was about to begin.

A Shot in the Dark

Five Months Earlier
Albuquerque, New Mexico

The surgery waiting room at the University of New Mexico Hospital had been filled by the crack of dawn with an entourage of Marc and Marina's friends and family. Everyone sat pensive and silent in low-slung chairs, or stood stiffly around the edges of the room, their backs to a wall. Marc shunned the comfortless chairs, choosing to remain on his feet.

Dr. Singh, the gastroenterologist, entered, followed by Dr. Gram, the surgeon. The two men presented contrasting appearances, Dr. Singh a short, dark, East Indian, and Dr. Gram, a robust, stocky German. Marc and Marina had come to appreciate them both during the course of several medical appointments, and trusted their expertise and judgment.

"We are about to go in there and take a peek," Dr. Gram explained, face-to-face with Marc, before acknowledging the room at large with a nod. "The procedure will take about an hour."

Dr. Singh softly added, "We'll know more soon. Meanwhile, I suggest that you try to stay centered."

Both doctors shook hands with Marc and departed.

A nurse entered next. "She wants to see her husband."

Marina lay on a gurney, hair tucked into a blue bouffant surgical cap, looking very young. She patted the cap with coquettish bravado, saying, "Do you like my hat?" alluding to one of Zane's favorite Dr. Seuss books, which she had read tirelessly with him many nights.

"I do. It matches your eyes. Always the fashion hound, you are."

"I need to take your kiss with me."

He bent to kiss her and held her hand as the sedative cocktail was administered, surprised by how quickly it took effect. She gave him a sleepy smile and was gone.

She had joked with him that she wanted Nirvana's "Heart-Shaped Box" to play in the operating room while she was unconscious, and he had promised to try to make that happen, impressed by the black humor evidenced by her choice of a song referencing cancer. True to his word, he gave the doctors her mixed tape—dark, moody, and edgy. He was told by a deferential tech that most patients chose Mozart or Yanni.

The operating room was chilly and brightly lit. Marina's body lay upon the table, draped in white, her abdomen exposed. A long vertical incision exposed her further, revealing stomach, pancreas and liver. The doctors, backed by several nurses, worked intently. Dr. Gram's gloved hand pushed and pulled at her liver.

"No wonder we couldn't find the tumor with the cameras," he said through his surgical mask. "It is like Nosferatu's hand upon the stomach, strangling it from the outside."

Dr. Singh peered at the perplexing tumor, eyes widening at the size, shape, location and complications of the mass. His mask swelled with his sigh. "So, there is nothing we can do. It is best to close everything up." He bent over Marina's sleeping face. "I am so sorry, my dear."

"Time to break the news," Dr. Gram said. "Will you take the lead? I'm usually not this emotional."

"Of course. Only thirty-four." Dr. Singh's voice broke. "I was the one who told them, after the endoscopy was negative, 'Hey, kids, go on and get married! Give me a call when you get back.'" His bitter tone was self-mocking. "'Congratulations!' I said. Yes, I'll talk to the family. I'll tell her husband."

The waiting room crowd stirred hopefully when the physicians opened the door and asked Marc into the hall. Their grim expressions told him everything he didn't want to know.

"I'm so sorry," Dr. Singh began.

Marc's stomach clenched.

"We found a severe gastric cancer of the diffuse type. Unfortunately, this kind of stomach cancer is not usually discovered with endoscopy, even with repeat endoscopies, and tends to advance very quickly. It involves the stomach walls and often spreads to other organs. In Marina's case, it has adhered to the pancreas. We will reconvene tomorrow to weigh treatment options. I'm so very sorry."

The doctor looked wretched.

White hallway, white ceiling and floors and lights, the doctor's white coat—so much white. Too much. The news percolated through the open door into the waiting room, a murmuring stream broken by the rocks of despair, from barely audible groans to granite projections of grief.

Dr. Singh took Marc by the elbow and led him away from the door, further down the hallway, and spoke in his gentlest tone. Marc asked him the question he most feared.

"Six months, maybe a year. Maybe... Maybe much less. It's hard to know." Singh shook his head. "This cancer is relatively rare as far as stomach cancers go, and it grows so fast that patients may reach stage three or four before they are symptomatic enough to seek diagnosis. Marina's case is stage four."

They hugged. Marc escaped to the nearest bathroom, cupped cold water again and again against his face. *No good. Still about to blow. Can't face that room full of people who love her.* He pushed out of the bathroom, spotted a storage room across the hall. *Time, need to buy time—right now.* An unbearably ironic thought. The storage room offered its own odd solace as he pulled supplies at random from the shelves, breaking, smashing, tossing equipment around, leaving the room a shambles.

Neon buzzed almost imperceptibly in the window near the end of the polished bar in the Gecko Bar and Grill. Dusk purpled the sky. The homeward-bound traffic of rush hour had given way to Friday night celebrants out to eat, drink and be merry. Some of them began to trickle into the place Marc had fled to after another day of medical consultations. He sat slumped, exhausted, on his stool. While Marina remained in Albuquerque's University of New Mexico Hospital, recovering from her surgery, he spent his nights in a modest motel nearby, turning to the Gecko for dinner and review. Vital decisions needed to be made soon.

Dr. Singh entered, rushed and short of breath.

"Rough day, eh, Marc? What are you drinking?"

"Diet Coke, I'm afraid."

"I don't usually drink at all, but…"

The bartender approached, drying a beer glass.

"What can I get you?"

"Shot of Patrón Silver and a water."

"That actually sounds pretty good, Doc," Marc said.

"What did oncology say?" Singh asked.

The bartender came back with glasses, lime and salt.

Marc and Dr. Singh raised their glasses. "To Marina's health." Dr. Singh banged his tequila back hard, sucked his lime like a pro.

Marc eyed him curiously and took a swallow of his Diet Coke before replying. "The oncologist was nice and blunt. They want to throw the chemo book at her. 'Intensive' was the term."

"Intensive is *very* intensive."

"She doesn't want to do it, is totally against it. What do we do? What would you do?" Marc asked, looking straight into Dr. Singh's dark eyes.

The doctor's face was shadowed by stress and fatigue. He waved a finger at the bartender. "I'd probably start drinking heavily."

"Believe me, I've been giving that great consideration." Marc stirred the ice in his Coke. "Marina told me that if she had known about this before we married…"

Dr. Singh winced. "Marc, I feel—"

"Don't. I would have married her anyway, do you understand? This wouldn't have stopped me from marrying her. She might have tried to get out of it, and that would have been a horrible mess. She *loved* her wedding, even the dopey shit I did to it. We're both glad we didn't know, okay? The die was already cast."

Dr. Singh nodded slowly. After a moment of reflection, he said, "Marc, we've become friendly through all this. Can I be frank with you?"

The bartender arrived with another tequila. Dr. Singh put a few bills on the bar, including a generous tip.

"I feel the same way," Marc said. "Shoot straight."

Dr. Singh played with his shot glass without drinking. "The prognosis for this kind of cancer is very poor, even if we pull out all the stops. If she does intensive chemo, she may never leave the hospital and she may die of some horrible complication. But that's the best and only real weapon we have. As a doctor, I'd say to follow the oncologist's suggestions."

He put a hand on Marc's forearm and punctuated his next words with light taps. "As your friend"—tap—"I'd tell you to get the fuck out of the hospital"—tap—"as fast as humanly possible"—tap. "Go home and love each other every day." He gulped his shot and followed it with the glass of water.

Marc stared, mouth agape.

Laughter burst from the other end of the bar, where a boisterous crowd was beginning to enjoy their Friday night.

The bartender returned to collect his money and the tip. "Thanks, gentlemen."

Yeah. Thanks for the tip, Doc.

Ding

September 6, 1995
Santa Fe, New Mexico

Tick. Tick. Tick. Marc was surprised to realize that he hadn't noticed the old wind-up travel alarm clock on the bedroom desk. When had it appeared? The desk was Marina's space, and he was sitting there a few days after the funeral, looking through paperwork very late at night.

Paperwork and bureaucracy accompanied death, as it did every stage of life. Birth certificates, death certificates, driver's licenses, marriage and professional licenses, draft notices—when you become eligible, or commanded, to kill foreigners—legally, with your government's blessing—why? First kiss, second base… What the hell is second base anymore? First marriage, third marriage, fifth kid. First divorce, first death of a wife.

In addition to the clock, a cinnabar lacquered urn sat on the desk, magnetically attracting his glance every few minutes. Marina's urn, her vessel, was a deep, dark red, almost black. He idly wondered how to spell it—ern, or earn, like earning money? Man, was he beat. He felt like a victim. At least he was feeling something, *doing* something. He'd initiated his little project, and now four smaller cinnabar jars waited, empty, behind Marina's. His task was to fill them for family members and Moonflute.

Moon had been there for him and the kids, supportive, serving those unadorned adobe-colored meals of hers—brown rice with fried tempeh and nuts, unpalatable veggie burgers on lumpy, whole grain bread, overcooked pinto beans and undercooked, cardboard-stiff, defiantly whole wheat pasta. Marc had let her do her thing; too much going on to get involved with Moon's cuisine. Chels and Zane didn't enjoy it much, but they were polite and swallowed most of it, though they would probably never hanker for tofu meatballs, and even less for raw Jerusalem artichokes.

Two days after Marina's death, Moon—Marc left off the *flute* now that they had become good friends—had sheepishly asked Marc for some of Marina's remains. A tiny amount—yes, *tiny* was the word of measurement she chose. *Cremains* was the word from the mortuary, but he didn't like either word. Sounded like vultures in the desert stuff. Ashes? Ashes to ashes.

He picked up the large urn and opened it slowly, wanting very much to avoid a Woody Allen sneeze moment, blowing the blow, ashes all over the place. He carefully, cautiously, using a teaspoon, heaped them into one of the smaller jars and tightened the lid.

But of course, it didn't all go as smoothly. A hay-fevered, bone-tired, widowed wreck, he was on the third jar when the spoon slipped and the whole amount fell onto the dresser top. Fell with a slight *ding* and created a gray and gritty powdered mess.

You can't think mess. *That's Marina, not a mess.*

Something glinted in the powder. He touched it carefully, filling the grooves of his fingertips with ash, then picked it up and brought it close to his face for inspection. A staple, the source of the musical ding.

I told you, you had staples inside.

He found a total of five staples while filling the urns that night— one for each urn, how convenient. He also found a bit of crimped metal, the remains of the elastic band that had secured his cremated ponytail. When Moon and the family heard about the staples, they all wanted one with their ashes, like sprinkles or a cherry on top. People did odd things in mourning.

He made sure to save a staple for himself. And the hair tie crimp.

The Closet

Silence ruled the house at night but its days continued to hum with the comings and goings of visitors.

Marina's absence was a gaping wound in the social body that loved her. They congregated to lick the wound, drawn to seek with eyes and fingers the evidence their minds could not accept. Absence of presence wasn't evidence of absence.

The sensation that her presence was merely elusive, not departed, was hard to shake; she was their phantom limb. To some, feeling her presence was a comfort. To others, it was unsettling. So it was that a group of women took matters into their own hands twelve days after her death, when Marc had gone up to the mountains to walk among the trees.

He'd left a scrawled note for Kata: *Out for the day, back by 6:00. Thanks*. Kata swept, mopped, dusted, and washed dishes downstairs, while a different sort of cleaning took place upstairs.

The nightstand was emptied of artifacts of illness—medicines, bottles, tissues. In the bathroom, Marina's toothbrush, hairbrush and comb, her toiletries and cosmetics, all were scooped into shopping bags.

The major attraction was her wardrobe. The women were guided by good intentions along with a sharp appreciation for Marina's taste in clothing. Nicole, though a size larger than Marina had been when healthy, would be able to wear some of the items. The other women, friends and relatives of various sizes and ages, wanted to be helpful and hoped to snag a memento or two at the same time.

Starting with the dresser drawers, they went through Marina's things. They filled trash bags with her personal belongings—satin lingerie, luxurious socks, lacy tights, nightgowns, negligees, silk scarves, kid leather gloves, tasteful jewelry. The more expensive items were left for Chelsea—the women weren't thieves.

From the closet came dresses, blouses, skirts, slacks, sweaters, jackets, jeans, and sportswear. They oohed and ahhed over her fine leather boots, her stylish shoes. The hangers and shoeboxes on Marina's side of the closet were quickly removed.

One boot box remained on the bed, something pink and fluffy sticking out.

"What's this?"

"Oh, my God."

"Try them on." The brazen suggestion was spoken in the brave tones of a willing conspirator.

Nervous titters filled the room when someone held up Marina's pink fur-lined handcuffs.

The boot box turned out to be a treasure trove of booty, not boots. What came out next put an end to the giggles.

"Oh. My. *God!*"

"No…"

"Yes, oh my God!"

A bright blue dildo, splendidly erect and gleaming, pointed toward the ceiling.

"Holy shit!"

One delicate hand held it aloft between carefully manicured fingertips.

"Reminds me of the Yucca Drive-In," Nicole said.

"Oh, God, you too? Misspent youth!" someone gasped.

"Stop, please, I can't hear this," someone else moaned.

"Youth isn't always wasted on the young," Aunt Elaine murmured.

"Eek!" A chorus of squeals rang out when the thing suddenly leapt to life, vibrating from the touch of an unnoticed button. Nicole scrambled to catch it, juggling, fumbling, red-faced.

"Shit! Sorry, Aunt Elaine!"

Several hands reached for it at once.

"Got it!" The buzzing stopped.

Nicole tipped the boot box over. Sex toys, lube tubes, another dildo, and vibrators in various sizes, shapes, colors, and textures rolled out, Marina's adventurous, playful sexuality spilling all over the bed.

"The hell with the dresses—I know which memento I'm taking home," someone said.

The rest of the group responded with dutiful giggles, but the wave of giddiness soon peaked and subsided into somber silence.

They were gone when Marc returned that evening—the women, the dildos, Marina's clothing.

No one had thought to consult him in advance, or at least, no one had had the guts to do so. They genuinely believed they were doing the right thing, but he never dreamed that Marina's presence would be so hastily scrubbed from their bedroom. From Marina's home.

Her closet door stood wide open. Her kimono, sweet with the scent of her, was gone from the bathroom door hook. *Damn them.* They had taken Marc's bedtime comfort habit of caressing his face in it like a child with a security blanket. He could tell no one of the anguish of that loss.

Yes, people did odd things after a death. Sometimes terrible, well-intentioned things. His only consolation was the suspicion that Marina had anticipated, even planned for, the grave robbers' discovery of the sex chest, an ideal prank from beyond. Like the Children at Play sign—Adults at Play.

"Good work, baby."

Grace

Marc allowed himself two weeks off from work. Or that could have been what his staff insisted on; he wasn't sure whose will had prevailed. He hadn't set foot in the clinic since Marina's fall into the coma, and was due to get back.

The fridge was still filled with more food than he could face, as generous deliveries kept pouring in. Kata found the means to redistribute much of it to local hard-luck families and shut-ins. Marc's appetite remained down for the count. The dogs accompanied him on long, aimless walks, chasing rabbits, lizards and each other.

The horses needed to be exercised; they finally had their chance when Armando came to visit, and insisted on saddling up for the animals' sakes. They ended up on a rambling, wordless ride, with Marc on Brown Horse, grateful for Armando's sensitivity in taking Winnie.

Chelsea and Zane had gone with Rosana to Albuquerque after the funeral, but that situation wasn't going well. Too many tears and sleepless nights. Too overwhelming for Rosana, whose default emotional state was tenuous. They were dealing with the aftermath of a family shipwreck, with everyone hanging onto scraps, tossing in the waves, no land in sight. Like the children, Rosana had come to depend upon Marina's steady, reliable presence. Marina's mothering filled a gap that yawned wide after she was gone, a gap that Rosana hadn't the resources to bridge.

Late one night, as a rare September thunderstorm pounded the clay and sand of Marc's road into a mucky soup, a knock sounded on the front door. His last visitors had departed hours earlier and no more were expected, especially at that hour. He turned on the porch light and opened the door to find an unfamiliar man standing with a bedraggled Zane and Chelsea.

"Daddy!" In a moment they were all over him, sobs escalating. "We missed you!" Chelsea gasped.

Marc stared in confusion at the shaggy-haired young man. Before he could ask *Who are you and what are you doing with my kids*, the fellow spoke.

"Hey, um, sorry to be here so late. Rosana said it would be okay. I was coming up to Santa Fe anyway, so she asked me to bring the kids. Gave me directions but not your phone number, and I forgot to ask. Good thing you're home. I'm a friend of hers. Daniel." He pronounced it 'Dan*yel.'* He tentatively held out a hand in greeting, looking awkward and uncomfortable.

"Come on in. Can I get you something? Don't have any beer, but a cup of tea? That okay?"

"Thanks, I can't stay. Took longer than I expected to find this place in the rain, and friends are waiting in town. But it was nice to meet you. And nice to hang with you guys," he added to Chelsea and Zane.

The kids gave limp goodbyes.

"Wait a sec," Marc said. "Kids, take off your coats, get into PJs. I'll come tuck you in."

"Can we eat something?" Chelsea asked. "We didn't have any dinner."

Marc gave Daniel a look. "Yeah, but PJs first."

As soon as the children left the kitchen, Marc whispered to Daniel.

"What's up with Rosana? She didn't call—is she in trouble?" His belly seized with anxiety, and it took an effort to keep his tone calm.

This time Daniel gave Marc a look. "Man, you know how she is. She's taking off to India. Says she doesn't know when she's coming back. An ashram or something." He shrugged, his gaze darting around the kitchen as he avoided Marc's stare. He shoved his hands into his pockets.

"Yeah, I know how she is," Marc said softly. *In* trouble? She fucking *was* trouble. He smiled grimly. He could kill her.

"Nice kids," Daniel said. "Um, sorry about—"

"Thanks." Marc cut him off. "Careful out there—the road gets pretty slippery."

Daniel nodded and disappeared into the wet night.

Unexpected resentment boiled up and over, and sympathy for Rosana evaporated. *Bitch! How could she—*

"Daddy, we really, really, missed you," Chelsea said, trotting into the kitchen, a fluffy bathrobe over her nightgown. She put her arms around him and was joined by Zane in his favorite Major Spaceman PJs. "Mom was... She tried hard, she really did."

Marc stroked her damp hair, swallowing the hateful words fighting to spill out. "I know, sweetheart. I know." He crouched to hug both children at eye level. "I missed you guys like crazy."

"Is Mom really going to live in India?" Zane asked. "Where the hell is India? Will we get to visit her there?"

The honest words out of his son's mouth opened gaping, new gashes in Marc's heart. Bad enough that Rosana had shown so little consideration for Marc's situation, as he dealt with Marina's illness and death while keeping his business afloat, and sharing parenting responsibilities. But now this? They just lost their beloved new stepmother to cancer and their mother abandons them? *Holy shit.* Holy shit. The grief of his own loss shifted as he was hit by the double-whammy of his children's loss.

Had Zane said *hell*?

"Your mother is an adventurous spirit." He gave himself a gigantic mental pat on the back for restraint. "We are all adventurers in our own ways."

"Marina was an adventurer," Chelsea said.

"She still is," Zane said.

"How do you know that?" Chelsea asked.

"She told me in a dream. She was with Major Spaceman. Something broke on their ship, and she was fixing it. She told me that when she got it fixed, she would come take me for a ride."

"That sounds awesome, buddy. Now, how about some grub? Pretty sure there's meatloaf in here," Marc said, opening the refrigerator. "And a hundred other things. It's like a magic fridge. Remember, Chels, those doll baby bottles that magically filled right after they emptied?"

Zane took a peek. "Yay!"

"Mom's fridge has brown rice, garbanzos, and not much else," Chelsea said.

"No garlic or onions? That doesn't sound like your mother's cooking."

"Really. She's on some kind of eating program, something from India."

"Too bad. No pizza, no lasagna." His stomach rumbled, a weird sensation, almost unrecognizable. He wondered when, or even if, he had eaten a meal that day. "Hey, I'm getting hungry," he said, surprising himself. "*Mangiamo pronto.*"

He began pulling covered dishes from the magic fridge. Out came a plate of chicken drumsticks.

"Those are for you, Daddy. Drumsticks for a drummer!" Chelsea said, pleased with her own wit.

"Rub a dub, dub, here comes the grub," Zane said, grabbing a couple of drumsticks and waving them over his head, face alight.

"Yay, God!" Today was the first time they'd said it together since Marina's death. *Too soon?*

"It's okay, Daddy." Chelsea comforted him, reading his face. "We can still say grace. Marina always laughed."

He smiled with effort. "Yes, she did."

"Yay, Marina!" Zane shouted.

"Yay, Marina." Marc and Chelsea followed gamely.

"Daddy?" Chelsea's voice wobbled.

His vision blurred. Down came the rain again.

Rosana's great fuck-up had gotten Marc off the floor. His children's losses were incalculable, the scars indelible, but he vowed to soften the marks. He would give them the best care he could provide. *Call Ruby in the morning—cancel my return until next week.* He would also take care of himself, for their sakes. He thought of the familiar flight attendant safety speech.

"In the event of a loss of cabin pressure, oxygen masks will drop from above your seat. Please place your mask over your nose and mouth and pull the strap to tighten. If you are traveling with small children, put your own mask on first."

A wisecracking attendant on one flight had made everyone laugh by advising, "If you are sitting next to a child, or someone who is *acting* like a child, please do us all a favor: put your own mask on first."

In that moment of crisis, he felt strangely centered, cheerful at the realization that he, their father, would be one hundred percent in charge of the children. No more shuffling back and forth between houses, at least until their mother got her act together.

The king-size bed was full that night as Marc read aloud from a favorite storybook, and they all slipped smoothly into the land of Nod.

Mask

Marc felt himself a stranger in a strange land, a stranger to himself. His bed, bedroom, house—his entire existence—had been transported to Planet Widower.

It didn't matter that he had seen it from the other side, had treated widowed patients and listened sympathetically to their spare and cautious confessions of loneliness. They were old. Death of a spouse had seemed part of the unfortunate but natural order. Husbands die. Wives die. But when they are *old*, not in their mid-thirties.

Had he suddenly become old without feeling the time pass? The face in the mirror looked old and young, fatigued and grieved. Widowed and alone. *I'm a widower.*

Old men might comfort themselves with memories of long married lives, and advice to do just that seemed to be the clichéd response from others who hadn't walked in the same grieving shoes. He had believed it, had certainly uttered it himself with compassionate sincerity. Humans protect themselves from the grief of others, justifying retreat from their feelings by resorting to the cruelty of hollow reason.

"It's for the best; she isn't suffering anymore. You're young, your marriage was short."

Left unsaid, but implied, was the assumption that the marriage's brevity ought to determine the depth and length of his mourning. Was mourning a competitive spectator event? *Is mine supposed to be a sprint?* Whose grief is more deserving, whose ought to last longer, and how much of a spectacle is expected from different classes of mourners?

Monotony and boredom set in. Marc experienced good days and bad, pain alternating with numbness. He felt disinterested in everything.

He woke each day in the familiar bed, the simple, comfortable room full of light. He walked into the bathroom, its small space crowded with memories of Marina—brisk little jiggles of her elbow while she brushed her teeth, the sight of her scar as she stepped into the shower, the heartbreaking, human beauty of her engaged in the most common activities, stroking lotion onto her legs, drying her hair...

And every morning he washed and washed his face with cold water, washing grief down the drain, but the well of it seemed endless. His eyes felt like goggles holding an internal body of salt water at bay. Pressure, crushing pressure, pushed at him as though he were on a deep dive, but it came from the inside out. And his dive mask leaked.

Masked at work, going through the motions, Marc understood that it was acceptable to look sad now and then, to receive the occasional condolences from those who knew what had happened, but he became proficient at turning the focus of conversation quickly back to professional matters. Then he masked himself at home for his children, who were frighteningly adept at fashioning their own masks, brave little man, and steadfast little woman.

Dr. Jefferson referred him to a child therapist, a twitchy sprite with short-cropped hair who moved nimbly from chair to floor like a child herself. The kids seemed to like her well enough, or at least they gave him that impression. But were they only masks talking to masks? Marc would bring PT coursework and journals to keep himself occupied in the waiting room, to avoid interacting with the other parents, invariably haunted-looking mothers. He also put off visiting with Dr. Jefferson, figuring he needed to attend to his own clinic, his own patients, but promised to check in soon.

"Gotta take care of biz, Jeff."

Ruby had snagged Marc, handing him the phone as he passed her desk to escort a new patient to the stationary bike.

"I know. I know. I'll call you. Got the kids full time now. Yeah... India...Yeah." The telephone cord reached its limit. "I promise."

"Who's helping you with the kids today?" Ruby asked, after he hung up and handed the phone back.

He thought for a moment. "Kata." A posse of women, some of the moms from school, had set up a volunteer childcare schedule for the after-school hours. "My mom and dad are flying in next week for two weeks—reinforcements."

"What's your plan?"

"Plan?"

"That's what I thought. You don't have one." Ruby pushed a button on the phone and spoke into the receiver, her eyes on Marc's face. "Hey, Andy, can you page Dez? We need her here in the clinic. Thanks."

She set the receiver down, poured Marc a cup of coffee, and stepped out from behind the desk. "We managed without you for weeks. Come on, treatment room one. Five minutes."

Marc followed.

"Sit." Ruby had clearly taken charge while he was away.

Dez entered, shut the door, and leaned against it, giving Ruby a knowing look. Her toned deltoids and biceps bulged as she crossed her arms.

"Okay, I'm outnumbered and outgunned," Marc said. "Uncle. Or Auntie. Whatever, I surrender. Got patients to attend to."

Dez began. "Here's the thing. You need more help at the house. The kids, Marc. They need someone there with them, *one* someone, not a revolving door of helpers, even very nice helpers. Someone to pick them up from school when you need to stay late. Someone to take them home, fix a snack, listen to them, hang with them, take them to appointments, give them a reliable routine. Someone you can trust. You can't do it all."

He started to interrupt, but Ruby shushed him with a brief explosion of throat clearing, and Dez continued.

"I'm coming this weekend to help you clear out your guesthouse. You're wasting prime living space on crap storage. My mom's having a yard sale; we'll take a truckload of your stuff to her place, hopefully make a couple of bucks. It's going to be a home again. Yeah, I know it's itty-bitty, but that's okay. Here is the woman who is going to live in it."

She handed Marc a slip of paper with a neatly printed name and number. "She needs a place to stay. She's *sane,*" Dez emphasized. "Not looking for a hookup or a sugar-daddy. Very independent, good with kids, fantastic cook, she's saving up for her own restaurant. Chen Ling. I've told her about you. She knows what she's in for, and she still said yes. Done deal." Dez flashed a broad smile of triumph.

He opened his mouth to speak, closed it.

"Where I come from, people say *thank you*. You're welcome," Dez said. "I know you won't call, so I told her to join us seven o'clock Saturday morning at your place, to help load the truck. She's a can-do gal. She'll be bringing her own bungee cords."

Dez squeezed Marc's hand and lowered her voice. "Gonna get through this with help from your friends, like it or not, love."

She opened the door to let him out. "Free to go, see ya."

Marc felt his mask slip, his chin tremble. "Thanks, babe."

As Dez marched away, he shuffled behind her into the lobby, pulling himself back into work mode. The older man on the stationary bike looked sweaty enough.

"Okay, Mr. Chavez, that's a good warm-up. Let's hit the mat."

Mr. Chavez smiled and mopped his brow. He dismounted, wincing as he limped toward Marc.

"We'll get you back in the game, Mr. Chavez. I promise."

Back in the game. The routine words of encouragement sounded strange, unnatural. *I'm still underwater. Keep it together.* Marc realized he'd been feeling out of exchange with his patients, going through the motions without his usual interest. They deserved more. He ended up giving Mr. Chavez so much more that the poor man, exhausted, asked to stop.

"Take a breather, brother." Marc sat down on the mat with his puffing patient. They shared sighs and chuckles, two wounded men with their game faces on.

"So, the Lions and 49ers," said Marc. "You watching the game tonight? Think the Lions stand a chance?"

Claude's Cure for Chaos

As Saturday approached, Marc's misgivings grew. Some chick he'd never met, never spoken to, would move in with him? Well, into the guesthouse. He appreciated Dez's initiative, but now he had to hide not only grief but an embarrassing little weed of resentment. Yes, he needed to get his life in order. But how much of it must he turn over to others, in order to do so?

The kids had gone to bed hours ago, and he still couldn't sleep. Insomnia, a fancy word for *can't sleep*. Not a big deal, he told himself, unless it continues for months. So far, it had been happening just a few nights here and there, making for a shitty workday. The staff said they couldn't tell, but the drag made him feel stuck in neutral. He had an eight-a.m. patient tomorrow, so he needed to be well rested.

Gusts blew around the house, straining the roof like a sail in a storm. He got up from bed and headed down to the kitchen. Met and Jet roused themselves to join him, the tags on their collars jingling as they slid wet noses into his palms. *Welcome to the pity party, boys.* They were good listeners, his dogs, but not great talkers, fortunately. They curled up companionably at his feet.

The rustic chandelier hanging above the table cast anemic reflections against the night-blackened windows. His attention was repeatedly drawn to the windows; the wind and the pops and creaks of the house left him uneasy. Or maybe not uneasy, but feeling battered, as if everything whirled around him, and he couldn't get anything to slow down enough to get a handle on it all. Chaos.

He thought of his old friend and mentor, Claude, whose heart had blown up in Moscow the previous year. Marc's own heart suddenly ached, missing him. Claude had given him a gift he called the Cure for Chaos, a system applicable to all kinds of thorny situations. Now, at three a.m., as Marc rattled around the house—nervous, distracted, and deeply sad—the memory of Claude and his cure drove him to find a notepad and a handful of No. 2 pencils.

Write it down, what you remember. Do it.

Claude's Cure for Chaos.

Number 1: Take a walk. That one was easy. He released his pencil and went to the laundry hamper to dig out a pair of sweatpants. He pulled them on, followed by a pair of boots, and tugged a thick hooded sweatshirt over his head.

"Let's go, guys." A canine adventure out in the middle of a windy night? They were game. "Coyotes beware," Marc spoke into the wind as they stepped outside, trying to get into the spirit of the jaunt. He was answered with enthusiastic tail wagging.

Ragged clouds raced overhead. *What's your hurry?* Marc wondered. *Where are you going?* The stars and crisp, crescent moon appeared fixed to a screen behind skittering, fraying bands of mist. He headed to the stables. It wasn't far, but it counted as a walk.

Number 2 on Claude's list was to look at things far away, to focus on objects and interests far beyond oneself. Marc stopped to study the sickle in the sky. Then the silhouette of the Ortiz Mountains, the stars, the guesthouse.

Thanks, Claude. I feel better already.

He let the dogs race around for a few minutes, then led them back to the house.

Number 3: Throw up on paper, figuratively speaking. Thoughts and have-tos, ideas and solutions, throw them on paper, rapid-fire.

Ruby's question—what's your plan—echoed in his mind. Did he have a plan?

He tapped a pencil against the pad. *I have a plan, certainly I do. And here it is, a problem and ten solutions. The problem: Be the best man and father I can be, love Marina, let her help me.*

The list of ten solutions, in no particular order, came tumbling out as fast as Marc could write.

Perform anonymous acts of charity every day
Exercise, take care of myself, eat well
Work hard
Prosper, make $
Win the game
The kids: take them everywhere

*Spend five minutes every day, five minutes only, talking/dreaming
with Marina*
Go to the Yucatán every year for the rest of my life
Recognize that it's okay to be happy and to be interested
Sleep

Marc looked at the list. He did have a plan. His shoulders relaxed. Claude to the rescue again.

The next step would be to prioritize the solutions. Be methodical. He stared at his list. The letters grew fuzzy, the words indistinct. A wave of drowsiness swept over him, and he slumped at the table. His pencil rolled off and continued across the floor. *Find it in the morning.* Eight a.m. coming up fast. He climbed the stairs to bed, *his* bed, and fell into a sound sleep.

When he opened his eyes to greet the day, it was with a renewed sense of interest. That, along with a single cup of strong coffee and a banana, sent him off to the clinic with a bounce in his step.

Three blasts on a car horn announced Dez's arrival Saturday morning. The woman was as punctual as Marina. Chelsea and Zane were still sleeping, but Marc had been up for a couple of hours. He'd brewed and finished a pot of coffee, so he started another one for his guests.

He went to the door to find Dez's cherried-out midsize pickup and a practical little white car; Dez was speaking with another woman and pointing to the guesthouse. She waved Marc over.

"Marc Hochstaff, Chen Ling."

Chen was clearly prepared for dirty work, in jeans, boots, and an old sweatshirt, her hair tied back in a bandana. She smiled in greeting and extended a gloved hand.

"Glad to meet you, Chen," Marc began. "I don't know what Dez has told you; it's not really an archaeological dig."

"Nice try, dude," Dez said. "We're definitely excavating here— that guesthouse is a pit. Come on. I told my mom we'd be at her place before nine. Early birds'll be there soon, before she's ready for business."

Marc opened the guesthouse, stepped inside. Hell, maybe it was an archaeological site. Pieces of exercise equipment and discarded office furnishings, boxes of old toys and clothing, books, videos, a dusty, neglected jumble. He felt a pang in his chest. Some of the stuff belonged to Rosana, some to Marina, and some to him and the children, all artifacts of past lives. The sight was overwhelming. He caught Dez's eye.

"Put your muscles to work," she ordered. "Time's a-wastin'."

As they focused on the logistics of moving equipment, Marc thought about how this activity fit into his Cure for Chaos list. Maybe it was part of taking care of himself.

No one spoke much as they grunted and maneuvered; between the three of them, the work went quickly. Chen was small, but strong and astute. Dez took charge of the boxes, eventually shooing Marc out to go roust Chelsea and Zane.

He remained wary about Dez's plan; how could the kids be expected to deal with another new woman in their lives so soon? And not a mom or a stepmom who would love them, not a Mary Poppins but—still, a nanny of some sort. Kind of a housekeeper, a neighbor, and a tenant, all in one.

The kids were up, hair and teeth brushed, and somewhat presentable by the time the truck and little car were loaded. They followed Marc outside to watch Chen fasten a tidy pattern of bungee cords across the back of the truck. She sprang down and removed her gloves.

"I'll be back to clean the guesthouse. This afternoon?" Her expression, on a brown face sprinkled with dark freckles, looked hopeful.

"Um, okay. Chelsea, Zane, this is Chen Ling."

Chelsea shot Marc a suspicious glare.

"Chen is thinking about living in the guesthouse."

Chelsea's face brightened. "Can we visit you there? I like that place, but Dad never lets us in."

"Because it's a mess," Marc said.

"Less mess now," Chen said, smiling. "When I finish cleaning, I hope you will visit me."

The knot under Marc's sternum loosened. "Hey, how are you going to unload the truck? Got help at the other end?"

"No problem—Armando'll be there. Hangover or no hangover, he promised." Dez winked.

Dez had been right about Chen Ling. As she settled into the guesthouse, a delicate organic relationship began to grow between her and the children.

Chelsea and Zane enjoyed the privilege of being taste-testers for the array of dishes Chen was developing for her future restaurant; they found their opinions about menu items treated with respect. The first time she went to pick them up from school, Zane grabbed her by the hand to introduce her to his teacher and classmates.

"My friend Chen, she's a *super* chef!" he'd said. Which led to Chen's cooking skills being pressed into service for school fundraisers, and not long after that, for private catering engagements.

Eat well was on Marc's list. Check.

Cakewalk

Holidays and bereavement go together like ass on cactus.

The first Halloween for Chelsea and Zane, without either Marina or Rosana to take them trick-or-treating, was somewhat salvaged by a Halloween carnival in the elementary school gym. Marc dyed his hair blue for the occasion and carried a trident as Neptune, god of the sea. Zane was Major Spaceman, Chelsea a sequin-tailed mermaid. It was the first time Marc had set foot inside the building since Marina's death. Even painted and masked, the other parents couldn't hide their pity when they caught sight of him.

"Come on, let's do the cakewalk," he said, leading Zane and Chelsea away from an incoming pity missile. Zane, a nimble scrambler, won the chance to choose a cake from a plentiful display on a nearby table. His choice sported poisonous-looking, dyed cherries atop a thick layer of multihued frosting, a grocery store cake nothing like the deliberately drab, but likely healthier, homemade competition. His messy smile was worth the risk of sugar shock.

As Marc was putting him to bed that night, Zane said, "I thought that cake would be good, Daddy. It wasn't, really. Thanks for letting me pick it anyway."

Marc hugged him. "We'll trash it. Maybe Chen will make some of those almond cookies you like."

"Yeah." He yawned. "I wish Marina could have been with us for Halloween. I miss her."

"So do I, sweetheart. So do I."

Marina had donned a sexy French maid costume last year just to tweak him about his "A Man Needs a Maid" wedding music stunt. He bit his lip at the memory.

"Good night, Daddy."

Chelsea reached for a hug. "Daddy, are you going to keep your hair blue for a while? I like it."

He'd forgotten about his hair. "Yeah, maybe. Think it's cool?"
"Yeah. You and your hair are cool. You are a *super*cool dad."
He was barely out the door before his eyes brimmed over.

The night was a bad one, and Marc couldn't stay in bed anymore; his legs were twitching, his thoughts racing. An urge to write came on like an itch.

He opened the top drawer of Marina's desk to look for paper and pencils, rattling the cinnabar urn, and there was her journal. He froze at the sight of its familiar cover, decorated with a sunflower at sunset, stars beginning to glimmer, and the crescent moon in the upper indigo corner. He lifted it with quavering hands, keeping the cover closed over the pages of Marina's words, and opened it to the back, where all the leaves remained blank. A song spilled from his fingers into her book, a drum beat between his ears.

> Driving north on New Mexico Route 14
> I never thought of October as very mean
> The sunset was amazing as I left my wife
> We were told she would lose her life.
> The scariest Halloween
> I have ever seen,
> The scariest Halloween
> I have ever seen.
>
> Driving back south on Route 14
> a November morning
> crisp and clean
> The sunrise was amazing
> as I returned to my wife
> on the scariest Halloween
> I have ever seen,
> The scariest Halloween
> I have ever seen.
>
> Took the kids out
> for Trick or Trick
> Pale, wide eyed

scared, excited demons
They showered me
with love, respect and candy
on the scariest Halloween
I have ever seen,
The scariest Halloween
I have ever seen.

That fright night with
jack-o'-lanterns smashed in the street
I lay frozen drunk
not drinking
numb to this world
awoke exhausted
with energy to spare
on the scariest Halloween
I have ever seen,
the scariest Halloween
I have ever seen.

One day while the children were in school, two months after Rosana's precipitous departure, Marc's telephone rang. Through a tinny connection from India, a stranger's voice asked if he would accept the charges for a collect call. He said yes.

Rosana said she was sorry, it had to be done, she'd be coming back but didn't know when.

"I know you'll take good care of the children," she said. "I'll write and call. Can you allow me to call collect? I'll get an address so they can write me. I'll call at two p.m. Mountain Time the first Sunday of the month. Thank you, Marc."

She didn't miss those Sunday calls. A good sign, he hoped.

Thanksgiving loomed heavily on the horizon. Heralds of heartburn began to arrive, masquerading as invitations to other families' celebrations, but Marc was accustomed to doing his own thing. He also wasn't in the mood for swallowing grief at someone else's feasting table. The quite understandable joy of others would be too raw. Too painful. He would have grieving company for his own table, where tears would be shed, not swallowed.

His parents, Marina's parents, and Nicole arrived the Monday before the holiday, each woman expecting to take charge of the kitchen, which meant an uneasy dance of compromise between the three of them, plus Chen, Marc, and even Chelsea, who was beginning to express her own culinary interests.

Chelsea took charge of the stuffing, making it Marina's way with clams and cornbread—the clams had been shipped from the Cape.

Zane and the dogs added unacknowledged but welcome chaotic interference to the kitchen, helping to distract and break tension.

The fathers retreated to watch television in placid agreement about keeping sports on, politics off. In the end, everyone got what they wanted to eat, and everyone made the best of a day on which giving thanks remained terribly, agonizingly, difficult.

Thank you, Marina, for coming into our lives, for the time you gave and shared with us. Thank you for your love, your faith, your loyalty, your humor, kindness, and beauty. We miss you.

As Marc went to bed that night, he picked up Marina's conch shell from its place on the nightstand. He stroked its familiar form and held it to his ear, a private bedtime ritual. Her whisper floated out to him, the sound of surf and love. Her journal lay nearby, unopened since he had written in it himself the previous month. The sight was comforting. He opened it as he had stepped into the freezing lake at Telluride: a deep plunge without hesitation. Her notes were sparse, concentrated in the early pages of the journal. Most of it remained blank.

3/30/1994

I burned my previous journal in a ceremony with Moonflute. It feels good to start a new one with these words from Miss Emily Dickinson:
"Hope" is the thing with feathers –
That perches in the soul –
And sings the tune without the words –
And never stops – at all –
I forget the next parts, no matter, we are on our way to NYC! Looking forward to the weekend. We both need to get away—what with Marc's reversed vasectomy and my gastrointestinal stuff, along with the R

factor (Rosana), school, the wedding, work and so forth, we're stressed! So, let's party!

4/1/1994
M & M fighting.
He shouldn't have to fix my issues. When third party is involved, discuss. If you have a problem with somebody you should deal with it
Apologies
give and receive them honestly, lovingly
I need to know that I'm special and valued at the moment
(Would I rather be right or be in this relationship?)
Personality, essence—learn personality glitches
"feeling overwhelmed, Marc, and I can't get a grip"
"I'm not with you, I need help, afraid"
Rules for fighting
When something sets you off:
1) STOP and ask if he is hearing what you say. If you are tired or he is tired, say not capable of hearing "I am intending to do this but now I can't" then write in journal what happened.
2) No name calling (verbal or physical abuse)
3) No dragging up of past issues in current issues; no mixing issues
        Example: Does he value me? Not okay to say I resent how you
        spend $ on kids.
4) Stick with "I" statements

4/11/94 NYC
Ate
1) Cinnamon roll, tea
2) Rice, steamed broccoli, cauliflower, carrots, whole wheat roll
    Felt horrible, threw up, felt better, slept well. Marc is emotional mess, drank a bottle of Absolut Friday, Saturday. Monday night drank 1 quart of beer, 2/3 Absolut. Very buzzed, very emotional.

Weeping, Marc closed the book and buried his face in his pillow. He was agonized by her agony and by the futility of their fight against that indifferent colony of cells. His body felt as if it would splinter and fly apart, and he didn't care. When he finally slept, completely spent, he fell into dark dreams of impotence, fear, and menace. The night was long.

Winter break from school meant an opportunity to take Chelsea and Zane to New York for Christmas and New Year's.

"Take them, Marc, always take them with you. Show them as much of the world as possible."

Okay, Marina. This is for you and them and me—for all of us. He imagined Marina's pleasure had she been able to make this trip.

Chelsea and Zane had been to New York briefly with Marc's parents during the wedding preparations two summers ago. This time he intended to show them the city's holiday magic with visits to the famous F.A.O. Schwarz toy store, the Rockefeller Center ice rink, and Carnegie Deli.

He found that he felt more himself in the city, though he recognized its charms as a temporary diversion. With despair close below the equator of his heart, hope high above, he navigated by the light of his children past the end of the calendar year and into January. They returned to New Mexico just ahead of an enormous, disruptive blizzard that buried the northeastern states.

The sight of the Sangres made him feel at home in Santa Fe in a way he hadn't before. Marina's presence was there, in the clear sky and the many things with feathers, the hawks that made his home their own. But the reminders brought a renewed sense of acute absence.

Winter

February fog shrouded the town as Marc headed in for an early appointment. He found the clinic lobby festooned with shiny paper hearts. Ruby wore a low-cut, ruby-colored top, dangly heart-shaped earrings, and some kind of fussy, red thingamabob in her hair. Her lipstick and nails, a brilliant red, matched perfectly. Shit, he'd forgotten it was Valentine's Day.

"Mrs. Martin just canceled," Ruby said, hanging up the phone. "She's sick and doesn't want you to catch it."

"Well, that's thoughtful of her." Mrs. Martin was the patient he'd come in early for. He checked his watch; there was time to get down to the grocery store and buy a bouquet of roses for Ruby's desk.

"Hey, I have to run a quick errand. Be right back."

Marc would be glad when this day of cardboard romance was over; he wondered how many acres of old trees were felled to make greeting cards for a single day's tradition.

Marina had laughed about this holiday, hadn't taken it seriously, but at the end of their last Valentine's Day dinner in one of the city's most celebrated bistros, she had admitted that there was something to be said for a day dedicated to romance, and that he, Marc, was supremely gifted in the romance department. His cheeks warmed at the memory as he waited in the grocery store line, clutching his red bouquet. Heartbroken.

After work he shot down to Evangelo's. A drink was in order, even if it was club soda with a squeeze of lime. Marc was surprised to find a familiar face, Dan McCannon, the attorney who had handled his divorce, sitting at the bar.

"What are you doing here alone on V-Day?" Marc asked. "Did the rest of us sour you on love?" The bar was fairly empty, populated by solo men; it would fill later, when the band came onstage.

"I could ask you the same thing, but I won't," Dan responded with an enigmatic smile. "Tonight I'm fishing for souls in this watering hole."

"Souls? What do you want with them? A soul and a nickel won't buy you a beer."

"Not drinking beer, my friend, just a Coke, and as for the value of a soul... Sit. Let's find out." He patted the barstool next to him.

Marc sat. "Diet Coke with lemon," he said to Nikos.

"So. You're here in a bar and you're not drinking either," Dan said.

"Not tonight, anyway."

"I heard about your wife. I'm so sorry."

"Yeah, thanks. Divorce and death are good reasons to drink, I guess. I drank when I was happy, when I was partying. Music, concerts. Then came cancer."

Marc gave Dan a brief explanation of Marina's diagnosis. "That night, after the exploratory surgery, I drank because I was scared to death. Just that night. Big slip. So easy to slip."

"You know, my thing with booze was odd," Dan said. "Airplanes. Two-to-three-hour trips and all those singles. My dad used to bring them home empty after business trips. Never any fucking T-shirt, just little vodka bottles. I took after him." He laughed, the sound dry.

"I'd have a couple at the airport," he continued. "Four or five on the plane—on half the trips I'd wind up in jail. Once for indecent exposure; don't even remember what I did. Cost me ten thousand dollars and I lost my job. What happens in Vegas happens in Vegas. But Lori stayed with me. Haven't had a drink since." He picked up his Coke. "If I do go to Vegas now, I drive."

"Holy shit, Dan."

"By the grace of God. We say that a lot. How's it going?"

"Well, I'm not so angry anymore—haven't thrown or broken anything recently," Marc answered. "I have help with the kids, thank God; out of their sight I break down, though. I play the clown with them, but they see right through me. It's a grind, people always asking, 'How are you?' Now I know how Marina felt. I'd ask her all the time, and she hated it."

He took a swig, remembering a particularly painful moment; he had been the one delivering grief to someone else. "A few weeks after my wife died, a friend of ours called. She'd been living in Austria and was back in New York. 'How are you two lovebirds doing?' she asked. 'How was the wedding?' We'd hoped she'd sing at our wedding, but this conservatory opportunity came up so she wasn't able to. Marina didn't tell her how sick she really was—didn't want her friend to miss an important career experience—and I couldn't reach her in Vienna to give her the news. Damn, my legs caved when she called."

And even now his equilibrium disintegrated. Shit. A couple of men down the bar looked his way, then away.

Dan draped an arm over his shoulder. "I want you to trust me. This is why I'm here, fishing for souls. I help run a men's group. We hold retreats at a mountain camp in Pecos. Twenty-five to thirty men, forty-eight hours. Marc, I tell you, many steps helped me to become a spiritual being again, and this was one. Our next retreat is the last weekend in March, beginning of spring. You'll always be affected by the memories of this past year, but if you come, hopefully the retreat will allow you to embrace life again. You're a good soul, a wounded soul. And you could use a spiritual tune-up."

Dan's smile helped dry Marc's soggy mood. Maybe a retreat was a backassed way of moving forward. He'd been white knuckling, trying to tough it out like a batter overgripping. Relax, accept the kindness of strangers. Friends too. Maybe it was worth a try. Maybe he didn't need to decide yet.

"Okay, you're convincing," he said. "I don't mean to blow you off; I'll think about it. Thanks, bro." He rubbed his face hard before standing to pull cash from his pocket, paying for his own drink and Dan's, and leaving an oversized tip. "Good luck with the fishing."

Marc drove home in the dark to a fragrant kitchen, and homemade, heart-shaped pizza covered in heart-shaped pepperoni, funny little valentines.

"Daddy! Look what we made!"

Weekend Warriors

March 29, 1996

Santa Fe, New Mexico

Friday had arrived. The last patient was enjoying electric stim and ice, Ruby had gone for the day, and Marc was facing the weekend retreat.

For weeks he'd felt like Monty Python's Holy Grail knights, terrified of a mysterious beast and needing to run away, run away. But was he running to something even worse? Check-in was at 5:30; it was 5:30 now, and he had an hour's drive to get there. Late already. And Dan wasn't going to make it. He had called to apologize, said his wife had broken her ankle.

Another good excuse to not run away, to try to grit his way through another day. He hadn't even packed a bag, though he had asked Chen to take care of the children. So, what would it be?

Dez walked in from the gym. "You going?"

"Didn't pack or anything."

"Big deal. If it sucks, so what? I'll take your patient off stim and lock up."

"Not really in the mood."

"Yeah, you're in a bad mood. Hard to tell the difference."

"I don't even have a toothbrush!"

"Bullshit. Your ditty bag's in the bathroom."

Dez disappeared, leaving him pacing and mumbling, and then popped back in to shove the bag against his chest. She led him out the door and to his truck, straightened his collar, and grabbed his cheeks for a kiss. "Have a lovely weekend, sweetheart! Bring me a T-shirt. Now get!"

Once Dez returned to the clinic, she picked up the phone and dialed.

"Hi, Mencore. How can I help you?"

"This is a friend of Marc Hochstaff's. He's on his way. Should be there in an hour or so."

"He's late."

"Sorry. He was very anxious, almost didn't get in the truck."

"No big deal. We actually like when someone's late."

Dez heard the grin in the man's voice, and imagined the devilish look in his eye as he addressed someone else at his end, "Hey, boys, we got a tardy." Returning to Dez, he said, "Thanks for the heads-up. *Ve haf vays* of dealing with ze tardies."

"Be kind," Dez said. "Oh, hell. Bust him good."

Marc made his way out of Santa Fe on the interstate through Glorieta Pass, driving slowly, distracted, overtaken by old clunkers and underpowered RVs. Forceful winds battered the pass; March in the mountains not only came in like a lion, it left that way too.

Eventually he turned off onto a paved road that led to an unpaved logging route through mountainous terrain, and that led to a rougher dirt road snaking up through the wilderness. By now, the sun had set and he was feeling his way through wailing trees. A faded wooden sign identified the Pecos Mountain Camp. This was it. He'd hoped to get lost, but damn, he must have been guided. He wryly cursed Marina. No reason to have found the place so easily while trying not to.

He parked outside a rickety fence at the end of a line of vehicles. Beyond the fence, illuminated by a dim, shaded bulb, stood a rustic structure. He couldn't see an entrance. He stumbled through the dark yard, clutching a plastic grocery sack containing his ditty bag and gym towel. Where the heck was—

A door creaked open, emitting a shaft of yellow light. Six men stood clustered just inside, staring silently out, arms folded, faces stern, heads shaking slowly, deliberately.

"You must be Marc," said the nearest man.

"I am. How'd you—"

"My name is James Stewart, Jim. Chief officer here."

"Nice to meet you," Marc said, looking forward to getting out of the cold wind. He extended his hand expectantly, but Jim simply stood there, impassive. As did the rest of them.

"You're ninety minutes late," said Jim.

"Got a late start."

"Well, you'll get an early start back home. If you'd like to try again, we'll have another retreat in three months. Frankly, I doubt we'll see you. You've disrespected our organization and the twenty-nine other men who made it here promptly. Thank you."

Jim and the gang turned away.

"Whoa, Nelly, wait a minute."

Jim stopped. "My name isn't Nelly. And, '*whoa*?' You talking to a horse? God punched you in the mouth, so you treat people like animals?"

"That's harsh."

"We can be harsh."

"Could I have a second chance, some way I could make it up to you? My wife died… My friend Dan McCannon hooked me up here. I trust him. I need help."

Jim's posture remained unwavering. "You serious about that?"

"Yes!" The word shot out tight, groveling. He didn't care.

"We know about your wife, your kids. Tough year. This'll be a tough forty-six-and-a-half hours. You disrespected us. Now you'll serve the staff and the brothers who arrived on time. Are you ready to do that, serve your fellow men, your fellow humans?"

"Of course. What should I do?"

"Come with me."

Following Jim through the door into a minimal lobby—rough-hewn plank walls, side table, coat hooks—Marc did a double take at the sight of a snarling cougar head on the wall above the table.

"Jose, Jose!" Jim called. "I have a tardy."

The way he pronounced *tardy* gave Marc a sinking feeling.

A small, tidy man emerged from behind a swinging kitchen door across the lobby holding an apron, a white box hat, and a cholo hairnet in a bundle. He tossed them to Marc, who caught them clumsily and examined the accessories in a moment of confusion.

"Oh, serve!" he said.

"Yes," Jim said. "Marc, you're going to join me and Pedro in serving the men. Now, if you're staying with us for the weekend, get the apron, hairnet, and hat on, in that order. Once everyone is served, we serve ourselves. You've missed most of the meal already."

Never having used one before, Marc fumbled with the hairnet.

Jose stepped over to assist him. "You haven't worked in the service industry, have you?"

"Not food service, but I have *served*; I'm very sorry to be late. I'm here now, and I'll be the best server you ever saw. Come on, Jose, let's get to work."

"Not to worry, Marc, we don't eat that much here." Jose grinned. "First we need your mug shot. Up against the wall, you redheaded mother," he ordered, riffing on an old country tune, catching Marc off guard. He took a Polaroid camera from the side table and positioned himself a few feet away. Before Marc could compose an expression, the flash fired, making Marc see stars.

"Okay, into the kitchen."

The hat kept falling off as Marc served ten staff members and the attendees—fellow runaways—dessert in the adjacent mess hall. The food was simple, and the men spoke little, their tones low and somber. As he moved through the room, conscious of being observed, Marc began to realize that he hadn't done much of this kind of attentive service since Marina's death. Sure, he gave his all, small as it was, to the kids, and just enough to his patients and employees, but as a sleepwalker. He was never fully present or engaged. Some of the men cast curious looks at him. He could see it dawning on them that he wasn't a staffer but a fellow client doing some kind of penance.

The hand reaching for the last cup was attached to a burly, deeply tanned arm bearing a familiar tattoo: a combination Zia sun sign and AA triangle. Where had Marc seen it before? He looked into the man's face.

"Dude!" the man said.

Marc blinked. It was the diver from the boat in Mexico—a New Mexican after all.

"Glad to see you, man! You belong here. You'll see."

Before Marc could say a word, a chair scraped and Jim stood to address the gathering.

"Good evening, my friends. I hope you enjoyed our rather meager meal. Although food will be available, it won't be the source of the nourishment you'll receive over the next two days. I want to introduce Marc Hochstaff. He has been indulgent. He was an hour and a half late getting here. His way of earning our trust again is to serve you during the few meals we'll have together. He's behaved appropriately in facing the consequences of disrespecting us. How was his service to you tonight?"

One man began to clap, as slow as a flamenco dancer signaling the start of a show. He was joined by several more and then the roomful, with a few here and there calling out, "Good, fine, great!"

"Should he continue to serve us?" Jim asked.

A Native man spoke up. "We all need to serve each other. But we don't need a waiter." Chuckles followed his words.

"Marc, did you mind serving the men?" Jim continued.

"Not at all. I'm proud to do so." Marc found a true feeling of satisfaction in the moment. Had he been jerked around? Yes. Had he deserved it? Yes. Was he in a space safe enough to let this happen? Hope so. He trusted Dan. Yes. Let the running away unfold.

"Okay, first of many lessons," Jim said. "Keep serving mankind beyond this weekend's meals." His lined face cracked an unexpected grin. "Every group has at least one tardy; thank you for playing that role for us today, Marc. The hairnet was Jose's idea; nice touch, Jose."

As Jose gave Jim an impish salute, voices rose in a hubbub of conversation.

"Fifteen-minute break," Jim announced. "Bus your dishes to the tubs in the corner over there and regroup in the main meeting hall to your right. Bring your guts and penises with you."

During the ensuing cautious laughter and clatter, Jim waved Marc over.

"We are men without masks here, including corporate masks. But I want you to know that Jose is the CEO of a company that supplies hairnets, uniforms, and equipment to the hospitality industry throughout the country. You might thank him for the gifts he gave you."

Marc understood. "I'll use them tomorrow and continue to serve, if you'll allow me."

"You'll be serving in different ways after tonight." Jim patted him on the back and strode away.

The meeting room was furnished in quintessential, old-fashioned hunter style, chiefly with a collection of trophy heads: elk, bear, bison, and cougar. Bearskin rugs had been scattered on the floor, and a few hung from the walls.

Marc found the grimacing stuffed heads to be disturbing distractions. He'd never been a hunter, never owned a gun, not even while living in the wild and wooly West of rural New Mexico, where guns and game went together like drinking and driving. He remembered being asked by a friend, "If someone threatened your home and family, would you use a gun?" He'd hesitated a millisecond in response. "No gun for you," had been his friend's caustic assessment.

In addition to the animal trophies, there were Navajo and Pueblo rugs, Native pottery and beaded leather objects, bows and arrows, knives, headdresses, and even a long peace pipe displayed as if in a museum. The paraphernalia was impressive and manly, symbols of war and peace. Definitely not a venue for Avon conventions.

The men settled themselves in a U-shape, sharing simple wooden benches oriented toward a low stage. They quieted as Jim took the stage and raised an arm.

"Ho," he said.

"Ho," the group repeated.

"I'd like a volunteer from staff to lead us in a blessing."

A pony-tailed man in flannel shirt, jeans, and boots stood.

"Thanks, Greg," Jim said.

Greg looked around at the men before bowing his head. The blessing was nothing like Marc had heard before in church, not an appeal to Jesus, or to the Holy Spirit, but to the manhood of all the humans present. *What did manhood even mean anymore?* He listened to the blessing, trying to absorb its message. *Fathers, brothers, sons, husbands, friends, lovers—*

Jim was speaking again. "This night will be long, as long as need be. We don't sleep much during these retreats, and you won't miss it. You'll be listening, sharing, discovering—relearning what was lost. You are kings and warriors, lovers and magicians. These are deeper and older identities than those that contemporary society has overlaid on you. We'll peel back the layers to find what you've hidden inside, the treasures and the shit, the pride and the shame, the courage and fear, love and tears. Let us begin."

He took time to meet the eyes of each man. "Each one of you will take the stage and address the group for ten minutes, telling your story, why you're here. If you want or need more time, or if you spend nine of your ten minutes broken down and weeping, we'll extend your share. This isn't the Academy Awards—no buzzers, no music to cue you off the stage. We're entering sacred time. Ho."

"Ho."

"One more thing," Jim said. "Have any of you heard of a talking stick?"

Heads nodded here and there.

"We give thanks to our brothers and sisters of the Northwest, our brothers and sisters in Africa, all our brothers and sisters near and far in time and space, for bringing order and respect to gatherings of humans. We give thanks for the talking stick, the speaker's staff. The staff confers the right to speak, and demands silence from the rest of the group. When it's your turn to speak, you take up the staff. Anyone wishing to ask a question may raise a hand, but we discourage interruptions. Clear?"

Silence.

"Now, every group has its own style of speaker's staff. We are no exception. I present to you the Mencore speaker's staff." He disappeared briefly offstage and then returned holding an enormous, white-boy, tan-colored dildo—at least eighteen inches by Marc's alarmed reckoning. *Holy shit!*

The men burst into howls of laughter. There were a few snide remarks, including, "No white boy has anything half that long!"

Jim stood patiently waiting for the outcry to die down before continuing.

"As I was saying, this is the Mencore speaker's staff." He raised it high, clutching the crazy, obscene prop firmly in his fist. "Many *hard* things have been said over the years with this... stick." He smiled a little. "Tonight, it's your turn. We'll speak in backwards alphabetical order by first name. Zacario leads off."

Zacario looked to be the youngest of the group, maybe all of eighteen years old. He took the dildo talking stick with a visibly shaking hand, and stood wordless for a long moment, not meeting anyone's eyes.

Marc felt sorry for him.

"I'm going to be a father," the youth began. "In three months, maybe less. And I don't know how." He gulped. "My father was killed in a gang shooting when I was a baby, so I don't remember him. My mom's boyfriends... They wanted her, not me. Sometimes they were nice to me in front of her to get what they wanted. A lot of times, when she was passed out or just not around, they... weren't so nice. I have two younger half-sisters and a half-brother at home. I worry about them."

The only sounds beyond Zacario's voice were a cough, a throat clearing, and a moan of sympathetic sorrow.

When Zacario finished his story, all the men extended their arms toward him, heads bent. Marc felt swept into a group message of love, support, strength, understanding, compassion.

The second speaker, William, blushed when he took the stick, and was welcomed by gentle laughter that stopped dead when he began his story.

"My Uncle Ern used to take me everywhere, and when we got there, he... he sexually abused me. He started by touching my dick." William eyed the giant dildo in his hand. "It gradually escalated to me touching him. After a year, I blew him. I was about eight."

By the fourteenth minute of his story, William was waving the stick as if beating his uncle with it. "Fuck you, you cock-sucking child molester!" he roared.

"My uncle died of liver disease and COPD. He drank and smoked himself to a painful death at sixty-two. Painful, painful death. My family wondered why I was so, so uninvolved, so apathetic about his *very painful* illness. I went to see him a few weeks before he died. Just stared at him, hoped he mistook me for the devil bringing his just rewards. It was a painful death, did I mention that?"

The tension broke for an instant.

"I never told the family; they've had their own troubles. Only my therapist, and now you guys. So, thank you. I'm going to stop and hand off the..." He looked toward Jim.

Jim thanked him, took the stick, passed it to Victor. The men stood as one, extending arms toward William, taking up Victor's first minute in a tremendous show of support. Victor's lost minute was given back to him.

Each story was riveting. Some devastating, some sharp and elegant. Tears fell down smooth faces, bearded faces, dripping unheeded to the floor.

Tim was thin, and much better dressed than most of the men. At the sight of him, Marc felt self-conscious in his straight-from-work clothes aromatic with sweat. Tim's hair was well groomed, his shoes shined. He looked like he ought to have the world by the tail, but as he gripped the dildo, he was clearly a nervous wreck, more so than any previous speaker.

"I grew up in a very small town in the Midwest, a pretty—well, *very*—conventional upbringing. I began to wear a mask before I even knew what that meant. It was instinctive, for survival, but I didn't know why. I know why now, and..."

He glanced around at the fierce-looking trophy heads, at the attentive faces below. "And I can tell you what I need to say without the mask. What I've never said to a straight man before. I'm gay." Tim's voice fell silent as he focused closely on the listening men.

"Before tonight, I couldn't have imagined saying that to a group of twenty-nine most likely straight strangers. Terrifying! My first boyfriend... He was beaten for coming out to a straight man. Had permanent nerve damage. I became an alcoholic. My AA brothers told me about this retreat and encouraged me to attend. I've been away with a lot of men in the woods, but this is different." He smiled and blinked.

"I hope I haven't terrorized anyone. Some straight men are afraid of gay men. We're all afraid, so afraid. I don't want to live in paralyzing fear anymore. I'm proud to be here. I know this retreat will help me to not... to not try to take my life again." He paused for a deep breath.

"I'm happy to have you all with me. *Men.* Men of all colors, all... you know." He eyed the dildo. "Please don't kill me in my sleep. Penis Power!" He thrust the dildo into the shadows above his head with a vigorous shake.

A moment of silence was followed this time by an outburst of love and enthusiastic acceptance. Big straight dudes with streaming eyes hugged Tim off the stage. They were an amazing group of men, each trying to live, to get through, to win. Marc felt part of a human story in a small and perfect universe in that room.

Two Roberts spoke, two Pauls, one Oscar.

Shit, we're getting close to the M*'s.* Michael was next. Maybe there'd be more than one—seemed like there were always a lot of Michaels. Turned out there were three. The third was Mike Smith.

Mike Smith was an angry man. He had been in the pen twice for beating his wife and kids, had been out a year, and sober for three. He wasn't very well spoken but he was sincere and emotional. Marc felt the group's love extend to Mike, all of them full of hope.

Fifty-fifty he'll make it, Marc guessed. *Please make it. Wife beater. Why was a T-shirt called a wifebeater?* In that moment of distraction, a red-faced and teary Mike hugged him and passed him the dildo talking stick.

"This is one big, heavy... talking stick." Marc hefted the thing, weighing his words. Began doing biceps curls with it. "Did some stand-up in New York in my twenties; wish I'd had a room filled with you beautiful people. I didn't. I also sucked." He allowed himself a nervous chuckle.

"I'm an only child. Always dreamed of having a great community, you know—wife, family, friends, people to work, and play, and love, and laugh with, people to trust, and count on, and give myself to. I married my high school sweetheart at twenty-eight; she was pregnant with our first child. My mother called her a free spirit. Months after the birth, her spirit got freer. Postpartum stuff maybe, I don't know. Two sides to every story; no, more like seven sides." He gestured with the dildo, glad to have something in his hand.

"Four years after the wedding, we were living in Santa Fe, had our second child. Within a couple of years, it all went bad, really bad. Divorced. I took it as a huge, personal failure. Always a saint when I had the kids, I got into a lot of partying and women after the breakup.

"A couple of years went by. I met a woman, an extraordinary woman, Marina. We met doing CPR, saving a man's life on the floor by my office. Fell deeply in love, married, and... she died a year later. Stomach cancer." He gnawed his lip, took a long breath.

"I drank, the night of the diagnosis, then went back to sober, except for one night in the Yucatán. Beautiful dinner by the beach with her, a couple of glasses of wine.

"So, wife number one has severe psychiatric problems. Wife number two, who rocked my world, died while we were still honeymooners. Lucky in love, I guess." The giant dildo drooped toward his knees.

"Our families thought we'd prepared for her death, but when her spirit left, the horror, depression, despair... Sadness, such fucking deep sadness. I stayed sober, thank God. My friend Dan said that this retreat—I called it running away—feels more like running *toward*. He was right. You all have my attention and respect."

Marc swallowed hard and handed the talking stick to Lawrence, followed by Louis, the diver from the Yucatán trip.

Bedtime was announced at the end of the stories, taking Marc by surprise; he found that he felt more exhilarated than tired.

"This is only the beginning," Jim said, wrapping up the evening. "Get a couple hours of sleep. Drum circle and sweat early tomorrow. Sweet dreams."

Fire and Sweat

Snoring and crickets had Marc sleeping fitfully with borrowed blankets on a thin mattress, as he bunked with several other men in a cabin. He strongly regretted not bringing fresh clothes or a clean sleeping bag—his shirt smelled gamey and they hadn't done the sweat yet. The weekend retreat to the wild would be extra wild in his case.

The sun was hours from rising when the men were roused by a pounding at the door.

"Up. Meeting room," someone called out.

The staffer waited outside as they shuffled around in the darkness, then led them by flashlight to the hall. A line was forming at the bathroom. Breakfast wasn't mentioned. Instead, once everyone had had a chance to take a piss and wash up, they walked single file over a needle-carpeted trail to a clearing, where a tent-like structure stood on a low platform.

"Enter the yaranga with bowed head, please," Jim said.

They stooped to duck through the flapped door. One man, a veteran in a battered wheelchair, was lifted and carried inside by two others. The interior was dim and cold, lit by a small central fire.

"Welcome," Jim said.

And so, it began, fire, drums, and chants. *Boom... boom, boom, boom*. Marc felt his pulse aim to sync itself with the simple drumbeats. *Thud... thud, thud, thud.* Once a drummer, always.

When his turn came to be drum guide, he couldn't restrain himself. He glanced around the circle at the men's inward-looking faces and their closed eyes, at the palms turned up in their laps. *Boom!* A rousing Cuban beat—syncopated, irresistible—leaped from beneath his hands. Eyes popped open all around. *Way to rock the yaranga!* they said wordlessly.

Sweat and tears streamed over his skin, sobs rose from deep within, from an endless well, only to fall again, this time on the outside, exposed to the world. Coyote screams of hallelujah burst from his throat. The hard floor under his ass vanished, the frozen stone in his chest melted, releasing his heart.

The men let him belt out his catharsis, and howled along with him. They shared it all, Marc and these men. Accepting and supporting, moving heads, necks, shoulders, hands, hips, feet, a vibrating wheel of energy, part order, part chaos. *I am still here, still alive,* he drummed. *My body and soul remember how to feel joy. Hallelujah!*

Thud. Thud-thud-thud. The men slowed and synchronized their bodies along with the drumbeats, and at last Marc passed the drum to the next man. Sunlight began to seep through the canvas walls of the yaranga. Life light started to spread through Marc's soul.

They had no breakfast that day, and only weak tea for lunch. The sweat would take place in sessions throughout the afternoon, following fasting. Marc's stomach growled. He drank plenty of tea and water, hydrating in anticipation.

The sweathouse was smaller than the yaranga. A fire pit sat a few yards in front of it, separated from the entrance by a low altar. As the men approached, they could see rocks heating in the fire. Bundles of sage and the pipe Marc had admired in the hall lay upon the altar. The men stripped to their underwear and entered single file.

Ceremonial time followed its own rhythm. When afternoon shadows began to cover the sweathouse, all the sweat work of the day came to completion.

An early supper was the first solid food they'd eaten since the night before. Marc donned his apron, hairnet, and hat to serve again. The men talked very little during the meal. They chewed slowly, savoring pinto beans, squash, and plain rice, as if they were feasting at a king's table.

"You are kings tonight as you sit together, honoring yourselves and each other," Jim said. "Know the king in yourself. Greet the king in each man you meet. Not only today, this weekend, but forever."

The men turned to each other, bestowing greetings with the reverence of royalty, and the affection of long-time friends.

The next round of activities took place in the main hall. Sometimes in small groups, other times all together, they worked through multiple exercises designed to build trust in each other and ease in accepting and expressing vulnerabilities. Ten minutes into an exercise about masks, a clown and a mime lurched into the room, a pair of crazed, masked muggers. Marc jumped up in reflexive fear, crashing into another circle.

"*Shit!* Sorry! Clowns, shit!"

The masked intruders each took Marc by an arm and pulled him to the stage. Anywhere else he would have resisted, but this— What was he supposed to do? He willed himself to neutrality, not passivity. Muscles sheathed but ready.

Jim approached him on the stage. "You're afraid."

"Yes, clowns and mimes, a phobia."

"We know. You fear the mask. You recognize the mask as a deception."

"Yeah, guess so."

"What do you think is behind the mask?"

"I don't know. It's just scary, weird, wrong. I can't explain it."

The grease-painted clown and mime brought their faces closer to Marc's.

"Look each of them in the eye," Jim instructed. "You know them. They're friends. Your friends, Marc. You don't need to fear them."

Marc stared at the clown, studying the eyes. "Holy shit. *Dan*?"

The clown nodded.

"I thought you..."

"I'm here for you," Dan said.

And so am I, indicated the mime in sign language, tapping his chest.

Marc looked at the mime again. "*Herb*?"

The mime nodded and shifted his feet in a familiar scissoring gait.

"We're here for you, Marc," Jim said. "Your friends are here for you. You won't always recognize us by our faces, so you must learn to look through the mask. You'll continue to encounter us out in the world, in our outside-world masks. Don't be afraid."

The clown and mime kept their grip on Marc's arms with a pressure he now understood as supportive, not aggressive. They smiled, still looking creepy. Seeing through the masks was going to take some work.

"Jeez, Dan, does your wife know about this clown dress-up thing?

The clown laughed. "Who do you think gave me the lipstick?"

Sunday was no day of rest for the weekend warriors, the runaways. They began with a silent meditative hike before breakfast. Everyone took turns assisting Chuck, the man in the wheelchair, when the trail hit rough patches. Speech was unnecessary. They coordinated actions, observing and working together.

Hairnet in place, Marc served lunch again. When he finished, he carefully folded the apron, hat, and hairnet, and put them with his ditty bag to take home, tangible reminders of service.

The last activity took place in the yaranga, where the men were asked to contribute words to live by. Marc chose Marina's version of the Lord's Prayer.

"She was brave, which doesn't mean she was unafraid. When she had to face the reality of dying soon, dying young, she reached for every weapon she could get her hands on, including the Lord's Prayer. But she changed the last line. She didn't ask to be delivered from evil. As evil as that cancer was, devouring her from the inside, she understood that there was no bargaining with God about it. She was beyond asking *why* that particular evil had come to afflict her, to take her from the world she loved, the people she loved, from me, her husband. She asked for deliverance from fear."

Immediately, the men began to intone the prayer, one known by many of them from childhood. When they reached the last line, *but deliver us from fear*, they roared it.

"*FEAR!*"

The word hovered above the fire in their midst, a burnt offering, before slipping through the smoke hole in the tent toward the heavens above.

The weekend's final gathering filled the main hall with the energy of post-cathartic men. Some stood deep in eye-to-eye conversation; some took silly photos of each other and of the dead animal trophies. There were boisterous eruptions of laughter, exchanges of contact information, assurances of further contact—a demanding, purposeful ritual, making damned sure their weekend's treasure would outlive these few hours. Lifelong friendships had been launched.

Marc found Herb crouched in a corner smoking a fine robusto, his solitude and silence a contrast to the movement of the room.

"Nice ash, man." Marc admired the nearly inch and a half of burnt tobacco clinging to the cigar's tip, a cigar-smoker's prized achievement, testament of calm.

"Right? Hey, hell of a weekend. You look peaceful."

Marc folded his legs to sit on the floor across from Herb.

The palsied, tattooed, train-wrecked, genuine superhero blew a train-puff of smoke and flashed his teeth. "A high start, man. Gotta keep it going."

"Yeah, I do. What next?"

"Tattoo. Something permanent like cement." Herb pushed his lips into a broad Billy Idol pucker. "Tattoo. Tattoo. Tattoo." He gestured with the cigar, an awkward gyration. The ash fell.

Both men stared at the gray dust. Herb pouted like his dog had just died.

"Ashes to ashes." Marc offered condolences.

Herb's expression lightened. "Dude! You don't have any tattoos, do ya?"

"No. I never really got it, know what I mean?"

"The pain?"

"No, that's no big deal. The permanence weirds me out. But I like all of this." He pointed to Herb's arms, which were covered in full-sleeve artwork. The designs were visual journal notes of Herb's life, memorializing cerebral palsy, the train, kicking addiction, falling in love.

Herb glanced down at his arms, appreciating Marc's appreciation. "Let me tell you, there is some serious spiritual shit in getting a tattoo. And I'm not talking a drunken sailor's *mom* on a heart."

"I think I'll get a big hawk across my chest, or a, what the chicks get low down on their backs."

"Tramp stamp!" Herb laughed loudly. "Show it off with your plumber pants."

"And a thong!"

"Marc, I'll introduce you to Giancarlo next week. We'll just talk to him. He's an expert artist. What he knows about Maori body art will blow you away."

Marc sat pensive for a moment. "Okay. Saturday morning next weekend? I don't know…" Could he do it? "What the hell."

The retreat ended with Polaroid 'after' shots to compare to the 'befores;' the contrast was astonishing. Despite curtailed sleep, limited food, rough accommodations, and stressful personal work, the images from the end of the retreat showed smoother foreheads, genuine smiles, jubilation, and determination. There were plenty of cigars too.

Marc put his Polaroids together with the gifts from Jose and the raven feather he'd picked up on the morning hike. He'd be returning to Santa Fe with a little less flesh, and a much lighter spirit, inspired by the power of ceremony.

Welcome to the Club

April 6, 1996
Santa Fe, New Mexico

Marc and his virgin skin arrived early at the tattoo parlor, a modest adobe on a back street off Saint Francis Drive. The very tiny yard was decorated with an oddball assortment of figures: a serenely smiling brass Buddha; a bronze dancing Shiva; wood carvings of Our Lady of Guadalupe; Saint Francis; Doña Sebastiana, La Muerte, in her death cart; a Northwest aboriginal style totem; one howling coyote; and standing proudly by the door, several pink plastic flamingos. The door stood ajar, and reggae music floated through the screen. He pressed the doorbell.

A man emerged a moment later, smiling in greeting, a wiry, tanned man whose astonishingly intricate tattoos were displayed by his minimalist undershirt. Silver hair pulled into a ponytail reached the middle of his back.

"Herb called; he's running late," said the man. "But we can get started if you want. I'm Giancarlo."

He ushered Marc inside, invited him to sit in a beat-up vinyl chair. "So, Herb said this will be your first tattoo, if you decide to go ahead with it."

"Yeah, I've never understood tats," Marc admitted. "Swore I'd never get one."

Giancarlo nodded. As it turned out, his salesmanship was grade A, his manner low-key. He was clearly a guy who knew the worth of his artistry and felt no need to push anyone off the fence and into tattoo world. You want it, fine. Aren't sure, come back some other time after giving it more thought. He paid sincere attention to Marc's story about his journey with Marina, about their love and her death. The tear in Giancarlo's eye sealed the deal.

They set to work reviewing styles and designs, which led to images of birds, which led to large birds, birds of prey, then to a gliding red hawk. The next step was to decide on the tattoo's location. Marc remembered Marina telling him about dreaming she saw a tattoo of a hawk on his arm as he wrote at the beach.

"I was thinking about my arm, but it's too out there—I don't want to show it off. I want this to be more private. Does that make sense?" Marc asked, hoping not to offend the artist, whose body imagery was clearly intended for public viewing.

Giancarlo raised his eyebrows. "In that case I could give you a *raperape*."

"A what?"

"On your bottom."

"Bottom of what? You want to do a *raperape* on my *ass*?"

"The style of body art I mostly have on myself is Maori. When you tat the buttocks, it's called a raperape. Just offering it as an idea." His eyes twinkled, but his contemplative demeanor returned a moment later.

"I served two tours in Vietnam," he explained. "Spent a few months in eastern Polynesia, where I got my first *kirituhi*. That's a Maori-style tattoo, a kind that's okay for non-Polynesians to have without causing offense. Traditional Maori body art is sacred, not for outsiders. It's important to know and abide by the cultural rules."

"Like the Pueblos here," Marc said. "I've been to some of the dances, public ones, but there are traditions that outsiders are forbidden to learn about. I get it. Some things are private." He thought of the men's retreat. Sacred space, sacred sharing, private.

"After discharge, I spent a week in L.A. and used my last dime to return to Polynesia. As you can see, I got more work done." Giancarlo extended a forearm to present the leafy patterns encircling and rising from his wrist. "Lived there fifteen years, married. Studied Maori body arts."

"What brought you back to the States?"

"My wife, Omma. She died of malaria. Forty-two years old."

"Oh… I'm so sorry. Thanks for telling me that."

"Yes, my friend. Welcome to the club."

Giancarlo got to his feet. "Ready? I like your decision about the Buddhist clouds. Everybody wants roses." He positioned Marc on a table.

Herb arrived, apologizing profusely for his tardiness.

"You know how we deal with tardies." Marc said. "We will— *Oww!*" Giancarlo had begun. "Ouch! Man, that *hurts!*"

"Yeah, I get a lot of that. Wait till we get to the back of the thigh." Giancarlo worked with methodical efficiency, his fingers gentle, but the needle hurt like hell.

Marc recalled Herb asking if his tattoo reluctance was due to pain and his clueless reply: "No, that's no big deal." *Shit, what was I thinking?* The pain was humbling.

"Congratulations, Marc. Great choice," Herb said, studying the pre-ink rendering of a hawk bursting through a ring of dark clouds around Marc's thigh. "Why your thigh?"

"Because he has good legs," Giancarlo quipped. "Especially the right one. And when he moves his leg, the hawk flies."

Finally, the hawk was complete, flying on Marc's quadratus medialis above the right knee. Next, the storm clouds would circumnavigate the thigh.

"How much longer?" Marc feared the answer.

"Till we're done. Two or three hours, maybe. Depends if you can handle it."

"He can handle it!" Herb said with a toothy grin. "Of course he can!"

"Turn over, face down," Giancarlo said. "The back of your thigh is more sensitive than the front. If it feels good to be kissed, feels even worse to be tattooed. Be glad it's not the tip of your dick. Sorry, man. But ain't it funny how that works, that dualism of anguish and pleasure. Breathe. Keep breathing." Giancarlo went back to work.

Marc was reminded of Moonflute guiding Marina through the fear, pain, and darkness of her journey out of this life. Breathe, she had said. Marc breathed. *Marina, be with me through it, baby. Be with me.* "Bring it on."

A few minutes later he was squirming. A few minutes after that, he began to drop multiple F-bombs while Herb and Giancarlo responded with sympathy and encouragement. The needle to the front of his thigh had been nothing compared to the back. His throat, chest, solar plexus—hell, even his balls—throbbed, but Marc realized the pain pushed well beyond skin-deep suffering.

Giancarlo paused now and then when the shudders beneath his hands reached crescendos.

They had all been there, the three of them, in the desolate land of loss. Talking it out was necessary but didn't anesthetize. Spiritual, visceral, emotional, and mental, all the domains of pain merged into a single abyss, a cavity of absolute anguish.

A scream tore from Marc's larynx. "Sorry, man, sorry," he blubbered. "Keep going. I'm okay."

"Don't apologize," Herb said. "It's fucking *hell*. You'll get through. Look at me, look at all this ink—and Giancarlo. We know, man. We know." Herb squeezed Marc's shoulder. "It's beautiful. You'll see."

Two more hours passed. Marc wasn't sure he could endure another moment; he felt like a child in the back seat on a long car trip when he demanded in a whisper, "Are we there yet?"

"We are there," Giancarlo said, lifting the needle away and stepping back. "Herb, get the mirror."

Ready? Ready!

A few nights later, the kids were tucked into bed, still in playful moods. Chelsea bragged about a math test.

"Dad, I had a B plus, but talked Mrs. Trujillo into an A minus. She's a pushover, but very nice. She feels awful about Marina dying, and about India. She knows I studied really hard. My first A in math, yay!"

Not to be outdone, Zane chimed in with, "Dad, I hit a shot from half court! I tried ten more times and couldn't reach, but, Dad, hitting that one—" His feet kicked under the covers with his excitement.

They admired Marc's tattoo, tracing the swirling clouds with careful fingers after he told them what an ordeal the process had been. His leg was sore and swollen from the weekend bombardment, but the ink was worth it. He flexed and extended his leg, making the hawk flap its wings.

"Cool, Dad. Birds rule!" Zane shrieked.

"Nighty, guys! Watch out for the bugs," Marc said, hand on the light switch, their elation contagious.

As he made his way up the curving staircase, he realized he was still smiling from the pleasure of seeing normalcy in his children's lives after all they had been through and were still going through. But he had one more thing to do. He'd been putting it off, hadn't felt ready. He was ready now. He climbed into bed with a pencil and a yellow legal pad, and jotted a few notes. When he was done, he lay back against his pillows with his eyes closed.

Four or five times over the past several months he'd had a beer, but didn't want or need a second. That was great.

He continued to use Claude's list, found it fun, a game.

He took the kids everywhere. The night they'd arrived with Daniel, paired with his discovery that Rosana was off to India, had kick-started his own life changes.

The writing he had recently begun was engaging, getting his creative juices flowing.

There was that wild weekend with the warriors, and Herb and Giancarlo and the tattoo. *My hawk*. Every day for the rest of his life it would be a permanent reminder of their shared journey. He had done the work and felt stronger, more effective, ready.

He jumped out of bed, pulled a business card from the desk, took it downstairs to the kitchen, and picked up the phone.

"Hello, is this Corbin Phillips? Do you channel the entity Michael?"

Zest

April 14, 1996
Santa Fe, New Mexico
    A lenticular cloud hovered over the mountains like a flying saucer lifting off.

    Today was definitely another shitty day in paradise, one of Marc's favorite Santa Feisms. The saying, peculiar to Santa Fe as far as he could tell, paid ironic homage to the city's perennial beauty. When clouds in the western sky scattered the setting sun's rays eastward, the Sangre de Cristo mountains glowed red-purple, theatrically so. From afar, they became a living mystery, a brief, fleshy incarnation that inspired cosmic dreams, before they lapsed into a slumbering silhouette. On an autumn day they were something else, pink earth showing through threadbare cobalt tree cover, with a heart-shaped patch of golden aspens stitched to one southwest-facing slope.

    The Sangres were gleaming with the remnants of winter snow, but the ski resort was closed for the season; he had missed his chance to get in a day on the slopes. His skis had been in storage all year. They— He blinked. Had he circled the same hill twice? Maybe not. But maybe he wasn't paying close enough attention.

    Rock rhythms resounded from the cassette player in his SUV. The lyrics about how good it had been living with someone, by the band Better than Ezra, turned his mind inevitably to Marina. Good, yes, it had been good living with her, hawks and all.

    Dust from the gravel road obscured the view in his rearview mirror. He drove fast, hitting bumps and making quick turns.

    "This had better be worth it." He spoke aloud to relieve his jitters. "I feel like a *60 Minutes* reporter. Yeah, Ed Bradley." Bradley was his favorite of all of them.

    More bumps. More bad driving. He sang along with the boys, belting out his search for— "Shit!" He braked hard, skidding, as a winged thing darted across the road. A shadow, only the shadow of a bird overhead. His heart pounded. *God, I'm braking for shadows?*

"You have to let me know. Give me something here, Marina, something big. You always told me I had a zest for life. If you tell me that today, well, damn, that would be… He pulled over to the rough edge of the road, turned off the engine, stopping the music, and closed his eyes. He saw her face in the rosy darkness, clear and radiant, just as he had first seen it three years ago above the body of a man who appeared dead. Together they had brought him back to himself.

"I have to know—don't leave me hanging. I trust you, you spooky, lovely love," he babbled, not caring what it sounded like. "Communicate! Give me the zest thing—that would be cool."

Marc rolled down the window. He lapsed into silence, hands on the wheel, listening to the wind whooshing through pine needles, an occasional vehicle whirring by in the distance. At last, he restarted the engine, turned down the music volume, and a few minutes later found his way to the address printed on the business card on his passenger seat.

A sign confirmed the street number, but no shingle hung out to advertise the services of *Michael the entity* or Corbin Phillips, the entity's channeler. Did channelers have professional credentials, titles or fellowships, strings of abbreviations after their names like docs and lawyers? Fellow of the American Academy of Entity Channelers—FAAECs. Shit.

He parked. An adobe home stood amid piñon trees, with views west toward the city. Its door gleamed bright turquoise, and two pots of scarlet geraniums sat on its porch.

Wiping nervous palms down the sides of his pants, Marc approached the door, where a patinated bell hung—a Santa Fe–style doorbell. He tugged its clapper string. The clang reverberated with surprising tenacity, echoing in his ears. The man who opened was an unassuming figure—forties, short gray hair. No tinfoil hat.

"Hi, how are you, Michael. I mean Corbin," Marc said.

The man's smile was relaxed. "That's me, Michael and Corbin. Corbin Phillips. I get a lot of the Michael-Corbin thing; I understand it can be confusing. Come in, nice to meet you, Marc. I hear you're a good guy."

Marc wondered who had put in the word for him. "From whom?" Still channeling Ed Bradley. He followed Corbin across the threshold into a tastefully decorated Southwestern-style living room.

"You have some fine friends in this town," was Corbin's quiet reply.

"Thanks. Sorry, I know nothing about you. What are we about to do?"

Corbin made calm, appraising eye contact. "This experience may seem odd if you haven't been around it much. I'll try to explain. As you know, I never met Marina. You'll be able to communicate with each other through me. It's like I'm on the telephone."

He put a fist up to his ear. "I tell you what she says, you tell me what you want to tell her, she hears. She hears *through* me. I am not her. Understand?"

Marc nodded. *Don't wisecrack—it'll piss off Marina—if she's here. So, here goes.* "I think so."

"Okay."

He knew that Corbin saw right through him, saw his uncertainty and skepticism, but the channeler didn't seem fazed. "My fee is fifty dollars per session."

"Seems inexpensive. You probably could charge thousands."

"Not what this is about. You'll see."

Marc handed him the cash, and they seated themselves across from each other at a dining table. Corbin closed his eyes. After what seemed an eternity of stillness, the man's face quivered.

"I am so glad you trusted me, Marc. You came; I knew you would. I've been waiting. I am *so* busy."

"Okay... Now this is, isn't..." Marc wanted to seem cooperative. "Busy doing what?" he asked.

"It's hard to explain. Things are different, you could imagine."

"I could imagine?"

"I help souls get from that life to another. Good work if you can get it. How are the children?" The words from Corbin's mouth sounded bizarrely ordinary.

"Uumm, okay."

"Are you with them? Stay close to them, always take them with you. Show them the earth!"

Marc's neck stiffened. "'Take them with you'? Hold on."

"You're going to be great. It was wonderful to share life with you, Marc. It's so big, so much bigger than you could know. When you see, you're going to be dazzled. You have a zest for life."

Marina's exact words. From Corbin's lips.

"What?" As if braced against a wall of resistance that evaporated, Marc's body slipped from the chair to a Navajo rug below. He raised himself onto one arm, searching Corbin's face. "What did you say?"

Corbin looked momentarily startled, his eyes wide open but unseeing; he remained in his channeling state.

"Marc, you have a zest for life. You'll love being loved; you'll have crazy life experiences. Go to Telluride. I'll get another body soon, and I won't be able to see you after that. There are many lives. Don't be in fear, no fear…"

"Marina… You have my total attention," Marc responded, still on the floor.

A carefree conversation between them ensued. Surprisingly, Marc found it easy to forget that Corbin was there at all—or was it the Michael entity—channeling her words. He felt lifted, his hands waving, animated by passions, joy, humor, love. Twenty minutes later, when the session wound down, he knew that he'd undergone a profound metamorphosis, one as mystical and real as a pregnancy's first declaration.

We are spiritual beings cycling through lives, deaths, separations and unions, guiding and following each other to endings that become new beginnings. We quicken in the warm, dark seas of our mother's wombs with the flutters of butterfly wings, the rhythm of dancing fish, moving into light and darkness and back again, losing and finding ourselves, losing and finding each other. Marina remained in his life and he in hers, granting each other beingness.

Marc departed from Corbin's house carrying a cassette recording of the session with Marina, a powerful surge of melancholy excitement coursing through his body. He paused before getting into his vehicle, lifted a hand to shade his eyes. Bright sunlight reflected from a myriad of surfaces in the world outside— grains of sand, chunks of granite, basalt, quartz, clusters of oily pine needles, a beetle's shiny shell, a raven's glossy wing. The electrical charge ebbed, replaced by an extraordinary and welcome flow of peace. Peace, infinite and self-replicating, filled every cell in his body.

The Life of Our Times

June 18, 1996

Telluride, Colorado

The lower Rocky Mountains, southernmost Colorado, towered deep green and formidable into brisk June skies as Marc drove his SUV loaded with cigar boxes through winding mountain passes. He glanced toward a lake to his right.

A magnificent eagle swooped toward the water, scraped its surface, came up empty, and soared fast, almost straight back up. Marc beamed at the sight, drumming his hands on the steering wheel to the rhythm of Pearl Jam.

He arrived in Telluride late afternoon. Traffic signs with blinking lights reminded him to slow down to 15 MPH. Tourists—young, athletic, and grungy—were out en masse, their numbers burgeoning in advance of the upcoming Bluegrass Festival. He flipped on the local radio. Max, a new friend and D.J., was signing off for the evening in his low, sexy baritone.

"Ladies and gentlemen of Telluride, I give you Green Day and 'Good Riddance.'"

Billie Joe Armstrong's earnest song of love, loss, and sweet good will filled Marc's ears. He paused at a fork in the road. The music held him in a tender mood as he arrived moments later at his cigar shop on a downtown back alley. He parked, glanced down at the tattoo peeking from the leg of his shorts, and gave it a rub before getting down to business—selecting cigar boxes and strolling into the compact shop.

A gilt-lettered sign above the door proclaimed Santa Fe Cigar Company, Telluride. He opened the squeaky door to poke his head inside, wearing a maniacal grin like Jack Nicholson as Kubrick's Jack Torrance, and bellowed, "Here's Markie!"

The man behind the counter, the spitting image of Jerry Garcia, hooted in reply. Abe Snyder, a former bandmate, had moved up to

Telluride from Santa Fe just in time to say 'yes' to Marc's business proposal, the cigar store. He looked happy with the move.

"Hi, Abe. How's business, bro?" Marc switched to his normal persona. The shop was like a cigar box itself, snug, golden brown, and woody. With the flavors and scents of romance filling his head, Marc was reminded of his wedding to Marina, when he had been given his first cigar.

"Hey, Marc. A little slow today, but okay." They shook hands. Bro-hugged. "What goodies did you bring me?"

"A lot of everything. About fifty boxes, some humidors, cutters, lighters, a few Cubans."

"So how was Cuba? Killer?"

"Killer, really. Sensational! You know I love the Caribbean. I went through Cancún. I was once a Mayan woman—in a past life, of course."

"Yeah, yeah, yeah. You have to be a real man to think you were once a chick," Abe said good-naturedly.

"Let's get the rest of the cigars out of the truck, then I'll buy you dinner at the Sheridan."

Abe nodded. They draped arms across each other's shoulders and walked to the SUV. When they finished restocking inventory, they ambled over to the Sheridan and ordered locally crafted beers, light and lemony.

Abe wiped foam from his mustache. "So, what's up with the investors?"

"Investors? That's formal of you. Our drinking buddies."

Armando Gallegos and Richard Frank, excellent friends, had agreed to go along with Marc's crazy-sounding business venture.

"Well, what did Armando and Rich say?"

"Busted my balls. You know Rich." Marc adopted an exaggerated New York accent to impersonate his friend. "Let me get this straight. You want ten grand from Armando and me for a cigar store way the hell up in Telluride; I don't even fucking *smoke*; and the whole premise of this business is so you can be closer to your *dead wife*?"

Abe guffawed. "What'd you say?"

"That's about it in a nutshell." He joined Abe in a belly laugh.

"What did they do?"

"Well, we kicked around some numbers. You know Rich with his spread sheets." Marc casually, deliberately, extracted two checks from his wallet and slid them onto the table.

Abe eyeballed the amounts and gave exactly the explosive reaction Marc had hoped for.

"Holy shit, man! Twenty grand?" He shook his head and rubbed a check between his fingers as if testing the ink.

"Let's not screw this up," Marc said, serious now, lifting his mug.

"To Marina," Abe said. They clinked and drank.

"How're you holding up?" Abe asked quietly, after a thoughtful pause.

"Okay, thanks." He hadn't told anyone about his channeling session; it felt too personal to share. "The kids miss her. They see a therapist, which helps. Rosana came back from India two weeks ago. Better, more relaxed, still not settled. They haven't stayed with her yet."

"Man, good luck with all that. You dating?"

"Not really. I walk down the street, all I see is old men smoking cheap cigars." He drained his mug. "Get me another beer; I'll be right back." He crossed the saloon to the men's room.

Dating. He replayed Marina's words from their last night on the Yucatán: *You're going to need the closeness of a woman when I'm gone.* And his own words to Armando, the first night with Marina at El Farol: *A gentleman doesn't tell.* He'd spent a few evenings with a woman, just one woman, since Marina's death. Young, idealistic, free-spirited—she had heard about his loss and took it as a personal challenge to rekindle his spark, an athletic endeavor. Mission accomplished. She woke his slumbering sensuality, made them both smile, but his heart was still in fragments and hers was as green as an early apricot.

"Your jowls wiggle," she had said in the midst of his energetic thrusting. *Jowls!* He stared into the mirror above the sink now, pushed his cheeks with wet hands. *Jowls? I stay in shape, I'm not exactly over the hill. Still in my thirties!* But the reminder of the age gap was a cold splash. Young eyes see with sharp young lenses. Young tongues may be innocently, unwittingly, cruel. He was old enough to understand that.

Being here with Marina—the picturesque town and hotel, the music festival, the mountain, its meadows and lakes…

"Keep it together," he told his reflection. Music swelled as he left the men's room to return to Abe. Three steps into the main room, he stopped midstride.

Sitting at the bar was Marina in a shimmering amber gown. His heart skipped three beats; he swayed, steadied, pitched forward—and up came her flat palm, as solid as the bartender just behind her. *Aspetta.* Wait. Stop in the name of love. She held his attention for an electrifying moment. There could be no embrace.

He cupped the left side of his chest and tapped twice, mouthing *Thank you.*

Marina tapped her chest three times, mouthing *I love you.* She gave him a childish finger-curl wave, kissed her fingertips, blew him the kiss—just as a mountain-sized mountain man crossed between them, breaking their laser gaze. The mountain passed and she was gone, her presence a transparent memory. *Marina, my Marina, my love.*

He rubbed his eyes, unable to move. This visit couldn't have been simple for her spirit to pull off. The universe had physics, ethics, a little playfulness. A strange thought, even for him, tickled his mind. Some comedian had been riffing on what it would look like when a man made out with a ghost. A grin spread over Marc's face as he imagined himself open-mouthed, tongue out, in the middle of the Sheridan Bar. *She saved me from that.*

He stroked the breast pocket of his shirt, stiff with a card in an envelope. He'd found the card tucked into the back of Marina's journal and knew he must bring it with him on this trip. Now he understood why. The image on the card was a majestic view of the Rocky Mountains and a meadow in glorious bloom. He pulled the card out and reread the message inside, written in her hand, hearing it with her voice.

To my Love,

On this day two years ago, we stepped into each other's lives and I found the light and love I searched for, for so many years. I can never thank you enough in words, only in acts of love and loyalty that endure beyond our lifetimes together. I often feel undeserving of your love, or that I don't know how to accept it. Sometimes it's too much for me, yet I need it so badly. I need you so. Please help me to celebrate the sacred in the everyday, as you do so well. Hold me in your heart, in your thoughts, in your being; carry my joy in you wherever you go.

Cherish the life of our times.

Forever and always,

Your Marina

He folded the card back into its envelope and approached the now lonely bar stool. There on the bar lay a rust-colored feather. Marc picked it up, slipped it into his pocket with the card. *Marina, you work in mysterious ways.*

Eventually he meandered back to the table, a wild smile plastered on his face, to continue the business celebration as if nothing had happened.

Something, definitely, had happened.

Six Pencils

June 30, 1996
San Diego, California

Marc sat writing and drinking espresso on the deck of a funky San Diego seaside café, his body fit and strong in new athletic shirt and shorts. "Wish You Were Here," by Incubus, blasted over the sound system.

Breakfast dishes sat pushed to the side on the thickly varnished table; five sharp No. 2 pencils lay scattered among the flotsam and jetsam of eggs and toast crusts. Bright sunlight bounced off the coffee-stained legal pad before him.

His hand raced over the paper, leaving lines of pencil scrawl behind. Fiercely focused, he occasionally paused to laugh aloud. When his pencil grew dull, he flung it aside and picked up a sharp one, repeating the action until he'd gone through all six. Energized, he jiggled and flexed his crossed leg, making the hawk tattoo beat its wings.

Dozens of seagulls circled, squawked, and cried around the café's splintered deck, as rhythmic as the waves sweeping against the pile supports below. Marc tossed his toast crusts to the water; the flock gathered them all.

Chelsea and Zane charged around the corner of the café deck, causing an uprising of seagulls. Their faces shone.

"Daddy! Let's go down to the beach now! Come on, come on!"

Marc gathered his paper and pencils, slid them into a beach bag with towels and sunscreen.

Take them, Marc, always take them with you. Show them as much of the world as possible.

They were with him as he worked and as he played. Today they'd squealed in the background as he'd written a new song.

Alone, the sheets are
quite clean
he is made really very comfortable
thin, hardly as muscled
as the day he received the tattoo
thigh lies shaky out of the
cool sheet
divorced one, buried one
strong daughter and
his great sun
the day is bright, the windows
are clean
the view is expensive
at this death scene
around the corner the
kids are getting lunch
day dreams of sunsets and warm water
the tattoo is folded where
it once was taut
the bird and the clouds
measure the passage of time
when he first knew of his
death and forlorn immortality
his sobriety and spirituality
calm him at this death scene
the pain is not so bad
more pain than this he
already had
rather excited, he had prepared
the lawyers and saints
and thoughts of his dad
love to see them all
one more time
this was selfish, ungraced
he was prepared
a prayer softly came to
this last breath, a white dream
at this man's death scene

Melody

August 16, 1996
Santa Fe, New Mexico

The Ortiz Mountains were a familiar backdrop to the southern view from Marc's home, their bony contours barely softened by sparse tree cover. Very different from the Sangres, much smaller in scale, but their dramatic, prickly protrusion from the plain gave the sense of a force to be reckoned with.

Today he was seeing the Ortiz up close and personal, driving through hills and foothills. Thunderheads rose to the north, dwarfing the mountainous edges of the high desert. A dust-dampening shower would be welcome.

He took off his sunglasses, squinted at the sign coming up on his left: Piñon Children's Day Camp. He turned onto the narrower and bumpier road to the camp—more like a trail—and slowed his SUV to a jogging pace.

A mile in, piñon and juniper crowding the roadside pressed back to reveal the camp entrance, where a farm gate hung open. A camp counselor in sunglasses and floppy hat was posted there, officiously directing the incoming parade of parents. She waved Marc ahead toward a dusty lot to the right of the stables. Several saddled and bridled horses stood placidly in the sun, tied to hitching posts.

Children were leading parents around by the hand, eager to show them camp activities; some hauled backpacks and sleeping bags, loaded up to leave. Marc parked, turned off the air conditioning, and rolled down the windows.

"Dad!" Chelsea ran toward him, clutching a long stick. As she came closer, he could see a pink and blue parrot painted on one cheek. Her hair tumbled around her face in curls, one lock braided with a rainbow ribbon. The piñon branch in her hand was decorated with feathers, colored glass beads, and shells. She immediately opened the car's front passenger door and plopped in, stretching the stick across both of their laps.

"Hey, honey! Let me see that." Marc cupped her face in his hands, admiring the paint job. He gave her a big smooch. "I love your parrot!"

"It's my tattoo, like your hawk and clouds."

Oh, boy, tattoos next. "What's this?" He peered down at the stick.

"What does it look like? A prayer arrow!"

"Really?" He lifted its tip for a closer look.

"My counselor helped me. We talked a lot. Well, I talked to her, anyway. She's a good listener. I talked to her about Marina and Mommy."

"That's cool of her. Above and beyond the call of duty."

Over Chelsea's shoulder he noticed an athletic young woman with flowing, shiny hair, her back to him, reaching into the trunk of a car. She leaned farther in, reaching deeper. Gorgeous legs, jean shorts. Nice calves. Nice hamstrings. Nice— He tried to be discreet, but Chelsea missed nothing. She tapped him on the nose with the arrow, curbing his distraction.

"What? Oh, honey, sorry. What is it?" He pushed the arrow from his nose.

"That's my counselor, Melody." She hollered out the window, "Hey, Melody, I want you to meet my daddy!"

Melody clambered out of the trunk, wiped her hands on the seat of her shorts, and turned toward Chelsea with an affectionate grin and wave. She re-tucked her camp T-shirt before trotting over.

Chelsea grabbed her hand and pulled her in for a kiss. Melody's wrist was decorated with brightly colored friendship bracelets.

"This is my dad. His name's Marc." Chelsea's intention was all too obvious.

"Honey, don't..." Marc said in a low voice, overwhelmed.

"Relax, you deserve each other," Chelsea returned sotto voce, matching his tone, her eyes wise and merry at the same time.

Marc gaped at his daughter.

"Hi!" Melody was standing at his window now, hand out in greeting. "I'm Melody Marcusi. Chelsea's told me a thing or two about you."

Whatever Chelsea had cooked up, Melody was handling it with grace and good humor. Marcusi, Italian?

He took her hand, dazzled, unable to come up with a snappy reply. "You have beautiful teeth." *Did I actually say that out loud?*

She laughed. "My dad's a dentist—comes with the territory."

Marc felt the hairs on the back of his neck prickle. "Ma-Marina—" he stammered. "My wife, she—"

"She had a beautiful smile. I know."

Melody's own perfect smile remained in place. Her eyes were an indefinable shade of pale gilded green. He stared into them, finding wildflower seedlings, cenote waters, delicate lacewings, and, as she patiently allowed him to explore, tenderness and compassion.

"Dad, I told Melody you promised Marina you would take me and Zane to Mexico. We have to go at winter break. Melody's a certified diver—she could teach me. I'm old enough to learn!" In Chelsea's enthusiasm, the tip of her prayer arrow hovered near his nose again.

"Chels, hon, that's months away. I don't know..." He faltered, turned to Melody to apologize for the awkwardness, but saw by the knowing amusement on her face that it was unnecessary.

"She has a point," he said, throwing caution to the wind.

Melody and Chelsea exchanged mischievous glances.

"Dad, Daddy!" Zane shot like a bottle rocket from the stable. "Watch me ride! Come on!"

Marc and Chelsea stepped from the car and accompanied Melody to the stable.

Melody took Chelsea by the hand, chatting. Her voice was musical, as lovely as her smile; Marc felt he could be happy listening to anything that voice had to say. He wanted to hear more.

"Can I ride too?" Chelsea asked, looking first to Melody and then to Marc.

They sought each other's silent permission over the top of Chelsea's head.

"I think you're ready for Lady Hawk," Melody decided. She untied a tall, spotted white horse from a hitching post and helped Chelsea to mount, as Marc boosted Zane onto a smaller sorrel.

Zane patted its neck enthusiastically. "This is my favorite! He's called Duende."

Marc and Melody followed the horses to the arena, their human strides falling into a companionable rhythm. Melody led him toward a shady spot to watch the children demonstrate their new skills.

The sand felt firm beneath his feet.

Somewhere in the forested mountainside, a hawk spiraled up and loosed a soaring cry.

Love and Blessings

March 15, 1997
Santa Fe, New Mexico

The Ides of March fell on a blustery Saturday. Marc was pulling out all the stops in the kitchen, whipping up an elaborate birthday feast for Chelsea and a gaggle of giggling eleven-year-old girls. His parents had arrived on an evening flight two nights ago and plunged immediately into grandparent duties, showering Chelsea and Zane with attention and gifts. Chen and Melody helped with decorating and kid wrangling. Moonflute arrived with an earnestly healthy cake as an alternative to the pink-and-purple-iced, plastic-ballerina-topped confection Chelsea had chosen at the supermarket with her grandmother.

Marc's minor anxieties about introducing Melody to his parents were forgotten in the joyful chaos of the party. When it was finally winding down, with sleeping bags unrolled amid jumbles of wrapping paper in the living room, his parents said their goodnights and went off to bed in the guest room while Chen departed with a promise to help with breakfast in the morning. Melody disappeared upstairs to the loft bedroom, her ascent followed by Moon's gaze. Marc accompanied Moon back to the kitchen.

"She's charming, Marc. When did she move in?"

"After Cancún, winter break. We all had a fantastic time! She's great with the kids. I know you're going to say it's too fast, too soon—and yes, she's young—but…" His words tangled in the need to justify himself to Marina's loyal friend. It hadn't escaped his notice that Moon had been watching Melody with particular interest throughout the evening, and he'd caught her watching him too, with raptor-like attention.

"I can see that she adores you and the kids. They look very comfortable with her. So, have you…?"

"What? You mean popped the question? Kind of, sort of, well—yes, actually, during a romantic stroll through Washington Square, when I took her to New York. We were staying with Sonya in the Village. The two of them sparked a great friendship; they talk on the phone weekly, and Sonya insists on singing at our wedding. Anyway, Melody said she wants more time living together first, but if we marry, she'd love to have Sonya sing."

Moon gave a satisfied nod, but Marc guessed that she wasn't finished with her interrogation.

"What's up your sleeve, Moon?"

It was a rhetorical question, but in response, Moon reached into the sleeve of her puffy winter coat hanging near the door and pulled out an envelope. "This is for you. It's from Marina."

Sweat dampened his forehead. "Marina?" He examined the envelope, confused, saw his name written in the familiar hand. "But how? I mean, do you know what it is?"

"Yes, and no."

He sank into a chair at the kitchen table. "Is this some kind of joke?"

Moon pulled up another chair and seated herself across from him, studying his face.

"Not a joke, Marc, nothing of the sort. An act of courage, more like." She clasped her hands together, steepling them on the table. "I know that Marina wrote it with love, but she didn't show it to me. She asked me to give it to you when you were ready to commit to marriage; she knew you would. You know, Chelsea sent me postcards from Cancún. So, I had a feeling."

She smiled. "This is the first time I've pulled the letter out since Marina gave it to me. It seemed like tonight would be a good time to deliver it. The one thing she asked is that you read it alone at her medicine wheel."

Moon stood to slip into her coat. "Thanks for inviting me, Marc. I had a lovely time."

They embraced, and he walked outside to see her drive off. The night air roused him for what he needed to do next. He climbed the stairs to the loft, where he found Melody nearly asleep. He knelt to kiss her. "I'm taking a quick stroll with the dogs," he said. "Stretch my legs."

She stroked his face. "Don't be too long."

The slumber party girls were still murmuring in their sleeping bags as he went back downstairs. He took a flashlight and the letter from the kitchen and called the dogs.

The night was dry, warmer than usual for March, and a waxing moon glowed. He settled himself in the sand and rocks overlooking his home, nervous about the letter, striving to calm himself by imagining Marina sitting with him. He opened the envelope, pulled out a single, folded sheet of paper, and directed the flashlight's golden beam upon it.

Dear Marc,

If you're reading this letter, the river of life has carried you to the next landing, a place of great joy, an engagement. I have such wonderful memories of being engaged to you, and married to you, my darling man. We lived a lot of life in a short time, a lot of deep engagement with each other, including sparring, pushing and pulling each other out of difficult places, forgiving each other our trespasses and frailties, being human with each other in the most intimate and holy sense.

This is what I wish for you in your next marriage, this and more, for you will have grown new spiritual strengths and suffered wounds I cannot bind, scars that will be traced by another woman's gentle hand.

Marc, I wish for you all the happiness you deserve. Do not let our loss shadow your new delight. I know you will not forget me. I know you will always cherish the love we shared. Bring your extraordinary capacity for love to your new marriage, with all the blessings I can give you. Love her with all of your big, beautiful heart.

Love and Blessings,
Marina

Whispers sifted through the dark living room as he ascended to the loft hours later. Melody's breathing told him she was fast asleep. He slid into bed as quietly as he could, reaching for her warm body with a long sigh. He was home again.

Dear Bubby-cakes

Melody stood in the cramped lobby of Moon's Luisa Street therapy office the following Monday morning, waiting for Moon to finish a phone call. The office door opened to an even more cramped room filled with a battered, messy desk, bookshelves, file cabinets, and overgrown potted plants taking over whatever they could cover. The place was warm, too warm for her jacket. She took it off, belatedly remembered that she was wearing a risqué, not-safe-for-summer-camp T-shirt—hoped Moon won't be offended—but it was a gift from Marc. *I Only Sleep with the Drummer*, boasted the green words across her chest.

Moon waved her in. "Thank you for coming, dear. Please have a seat."

Melody took the well-worn chair Moon indicated, too tense to relax. Marc's therapist friend had called and asked her to come in without explaining why; maybe it had something to do with Marc.

Moon fastened half-moon reading glasses onto her nose, turned to a metal cabinet and pawed through files.

"Ah! Here it is." She held out a white envelope with a thick seal of red wax.

"You don't need to read this here, but it was important that I deliver it to you in person. I haven't read it myself, so I can't discuss the contents, I'm sorry." She peered at Melody above the glasses, reading her T-shirt.

Melody's face burned. "It's from Marc—the shirt, I mean. You know how he is."

"I only sleep with the front man, myself." Moon's eyes twinkled. "Marc is a dear friend, sweetheart. He's been through a lot; I'm glad to see he's found happiness with you. I understand he's proposed, and like a sensible girl, you asked for time to consider."

Melody smiled shyly. "My mother thinks it's a little crazy. She says I'll be swamped with housework and childcare. But... I *am* crazy." She laughed at herself, a quick nervous release. "I'm crazy about Marc. As for the kids, they've curled up in my heart in a way I can't explain. I met them before I even met him. We just connected. So I'm sure what my answer will be."

"That's good to hear," Moon said with an encouraging smile in return. "Well, good luck. Keep in touch."

Melody found herself ushered out the door, clutching the letter. She sat in her car for several minutes, wondering whether to open the envelope right away. Was it some kind of pre-nuptial agreement? Was he that kind of man? She picked distractedly at the red wax and turned the envelope over to look at the address. It wasn't Marc's penmanship and was simply addressed to *Marc's fiancée.* She took a deep breath and started the car. Marc would be working late today, and the kids were in school. She headed up the mountain.

There'd been more snow this year than last year, meaning better skiing. She and Marc had taken Chelsea and Zane to Taos for skiing lessons several weekends in January and February, which gave the kids plenty of time to enjoy the slopes while she and Marc took time for each other. As she followed the winding road toward the Santa Fe ski basin, she thought of the pristine snow, the clarity of the sky, the fine winter air, and tried not to think about the letter.

At last, she found what she was looking for, a turnout with only the tracks of other vehicles in the snow and not the cars themselves. Solitude. She parked, and carrying her purse and the letter, she followed a trail to a dry boulder. There she broke the seal on the letter and pulled out a handwritten sheaf of papers.

Dear Bubby-cakes,

You may have known me, or thought you did. Are you my sister, my friend? Maybe we never did cross paths, and I write you as one imperfect stranger to another, my husband's next wife. My dear husband, who calls me Bubby-cakes, Dollbaby and Sweetheart—I hope these are familiar terms of endearment to you from your fiancé, my husband. Heart of my heart.

It is because he is all that to me that I write you now, as he sleeps exhausted beside me on a full moon night, snoring lightly, a pillow clutched over his chest, none under his head. (Do you know that he does that? He says he thinks it's an unconscious, primitive and self-protective gesture, covering the chest. I've never seen anyone else sleep that way, though.)

I wonder if you're living with him now, sharing not just his bed and his romantic attentiveness, but the mess, the intimacy of kissing in the morning before opening your eyes or brushing your teeth.

Do you love his order and his chaos, his thoughtful, reasonable mind and fathomless heart?

Do you appreciate his tears?

Do you cherish him?

I love that word: cherish. To love and to cherish.

I hope you'll forgive my muddled words and take my intention to heart. Here goes—random notes, girlfriend to girlfriend, wife to wife:

You and I both have former wives in our lives. It's tough enough to step into the life of a man with an ex-wife and children, marry into a family wounded by a traumatic breakup, navigate the complexities of the on-again-off-again mother of your husband's children, honor the feelings and ties that came before you, and that still flow onward into your life.

You, my sweet friend, are taking on that and more, an ex-wife and a dead wife.

That would be me.

A dead wife.

I am only capable of writing this because it doesn't yet feel real. Or it didn't, until butterflies filled my chest tonight as I saw him sleeping, their wing-beats jittering, cold and hot, and I could not shut my eyes. What can I do to help him be happy when I am gone?

There's so much I wish I could tell you in person. I would take your hand in mine and study the shapes of your fingers, imagine your touch on his cheek—God, it hurts to think about that—but I have no choice. His life goes on, so must his happiness.

If Marc has chosen you to marry, I know you have a sense of humor and an open mind. You are a courageous, strong, loving and adventurous woman, to take on this man and his wonderful children. So very, very lucky—yes, I envy the life that you'll have together, I can't help it. I am no angel. Do NOT let mythologizing of the dead turn me into an albatross-angel around your neck.

Has Marc told you that I struggled with addiction, and how he helped me when I fell off the wagon? I was arrested for DUI. He attended the sobriety meetings with me, all of them, every day for a month. Okay, he wasn't just being supportive—he was also protective—it was me and a roomful of drunk guys. But still! Before I met him, I wasted so much time partying, getting wasted.

I thought I had time.

I'm here to tell you that as long as I live and breathe, I am human and imperfect, doing the best I can with the hand I was dealt. For your sake and the sake of your new family, let me be your imperfect friend, not the "perfect" dead wife you measure yourself against. Don't do it and don't let anyone else do it to you.

Be your own flawed and precious self, for that is why he is marrying you.

My hand is shaking now. I'll write more tomorrow.

Melody realized she was holding her breath. She exhaled, a shuddering translucent cloud, gone in an instant.

She pulled out the next page.

Dear Dollbaby,

Days have passed since I started this letter. It's a beautiful summer, my last summer, I know that now. Past the solstice, the days are growing shorter but are still glorious. I'm looking forward to a picnic in the mountains.

Melody looked up from the letter, imagining this snowy, peaceful spot in the summer, perfect for a picnic. A chill shot through her, nothing to do with the air temperature. As if... She swiveled her head, searched the trees, saw no movement, heard no footfall, no creaking branch or flitting bird, and yet—the distinct sensation of another's presence was intense and overwhelming. All she could do was sit, eyes and ears open, absorbing the stillness of the field of snow.

At last, she was able to turn her attention back to the page.

The children are doing as well as can be expected, but they will need so much compassion and love. It's said that three times is a charm—I hope, for them and for Marc, that you are that charm, bringing love and light to their lives, and that the three of them charm and delight you. I hope you love them as your own.

I also hope you are blessed to experience the mystery of pregnancy and childbirth yourself. That's something I wished for and missed. Miss...

More things I hope for: that you will visit the magical place of Tulum with its cenotes, where Mother Earth speaks through the water if only we listen to her.

I hope you'll watch Young Frankenstein with Marc and the children many, many times, and love it as they do.

I hope you'll go to a drive-in movie with Marc and make out like lovesick teenagers. I wanted to see a flick at the Yucca Drive-In—was meaning to, but the shows stopped. Do what you want to do—don't wait. Don't wait!

Travel, take the kids with you, see the world. Share Marc's zest for living. Visit Corinne, Marc's French ex-girlfriend, and her fiancé, in Saint Tropez. I had a change of heart about her... Didn't get the chance to patch things up. She's really one of Marc's great friends.

I hope your wedding is all you wish it to be, and that Sonya sings for you. Watch out for practical jokes!

Okay, girlfriend, I guess this is it for now. Moonflute will make sure you get this letter when the time is right. She's helped me so much. She'll help you if you ask.

Don't be afraid to ask.

Please write me back—it's a comfort to imagine you doing that. Write me, and burn the letters at my medicine wheel.

Your friend from out of time,
Marina

April 2, 1997, Dear Marina...

Melody did write back. More than once, a private observance she revealed to no one, not even to Marc. Marina's act of faith, writing a letter to a stranger she would never meet, offered and granted solace, a gift Melody honored. She shared fears, confessions, hopes, and dreams with her imperfect friend, finding serenity in the ritual. Letters rose skyward, prayer arrows of smoke, shedding ash upon the medicine wheel.

Your friend from out of time,
Melody.

Sand and Shells

Twenty Years Later Minus One Day
Santa Fe, New Mexico

Twenty years later minus one day, Marc sat at the kitchen island of his northside Santa Fe home, pencil in hand, writing again. It was two o'clock in the morning. His extravagantly gorgeous black chow puppy, Zsa Zsa, sat at his feet, adorable and adoring, licking his calf with her blue-black tongue.

Light puffs of snow sailed past the stretch of south-facing window framing the darkened panorama of Sun and Moon Mountains. The view of those voluptuous forms, as subtle and lifelike as the breasts of a sleeping woman, was naturally a top selling point for this graceful, comfortable home in the foothills, Marc and Melody's residence for several years now. Marc found the sight an uplifting and calming reminder to look at things far away.

He had gone to bed early with Melody, joking about the exciting Friday night they were happily avoiding by staying home. She was sleeping through the rhythmic hiss of her CPAP mask, but Marc dozed in fits and starts, restless.

Eventually, he slid out from under the covers and went to the kitchen to throw words on paper, a random mess. He couldn't read his own jagged pencil slashes on the yellow legal pad. Finally, he copied out the letter he had composed to himself, skipping salutations, going straight to his thoughts.

When was Marina's birthday? I think it was close to her death date but now I can't remember, what an asshole. Funny, I guess, what we lose and what we remember—her smile, unforgettable after all these years. The way she handled her death and my future. The gifts she left—spirituality on our own terms, passion for life, boundless love. Her generosity. Her blessings for me and the kids and Melody, my

Melody, my wife and best friend in the world. Our twentieth wedding anniversary coming up, a truly momentous occasion.

Marc's pencil trembled over the paper; he wiped an eye and pressed on.

Would we even be celebrating this anniversary without Marina's— what— interventions? I called her a witch once in Playa, and I still wonder... Witch, angel, spirit—yet so very human.

It's not that I am obsessed with Marina, or that she continues to look over my family and me. It's not that my love for Melody is any less than my love for Marina's memory. And it's not that I still smile at a hawk passing way too close, or at the blurring line between water and sand.

How can I compare the love I have for my "big" kids, with the love for my six-foot-two, eighteen-year-old twin boys? Shea, named for the stadium I grew up in, and Leo, after my wondrous, dystrophied cousin, both about to graduate high school and head off to college, a couple more redheaded Italian boys out in the world, look out, here they come!

To quote Walt Whitman—well, some of the lines I can remember, anyway—

"As to me I know of nothing else but miracles,
Whether I walk the streets of Manhattan
Or wade with naked feet along the beach just in the edge of the water
Or birds, or the wonderfulness of insects in the air
These with the rest, one and all, are to me miracles,
The whole referring, yet each distinct and in its place."

Miracles. I think of the pleasures and pains of these past twenty years, fantastic fortune, great highs, low lows, illness, health.

Melody: beautiful, fragile, tough, amazing woman. She went out of her way to befriend Corinne, and Corinne's husband, Yannick; they have spent nine of the last ten Christmases with us. Out of the blue, the girls are thick as thieves...

The home we bought near Playa del Carmen, Mexico, during the good days, and had to sell during the bad. My community of friends, guides, and family, who have given me so much love and support, compassion and companionship, advice and forgiveness. Who have enriched my life. No. Who have made my life.

Cheers to the power of people together, and to the inherent power of ceremony. In Madison Square Garden, in church, in a meeting or a runaway retreat, in a movie theater, instead of home alone watching The Price is Right. *The hormonal, physiological connections we make in a group bind and transport us. There is power in the doing, the participating, bearing witness to each other. Holding light in the darkness for each other.*

My time with Marina through her illness, fear, acceptance, finality, Telluride—I became a better man for it, but why does someone have to fucking die?

We all die.

I rose to the occasion, got through it walking tall. Okay, did some crawling too. I kicked ass and feel proud of myself for that. Marina's fortitude helped me to become stronger than I knew I could be, and I carry that strength with me still.

Melody, my children, my mother, the health challenges we all have faced—I know that I am capable. And I know that I am a spiritual being, I have a body filled with spirit and that spirit goes on. Marina showed me. I now (conveniently) believe in other lives.

To know of other lives, or at least to imagine them, makes it possible to look through the masks around me, to recognize myself in other faces.

And the magic that helps guide us, I know it, I feel it. I wish that everyone could feel it too.

We can be surrounded by angels and not see them, yet they are there, they are here. Be aware.

"Why, who makes much of a miracle?"

Just ask Walt.

Marc folded the letter and slid it into the pocket of his jacket hanging near the front door. Below the jacket stood an antique Italian cradle, now a repository for puppy paraphernalia. He stroked the smooth wood, gave it a gentle nudge. Sunrise, sunset, sunrise. He should be up and out the door in a few hours before anyone else awoke. Get a little sleep, rest your head.

Marc usually had patients scheduled on Saturday mornings, but not this Saturday. He drove alone through the city and south onto Highway 14. Clouds stretched and rolled like the ink on his leg, loosing a brief flurry of wet snow. Gritty gusts of spring would soon descend; he aimed to be there ahead of them.

The Cerrillos house remained uninhabited. It had been on the market for years now, owned by some realtor with apparently little interest in selling. Marc steered down the rutted drive past the Children at Play sign he had put into the ground at Marina's behest. It stood at the same crooked angle, its words mere ghosts on the metal, sandblasted and bleached beyond legibility.

He parked and climbed the rock formation to Marina's sacred space, inhaling deeply. The morning air was damp with the fragrant breath of the mountains.

At the top of the hill he knelt. Marc made this visit annually, with Melody's blessing, and always found more shells added to the sandy circle. He wondered who brought them. A low marble memorial carved into the shape of a stylized hawk, now fallen, presided over the site.

Marc dug with bare hands and tucked his letter into the sand. He stood the sculpted bird upon the buried message and piled stones around it, but the monument kept toppling. At last, he managed to prop it nearly upright, poised for flight. It would hold for a while.

He rocked back in the sand, picked up a conch, and listened. Once a year, in the midst of the desert wind, he listened.

© Tamara Lichtenstein

Michael Hoerning was raised on Long Island amid an extended Italian-American family. Talking with his hands came naturally, as did working with them—cooking under his grandmother's tutelage, drumming in cover bands, making a career in physical therapy.

He received his education at SUNY Stony Brook and NYU. Along the way, he managed a bar at the age of seventeen in North Carolina, produced musical acts in Harlem, wrote for a sketch comedy troupe on New York's Lower East Side (the only member with a favorable day job, he was able to rent storefronts for gigs), became a tobacconist, and spent a couple of years practicing physical therapy in Rome, Italy, starting with the Team Roma soccer club.

He is a long-time resident of Santa Fe, New Mexico, where his practice continues. Sand & Water is Hoerning's first novel.

CPSIA information can be obtained
at www.ICGtesting.com
Printed in the USA
BVHW071608251119
564690BV00001B/62/P